DAYS OF AWE

C.L.Quinn

Blak Kat Publishing
May 2016
All rights reserved

106 years have passed since the Days of Innocence.

Prepare to meet the world mankind has built since then.

The Grand Destiny has Arrived…

Readers, as in Days of Innocence, to help you with this story, this is a brief summary of the guardians: 10 vampires, 10 humans, 10 supernaturals, and the healer, Crezia. Five humans are introduced in this tale.

The Vampires:

Children of the Sun:

Cairine- Bas and Park's daughter
Maccabee- Bas and Park's son
Caedmon- Eillia and Daniel's son
Fia- Tamesine and Marc's daughter
Bryson- Tamesine and Marc's son, Fia's twin

Children of the Moon:

Eras- Ahmose and Starla's son
Shani- Ahmose and Starla's daughter
Ife- Ahmose and Starla's daughter
Brigitte- Ahmose and Mal's daughter
Talib- Chione and Donovan's son

And in Boston:

Crezia- Mies and Sarah's daughter

The Totems from Patagonia:

Su'ad, Abasi, Bura, Ari, Pilar, Darwishi, Indah, Lemah, Banyu, and Nur.

The Humans:

Jackson, Sally, Jessie, Taylor, Dean—college friends from *Days of Innocence,* who discovered they were chosen warriors on an unexpected trip to Patagonia.

One

Birds cooed on the edge of the balcony, a variety she hadn't seen for three decades. Leaving the cool interior of the apartment, Cairine walked out slowly so she wouldn't startle them, a ready smile for her unexpected visitors.

"Well, hello, my darlings. Where in the world have you come from?"

She had no doubt that they were here because they sought her. *How beautiful!* Fluffy white feathers dappled with peach tones that looked like sunrise on a soft summer morning (*yes, she still remembered!*), bright eyes and a streak of dark along the base of the neck.

Turtle Doves, four of them, here, on her balcony on the sixty-fifth floor of the Stratos Tower. *At night*. Unheard of.

"We didn't think any of you had survived. I am so thrilled that you have. Come into the interior. You cannot stay here, the winds will come soon and blow you away."

As if they understood her command, the four doves lifted elegantly on silent wings and flew through the forceshield that kept the cool air inside. Environmental controls held the apartment at a steady 72 degrees.

"I think I can order up some corn or seed. I don't know where you've come from, but you must be tired and hungry."

A low chime interrupted Cairine as she headed to her galley for something appropriate for birds.

"Figures," she commented and held a finger up to let the doves know she'd be right back, well aware they had no idea what it meant.

"*Answer*," she called out when she entered her living space again, and a wide monitor on the wall showed a man waiting in the hallway. A slow smile came.

"Talib! *Allow access*."

A low hiss preceded the door's movement as it slid back into the wall, then a head with glossy black spiked hair poked in.

"Cari?"

"Get in here, Talib!" Cairine hurried to hug the slender, well-muscled man. It had been at least fifteen years since she'd seen him last, the hug long and close. "You smell so good. What is that scent?"

Pulling back, she watched him shrug, something she clearly remembered common for him. "My mate gives me these herb packets to carry. She says they ward off bad spirits."

"It's lovely. How *is* Su'ad?"

"She's perfect." His eyes went to the galley. "I see my friends made it."

"*You* sent them? From where?"

"Home. They are the last of their breed, and I've been protecting them, but things in the south are heating up too much."

"Oh, my friend, it isn't any safer here. All indications show that my big buddy may blow soon. When it does, it will take everything we have to try to contain it. Honestly I really don't know if we can. Right now, we are all spread so far. You know that for many decades we vampire guardians have been assigned at ten different points around the globe along with one Totem and one of the five human soldiers we have?"

"I do. That is the other reason I've come. There is a disturbance flowing through the ether. You're right to be concerned."

"Chione and Donovan were here two weeks ago. Talib, I've never seen them so quiet. And over the years, you know we've had a lot to worry about. This event may be imminent. Chione said that when the time is near, the final five humans should be revealed."

"The portents are there. I think we should put everyone on alert. They need to be ready at a moment's notice."

"I have to agree. Now, though, in celebration of your first visit to my home, I want to take you to the finest dinner in the mountains and show you some of our views. I've been working nonstop for twelve weeks, and you are exactly the break I need. You *do* have time to stick around for a few days, don't you?"

"Of course, Cari. You are not the only one who needs a break."

"This is a welcome surprise, Talib. Let me settle my new roommates and grab my bag."

Talib looked around Cairine's apartment as he waited for her to arrange food for the doves. Wandering slowly through the immaculate, although sparsely furnished rooms, he thought about the years since he'd seen *any* of his friends, let alone this beautiful woman he'd half loved as a young man. He smiled as he fingered an anatomically correct nude figure of a man formed in smooth metal. Of course, he'd never had a chance. Her youthful heart had belonged to his friend Eras from the first time she'd met him and knocked him on his ass in that soft sand on the beach in France they had all come to love.

He missed the simplicity of those days. Even now, after over a century, he still *missed* those carefree days.

Slipping past the air barrier, he moved to the balcony railing to view what was unique for someone who'd lived in the forest for eighty years…a dense, elevated city. Skyscrapers continued down the mountainside, subtly lit with efficient lighting so to disturb as little of the night sky as possible. It was striking to behold, but he would be happy to return to his forest that, because of magics, remained hidden from the rest of the world that he admitted still overwhelmed him.

"I'm ready, Talib." Cairine joined him. After watching the scene with him for a few silent moments, she took his arm. "I never get tired of this view."

"It's because you're responsible for it."

"Partly. And because I was able to save so much green space."

"Yet it's all still in danger."

Cairine's sigh was soft. "Yes. There's that. But tonight, we celebrate. Tonight, we're together without a mission, just two friends getting a nice meal and catching up. This is a perfect evening to do so."

"Then shall we?" Ever the gentleman, Talib offered his arm.

"We shall."

The elevators attached on the outside of each building, clad in unbreakable poly-fiber carriages, moved down over sixty floors in seconds to stop with an almost indiscernible landing.

Cairine waited as Talib adjusted his step. He wasn't accustomed to the speed of the elevator. She led him toward one of the community lift-cars. Eighty lift-cars waited in garages along the mountainside, several outside of each building. No one needed private vehicles on the mountains anymore, and the vertical take-off airborne cars could take them up or down the mountain within minutes.

Mostly automated, the car responded to Cairine's verbal command to take them to a restaurant built at the peak of this mountaintop with a view of the Rockies she considered unparalleled. She might be a bit biased. This was her mountain, had been home for her for the past one hundred years plus, and, with fortune smiling on her, would always be. Rising smoothly from the ground in a perfectly controlled ascent, the lift-car took to the air.

Talib released his held breath, his eyes darting from her to the landscape as it passed quickly.

"Exhilarating, isn't it?" he said abruptly, his voice tight.

"Is it too fast? I can slow it down."

"No. No, Cari, it's fine. We just, um, still move at a slower pace in Patagonia."

"I kind of envy that. Here, I think we often move so quickly, we miss things we shouldn't. Nothing is like it was when we lived our uncomplicated lives in France and Africa."

"The world moves on, guided by time. I agree, though, too many have lost the human touch."

Cairine leaned out her open window. "I think that happened a long time ago. If we can't stop the foretold events, we might go back to how our ancestors lived hundreds of years ago."

"That wouldn't change much about the way *my* tribe lives." Talib laughed, his fingers curled tight around the handle of his door for support.

"See. You are already prepared when the rest of us will be lost. I really missed you, my moon brother. And the whole of our brothers and sisters. We need to have a party before it all blows up."

"While I agree, I want to hear how *you* are doing right now, my dear friend."

"Really quite well. I've no complaints. I want to hear about everyone in South America, too."

Talib nodded as he looked behind at the series of tall buildings that stair-stepped down the mountainside.

"Cari, isn't this where your cabin used to be?"

"Yes. It still is, nestled in a protected veil of magics. I go there a lot, but when the tower cluster became a reality, I took over the project to control and contain its advance. I love these mountains, and while I knew the area was perfect for the city, I had to protect the wild spaces so that the mountain lions and other animals still had a place to be. I would be a poor earth sentry if I hadn't. So I saved my cabin that I got from Jackson and most of the mountainside around it. If you look over there…"

Cairine pointed to a darkened area below them. "No lights. That's my place and the home of a lot of happy wildlife."

"But you live in the tower."

"Largely, yes. I manage everything from there. I love my cabin, but I also love that skytower apartment. Most of the humans who live in the building don't know I'm there since I occupy the top six floors exclusively. The buildings main elevator doesn't even go up past the floor beneath me."

"Good fortune."

"Intentional. I may live closer to my human neighbors than most vampires, but I still maintain separation. They're smart enough to figure out something about me is different if I let them."

"It appears to be working." Talib gasped as the car shifted suddenly to the vertical drop that would place it directly in front of *Skyborne*, the nightclub and restaurant frequented by most of the mountain's residents.

A sprawling one-story building filled most of the mountaintop, lit with soft rose and blue lights around the perimeter. Stepping gratefully from the lift-car, Talib tamped down the desire to drop to the ground and kiss it in relief. He was vampire and he knew that even if the car had failed, he wouldn't have been permanently injured, but he had never been comfortable with flying cars. In his mind, cars shouldn't fly.

Talib saw Cairine's amused expression. Shrugging, he grinned. "I'm a pussy."

"It's okay, love. I *like* pussies." She watched a slow smile widen on Talib's face and punched him in the arm.

"You know what I mean. Don't be crass, you're not good at it." Grabbing the same arm she'd just slammed her fist into, she pulled him toward the beautifully illuminated glass building. "My treat, of course."

Swiveling, Talib's head moved to take in all the sights and sounds of this busy club. "It has been almost exactly thirty years since I left Patagonia, Cari."

Quiet for a moment, she imagined the isolation, so different from her life here. Nothing would make her change her decision to stay in these beautiful mountains that she loved every bit as much as her native France.

"It must seem overwhelming for you. Well, you are in for an exciting night. The food here cannot be surpassed anywhere on this earth or above it. *Skyborne* is owned by two women who have been partnered for twenty years, and I tell you, their love rivals that of long term vampire relationships. Cassie travels the world in search of authentic cuisine and Pia incorporates it into their menu, which is constantly changing and evolving. I eat here nearly every night and never get bored."

"Lead the way."

As they moved to the entrance of a busy dining room with glass tables and crystal quartz lighting that left a subtle glow all around the upper perimeter of the room, Talib noticed Cairine nod to a tall redhead who smiled slyly. Weaving through the tables, the woman joined them and stopped directly in front of Talib.

"Oh, darling, where have you been keeping *this* one? He looks like the entrée I need to devour tonight."

"Hands off, Serena. He's wed to a woman who could tear you apart in two seconds."

Smiling, Serena took Cairine's arm and pulled her closer. "Well, then, I'll just have to snuggle up to you."

Serena kissed Cairine on the cheek and waved as she sauntered toward the next guests.

Leading Talib across the wide expanse with noisy diners, Cairine dropped into a padded chair in front of a glass table lit from beneath with tiny pinpoint lights.

"Please sit and check out this view."

Talib lowered himself into the comfortable chair and scanned the scene outside the seamless glass wall. It was breathtaking. On one side of the view, the seventy story buildings that stair-stepped down the mountainside, all softly lit, following the line of the landscape, formed an artistic sweep of homes. Directly ahead, sweeping vistas of the valleys below and adjacent mountaintops, all lit carefully to protect the natural balance of the Rockies, showed stunning engineering brilliantly intertwined with nature.

"You've really created a special place here, Cari."

"Not alone. Jax and I put together the best team of architects, engineers, and graphic artists I've ever seen. I wanted to make sure we provided homes for the residents, but kept our damaging footprint low. These buildings are fully self-sustaining like most of our urban skytower cities. We've maximized every resource and I have to say, I'm incredibly proud of our success."

"You should be. I think Su'ad would love to see this."

"Talib, you and Su'ad are Earth warriors, you need to get out and see this world. Staying locked in your country, in the Totem community, won't feed your power. You two should buy a jet and visit all ten of your fellow warrior's locations."

"They *do* cover the four corners. When Chione and Donovan told us forty years ago that we would be assigned to duties on ten different stations around the globe, we had no idea that it would be so long-term."

"Too many things going wrong with how humans handled life and living. Had we not intervened, there would have been one or more nuclear events, the governments would have never been able to provide essential services and food for so many billions. The population explosion needed someone to handle it, and that had to be us."

"It was part of our destiny, I get that. Everything is primarily under control now, except for the earth's natural engine."

"And *that* is frightening."

As a humanoid a.i.bot server smoothly slid to the table on maglevs to drop off a slim bottle filled with a pale blue liquid, Cairine lifted the small glass already placed in front of Talib and filled it to just below the rim.

"This, you must try. It's called *giera* and I guarantee you've never tasted anything like it before. Your tongue will thank you."

Fully trusting Cairine's judgement, Talib poured the liquid into his mouth and held it there before he swallowed it to experience the full favor. Sweet, with a sharp spice that tickled his tongue and cheeks, the slightly viscous liquid slipped down his throat. His eyes wide, and a little teary, he lifted them to look into hers.

"Whoa, that is…uh, bracing."

"Unique, isn't it? The first time you drink it, it tastes and feels a bit sharp, but you get addicted quickly. Pia was a chemist before she and Cassie opened this place. She holds patents on fifty or so unique foods."

"Su'ad would love this. Yes, Cari, I think perhaps I'll bring her to visit. You're right, and since our destiny may arrive soon, we should take some time to travel through the world and experience it before everything erupts."

Cairine sipped her *giera,* her eyes moving over the landscape spread below, then back to this man she'd known her entire life. He was just as gentle and soulful as when he was an innocent boy.

"Yes, my friend, you should. I can't believe it's been over a century since we used to meet on the shores of the Mediterranean."

"Time doesn't wait for anyone, does it?"

"No. Even with our long lives, I feel as if I won't get the chance to do everything I want. I still can't imagine how it must feel for ordinary humans who only get eight or ten decades. Even with all the medical advances these past years, it isn't enough."

"Preaching to one who agrees, my friend. How about we finish dinner and you get me back into one of those death cars and show me these mountaintops?"

"Deal."

Two hours later, Talib drew a deep breath and took his seat in a different type of lift-car, this one open on top with seat belts that clipped over both shoulders.

"Touring car. Literally," Cairine explained as she clipped her belt. "No better way to see the landscape than this. Jackson designed it thirty years ago."

"I think I got the word right in the restaurant."

"Talib, I promise you won't die in this. They have an extremely high safety record."

"Extremely high. That means *some* went down."

"Well, it won't go down with *us* on board. We're magic, right? Oh, Talib, look to your far left!"

The sky was on fire. Auroral displays were common in the mountains and tonight, bright blues and greens danced across the black night for her visitor.

She watched Talib as he sat stone still, his gaze locked on the celestial colors that wrapped around them as the lift-car swayed gently, suspended in air.

"I feel as if I could touch it."

"You can't get this view from the ground," Cairine pointed out, her eyes sparkling.

They stayed in a slow advance mode as the lift-car circled the lesser inhabited areas of the mountains, then the skytower city where Cairine lived. In its own way, the towering buildings were just as lovely as the landscape. Built to blend in with the mountains, one could be forgiven for thinking the slender obelisk shapes belonged there.

Cairine exclusively occupied the top 6 floors of her building, all of which were protected against the light of day, except the rooftop, where she grew personal gardens of fresh vegetables and fruits.

Cairine sighed. "It's near daylight."

"I know. I would like to stay in town for a week, if that is okay with you. I would not wish to interfere in your life or obligations."

"Talib! Any of my brothers or sisters are welcome anytime for as long as they want to stay. There would never be a time or event that would change that. I have twenty-two extra rooms just above my apartments. You have your pick."

"Thank you, but it was only proper to ask. I remember the young woman I played with on a sunny beach many years ago. She was the most generous hostess, so I knew that you would welcome me as I would always welcome you."

"Always. Let's get back, I'll arrange a last snack before we go down to rest, and make sure that your doves are set. They can roost on the enclosed deck on the roof. It has a shelter in the front half that will provide sanctuary, and on calm days, they can seek the sky."

"Bless you. I knew I made the right choice."

The lift-car dropped them in front of the elevator and once back in Cairine's apartment, she placed an order in the galley for food prep, turned, and took Talib's arm to lead him to a stairwell outside the door.

"Let me settle you in. I set the FP to have our snacks ready in fifteen minutes."

"You have one of the food printers."

"You don't? Oh, Talib, if you take nothing else back with you, take one of these FP units. For anyone, they're great, but for vampires, it's a revolution. Nearly anything you want, anytime you want it. The unit can reproduce an incredible variety of food with minimal time or waste."

"I'm sold. Food is an issue in the rain forest these days. Access can be spotty, or require long drives to procure what we need. Crops fail sixty percent of the time due to drought."

"That won't be a problem with these units. Your tribe is still growing, so you must have them. I'll provide three units for you along with supplies for a full year of production."

"You are my angel."

"I do well in the celestial department, I admit it. Let's get you set, and enjoy our final meal of the night."

Thirty minutes later, bellies filled, laughing, Talib followed Cairine to the top of the skytower carrying the turtle doves he'd sent to her. The Totems who lived in Patagonia had a true bond with all animals, land, water, or air, and had sent them forth on Talib's request. It was too warm now in South America for the birds to remain healthy, and since they were four of only a few left, he felt a deep responsibility to try to protect them.

"Here, these boxes will make perfect homes for them. This shelter withstands any wind, and when the air is calm, they'll be able to fly anytime they want. My FP can produce all the seed they need. Talib, they'll be happy and well here."

"Then my choice was right. So many have been lost, we must save all we can."

"Absolutely."

Talib's empathic skills had heightened since living with the Totems and he sent a message to the birds that this was sanctuary. Cairine watched with amazement as they flew the short distance from his hands to the boxes she'd indicated, and landed smoothly on top.

"Beautiful. They'll be perfect guests. Come over here for a moment." Cairine led Talib to an intricate railing that looked like ancient iron, although he knew it was likely made from a new material a third the weight and ten times stronger. These buildings were engineering marvels, to stand so tall and strong against the mountain winds.

Leaning against the top of the rail, Cairine closed her eyes and breathed deeply. "This is one of my favorite places in the world. It's so quiet and lovely. As a child of the moon, I know that you can tolerate sunlight briefly. Sometimes, though, even though I'm *not* a child of the moon, I push my limits and stay just long enough to peek at a rising sun, or come up just in time to watch it drop. It's a risk, and I *have* won a few nasty burns, but it's worth it to see the sun again. Like the birds, this is *my* sanctuary."

"We need it more than ever. The Mother Earth is struggling, but so are we."

Sliding an arm through Talib's again, Cairine pressed against him. "We've had spectacular lives. Every one of us has contributed to her survival through the past many decades. I am so very proud of all our brothers and sisters. When our day comes, we'll be ready."

Talib nodded and kissed Cairine on the top of her head, a hand sliding through her silky strawberry-blonde curls. "Namasté. Peace in our time."

"Word, brother. We do all we can to ensure it, but living creatures are volatile."

"From the beginning of time."

Quiet, happy to just stand close, to share this moment with each other, the two vampires watched vermillion creep into the eastern sky.

"Time to rest." Cairine pulled away and led Talib to the guest rooms. "I'll see you tonight. Anything you need, the FP can provide. All other amenities are in your room or one of the closets in the hall. When you rise tonight, just come on down to my apartment and come on in. If I'm not up, order something from the FP and I'll be there in no time. Talib, I'm *so* glad you came. Rest well."

Half an hour later, one floor below, she sighed in contentment as she slipped on a satin gown after a quick shower. The smooth fabric stuck to her moist skin as her fingers moved along her naked belly while she wandered into the galley.

"Tea, chamomile, hot, with sugar."

A soft chirp announced the beverage, prepared to her preset parameters, ready on the ledge of the FP unit as a clear access door opened.

Reaching for it, Cairine gasped as arms slid around her waist, and lips pressed to her neck. Turning carefully, she grinned.

"Otto! I nearly spilled this tea!"

Keeping her eyes on the huge man unexpectedly holding her, she set the teacup back on the ledge.

"What are you doing here? Not that I'm not thrilled to see you."

Her eyes slid over Otto's tall frame, past the dark beard that he hadn't had the last time she'd seen him, lower to a tight tee shirt spread over big arms and jeans so tight, the bulge below the z-closure was fully outlined.

His left bicep flexed as he slid his arm under the satin gown to replace hers. "Special flight. VIP wanted to leave early, so I got the gig to bring him home. I have tonight only, and then I have to fly back to the station. Guess what I want to do?"

Cairine jumped into his arms, her long legs around his waist, she buried her fingers in his thick hair as she pulled him close. "Oh, God, yes! Two months is too long! A girl can only get so far by herself."

Otto growled. "I need that illustrated, please."

He set her on the floor, then whipped her up again, this time thrown over his shoulder like she'd seen in old movies where men liked to prove their masculine strength. While that wasn't exactly true in this case, a sexual thrill ran from her breasts to her core, especially when his other hand moved along her buttocks under the gown and sought the slit between them.

The wide hallway led to her chambers, the largest room in the apartment, cloaked in champagne tulle fabric from the ceiling to the floor. Once he set her bare feet on the cocoa carpeting, his hands moved back to her.

Cairine closed her eyes to immerse herself in the sensation of Otto's fingers curved around each shoulder as he slid the straps down, the fingers moving on to her waist, the satin brushing her skin on its way to the floor. She opened her eyes again when the fingers were suddenly gone to see that he'd stepped back.

Bright white teeth highlighted by the sexy beard she found she liked, showcased his tongue as it slid around his lips. He took one more step backward to scan the most beautiful body he'd ever seen.

"Please show me *how* far a girl can *get* by herself."

Backing away, Cairine knew he watched her bare buttocks as she walked to the bed, and leaned over to pull a curved silver rod from a drawer in the nightstand.

"I'm going to need this." Then she snatched a tall bottle from a shelf above it and looked back at Otto, still standing where she'd left him, watching every movement.

"And this." Carrying the Scotch and vibrator to the bed, she crawled up into the center and knelt, her expression serious. "First, I get comfortable." A slow grin came. "It's going to take a while." The grin died, but her eyes glittered.

Otto forgot to breathe. He wanted to stay right where he was and watch this stunning woman bring herself to orgasm, but he was pretty sure he couldn't make it that long. Patience wasn't a virtue he possessed, but he was going to give it his best attempt.

"I've been pretty deprived." Cairine moved her fingertips over her chest, the tips lingering on her nipples, then moved down to caress her flat belly. When they slid between her legs, she smiled again, and laid her head back, her eyes closed.

Otto started forward, but stopped himself a few inches from the foot of the bed.

Cairine's body collapsed and she fell back against plumped up pillows, her eyes still closed, the fingers of her left hand moving along her slit, as her left hand reached for the vibrator.

"No," Otto barked, instantly on top of the bed, his hands on her thighs. "The only thing getting inside you is me."

Cairine lifted her head, grabbed the vibrator, and pitched it across the room. "It's about time. *Now*, I'm ready to play. Welcome home, Otto."

Shaking his head, Otto pulled his shirt off and slipped from the bed just long enough to remove his boots and jeans. Naked now, he moved around the foot of the bed and crawled up until his mouth was just above Cairine's privates. Staring openly, her own tongue moving along her lips, she scanned each hard muscle as they flexed with his movement. Dense dark hair covered his chest. Sexy, all male. *Human, but near perfection.*

When she felt his tongue move along the slit, nipping along the path, she dropped back to the pillow and groaned. "You have to find an earthbound job. You can't stay away for months at a time," she whispered, as he moved closer and buried his tongue inside her. "Oh, fu…"

Her own gasp shut her up as she lifted her back off the bed. "God, Otto, I'd swear you practice while you're gone. Where did you learn that?"

He lifted his head to look at her. "I *do* practice."

Brows drawn, she raised her closed lids to meet his eyes. "You better not."

"The only woman I've touched for ten years is you. The only woman I *want* to touch…ever again. What else is there to do on those long nights on Mars? Centuries of vids with some interesting ideas on sex. Here, let me show you."

Lifting her buttocks off the bed, he began a series of little attacks, bringing her to the moment before climax and then stopped. He traveled down one thigh and around to the other one before he began again. The motion of his mouth combined with something hot that suddenly touched her there made her jump as intense pleasure spread through her to her belly.

"What was that?" she whispered.

"It's an organic stimulator. Just let it work."

It *did* work. An infusion of heat that only got hotter when Otto's tongue slipped on the viscous fluid pushed her to another strong orgasm.

"Now, let's try it together," he said, lowering her back down. "Would you like to help me?"

Cairine pushed up onto her elbows as he passed a small iridescent blue tube to her.

"Cover me with this." Otto held his fully engorged cock in his hand.

After a moment, curious, incredibly aroused, and in spite of the two orgasms he'd already brought her, she moved back up onto her knees and squeezed the tube. The same remarkable fluid burped out into her hand in a large glob. *Enough*, she thought.

Although she thought she was already as stimulated as possible, the act of taking Otto's cock in her hand and massaging the gelatinous material along his length nearly put her over the top again. She stared at the thickened cream she massaged along his length.

"Lay back."

Once she was flat against the mattress again, Otto suspended himself over top of her. "Baby, I'm about to agree with you. Maybe I *should* find a grounder job."

"For now, you know what to do, Sky King."

She didn't need to ask twice. Otto surged inside her and within moments, he exploded into her, taking Cairine right along with the intense orgasm they both had needed for a long time.

After, wrapped in each other's arms, both spent and satisfied, Cairine kissed Otto's chest and buried her fingers into the thick hair. "You'd never be happy on the ground, my darling Otto."

Moments passed while he stared at the ceiling's soft lighting that imitated candlelight. When he finally spoke, it followed a strangled sigh. "Yeah…"

Months apart culminated in weeks of aggressive sex, their need to be together, to become part of each other again after such a long absence, so powerful.

Otto nuzzled into Cairine's hair, the softest thing he'd ever felt. Her scent always undid him, made him need her more than anything he'd ever known in his life. Now, ten years into their relationship, yet not ten years older due to her crazy vampire blood, he had known from the beginning that he never wanted to let her go. He wasn't sure how *she* felt. Closing his eyes, he decided that moment…it was time to find out.

"You really can't stay longer than tonight?"

"Sorry, doll. The station is at capacity and they need all hands on. The only reason they had me fly back this soon was because the passenger is the ambassador for European relations. He has a lot of pull."

"Umm…" Daylight was tugging at Cairine, and she couldn't open her eyes. Turning into Otto's warm body, she snuggled close. "Don't leave one moment before you have to."

He lay still for a long time after she'd fallen asleep. That was his intention.

Talib woke, and looked around the dimly lit room, confused. It took a moment to remember that, for the first time in decades, he wasn't home in the forest with Su'ad by his side. Lying in the padded, comfortable bed, he didn't move for many minutes. Overwhelmingly, one feeling struck him. Emptiness. He missed his mate pressed against him, or running her sharp claws along his spine to wake him.

Finally, he forced himself to rise and went into the well-lit, fully supplied lavatory with a shower that looked like a waterfall.

Still naked, he looked for the controls to prepare the shower when he remembered something Cairine had told him last night. *The rooms are voice command now.*

"Water, warm." Within seconds, the shower came alive, a strong pulsing arc of crystal clear water cascaded into the tiled bathing space that was larger than his bedroom back home.

"Su'ad, you would love this," he said out loud as he dunked his head under the generous spray. He missed his home and his family, the community of supernaturals he'd grown to love, but he thought that it might be time to bring some of these modern features to the Patagonian rainforest.

Dressed and refreshed, Talib skipped down the stairs to Cairine's apartment and entered without touching the announcement chimes as requested. Subtle lighting glowed around the edges of the living space, the balcony still closed off with the UV barrier. It was quiet, so he figured she was yet to rouse, but he was hungry and moved toward the galley to start first meal.

After choosing six dishes that he didn't recognize, but sounded interesting, he waited for the little panels to open with his choices prepared and ready to eat. Leaning against the countertop, his arms folded, Talib heard a yawn and looked toward the doorway to welcome his friend.

Someone entered seconds later, but it wasn't Cari. The man was human, big, barefoot, wearing only very thin white shorts that hid none of his genitals. He was scratching his chest and yawning again when he looked up and saw Talib. For several long moments, they stared at each other.

Finally, the human moved forward with an easy smile, his hand out in the ancient practice of handshake.

"Hey, there. Morning. Um, I didn't know Cairine had a guest."

Talib hesitated before taking his hand. So she had a roommate. He found it interesting that she didn't tell him that someone was living with her.

"Yes, I just arrived last night. My name is Talib."

"Talib. I recognize the name. Aren't you from South America?"

"From Patagonia, yes. And I am the one at a loss."

Reaching for the chiming FP, Otto pulled the plates out and set them on the table. Turning back, he removed the remaining plates. "Sorry. Otto Peretti. I'm Cairine's..."

"Friend. Otto is a *close* friend."

Cairine came up behind them and slipped around Otto's large body. "I see you two have met. Talib, Otto has been my blood-bond and lover for the past ten years or so. He pilots shuttles between the orbital bases and Mars, and showed up unexpectedly last night. Otherwise, I would have already introduced you to each other."

Smiling, Talib took Otto's hand and held it for seconds longer than necessary, his eyes moving over Otto. He knew that Cairine hadn't been with Eras since that first year they'd all went out into the world. And while he knew she wouldn't have been uninvolved with a man for all the years since, it was strange to see this huge human in her home. He'd always thought that she and Eras were meant to be. But here he was, the man she'd chosen to share her life with, human, and it looked like quite accomplished.

"I am honored to meet you. Cairine is quite extraordinary."

Otto glanced at her, and Talib could see the devotion in his eyes. So he was in love with her. He wondered if Cairine reciprocated, but she wasn't transmitting any clues to him. He stood silently, watching them.

After an awkward silence, Cairine tugged Otto and Talib to the glass table where Otto had placed Talib's plates. "Eat. I'll prepare everything else. Otto, you've been offworld for a long time, so I'll order all your favorites. And Talib, I'm going to introduce you to all of *mine*."

As she turned to the FP, Cairine rolled her eyes. Talib had always been the most private and sensitive of her vampire friends, but she was surprised that he seemed uncomfortable with meeting her lover. He *had* to know that she'd have someone.

And Otto, her overgrown space cowboy, had a wild streak and mischievous sense of humor. He was likely to play with Talib's discomfort.

A tickle began in her belly, though, that she was here in her home with two men that she loved with all her heart. While she was never lonely, Cairine missed her family. The years flew by, everyone so busy and on opposite sides of the globe, she considered the question on her mind: how long had it been since most of them had been together? Forty, or was it *fifty*, years?

Just as she finished placing the food orders, the chime for her apartment interrupted.

"*Answer*," she called out, as she headed back into the living space. Smiling, she saw another man that she'd loved for a long time grinning into the camera.

"*Allow access*."

The door slid into the wall and Jackson hurried through, a small crystal tablet in his hands, and a ready welcome. "Hey, gorgeous!"

He still wore the short afro cut that he'd had when she first met him over a century ago. A trimmed beard and series of crystal earrings up the earlobe of his left ear were the most noticeable changes. Other than that, little had changed in all those years thanks to his daily doses of Cairine's blood. His smooth mocha skin tight and unlined, he was still fully human.

"Hey, handsome. I thought you were in L.A."

"Just got back earlier today. Glad to see you, but we have a lot to go over. I just coordinated the data for the past three months between L.A., Seattle, and Yellowstone. You need to see this."

"Shit. A crisis first thing. Well, come eat with us, and then we'll retire to look at your numbers."

Jackson followed her into the galley. First he noticed Otto, who he hadn't expected. "Hey! Thought you were on Mars." Then his eyes moved to Talib. "Holy hell! There's a face out of the past! Talib, isn't it? Cari, you have a full house tonight."

"Three hot guys. What more can a girl ask for? Take a seat, Jax, I know what you like."

Entering several more food choices into the unit, Cairine looked behind her. The men were already reaching for the food on the table, Jackson easily engaging the other two who were strangers to each other in casual conversation.

This was what it was all about. The destiny thing they'd lived with all their lives, the expectation, the battle, wherever or whenever it would come. These beautiful souls, loving men who really cared about this world and all life on it, and beyond. Those doves, likely the last of their kind, and all others who struggled to find a small spot on this overcrowded planet; humans, supernaturals, vampires…all life.

Whatever information Jackson brought with him, the tone in his voice, the serious look in his eyes…it wasn't good.

Two

IN PARIS

The brutal blow landed on Taylor's shoulders, forcing him forward so hard, his head struck one of the hardwood posts holding up the roof of the pergola. Pushing back to his feet, he recovered quickly and spun out of the path of a roundhouse kick that might have ended the fight. She was coming at him with all she had.

Good. She needed the practice and so did he. Coming from behind her, Taylor got a good grip on her to lose it seconds later when she flipped him up and over her head to land flat on his back, out of air and out of time. Unable to breathe, he was done.

He lifted a hand, his words finally making it out past labored gasps. "Fia, stop! I give!"

Fia lowered her hands and stood in front of Taylor as she reached out to help him stand. "Pussy."

"Bitch."

"Human!"

"Barely. Anymore, anyway. Give me a few more months, and I think I can take you."

"You think that cocktail will make you true competition for a vampire?"

"I think that Rodney's proof anything can happen."

Shrugging, Fia pulled her gloves off. "You're probably right."

Her eyes moved over Taylor's new body. He *was* fucking huge. Before they began the sparring session, he'd tugged off his muscle shirt since the air had continued to warm now that summer was closing in. His smooth chest had all the right curves, hard pecs, and the desired six pack. She'd done all she could for the past few months not to notice. In the years since they'd been assigned here, she and Taylor had worked well together, with excellent clinical results, but they'd always butted heads. Two strong personalities in one room was rarely successful.

Chione had called six months ago to explain that they needed to begin giving him the super-cocktail of multiple First Blood vampire's blood. It would change him into the same kind of human-vampire hybrid they'd discovered through giving the cocktail to Rodney for decades. Rodney wasn't 100 percent human anymore, and although he wasn't vampire, he had all the power and strength of one. But he could live in daylight.

Chione, in her role as protector and guide for the children born to fight for the earth, had said he was chosen for this destiny by the powers-that-be. Taylor, shocked, had agreed, and been taking what he called the "vile vial" since then. The results had been as expected, and he'd developed several interesting powers and the exceptional body of a first blood vampire.

"Ugh!" Taylor reached for his shirt. "I'm hitting the showers. I'll make it in today, but it might be a while. You hit like a girl!"

"Thank you." She knew what he meant. Taylor still clung to a lot of the things he loved before he joined the vampire community over a century earlier. He easily admitted to her that women had always been able to best him, emotionally *and* physically, and that had not changed when he came to Paris twenty years ago to work with Fia in the WHO.

"You remember that," she called back as she turned to pick up her own gear.

"Like I'm going to question the prime director of the World Health Organization. Who happens to be my boss."

"Smart man."

"So I'll see you in a few hours. I may be in the process of converting to this weird hybrid Chione and Donovan want me to be, but I still hurt like a mother when you put me down like a dog."

"Oh, Taylor, man up. If you're going to have vampire skills, take the beating like one."

"I said it before. Bitch."

"Takes one to know one." Fia grabbed her pack and blew out of the garden. Slowing down before she reached her cabin, she started laughing and spoke out loud to herself. "Why the fuck do we act like teen-agers? I don't know why they put us together. God, we're not good for each other."

She hadn't realized she'd spoken aloud until a deep voice answered her.

"Bull. You two push each other to be better, and it works. I haven't been here too long, and yet I can see that."

Fia pitched her pack onto a bench and turned toward Ari. After a long minute staring at the koi swimming in the little pond Ari insisted on digging into the garden, she looked into his odd-colored eyes. "Maybe. How are you feeling?"

"Improving daily. I have been able to take short flights over the sea the past two days. Thank you for devising that remedy. I've never been sick before this."

"New country, new world, for someone used to the isolation of the rain forest. You were bound to react to the bacteria and viruses you've never been exposed to. Happy to help, Ari. It's what I do."

Fia searched the slender Totem whose spirit animal was a hawk. "Ari, just remember to be careful. There are always eyes here and very few places without surveillance vids."

"I know. I only change forms on the sand in pitch darkness. Taylor has been going with me sometimes as look out. He's a good man."

Fia rolled her eyes again. "Yeah, yeah, he's a prince. Okay, I'm getting cleaned up and heading to work. You feel up to taking a partial shift tonight?"

Ari nodded. "I'll get something to eat and come in with you."

"Nifty. Meet me back here in half an hour."

Later, leading Ari through the lab, Fia explained some of their work to him as they walked down the long hallway.

"This is a level 5 Biohazard facility. We handle new and unknown pathogens here to determine nature, origin, threat assessment and containment."

"Great. More contaminants. Since I'm avian, I wonder why the Guides sent me here."

"Ari, we know that they receive their commands from the Powers. You are supposed to be here and you *do* have a place. Remain confident of your role. We all have one to play when the time comes. Chione told me once that all we have to do is remain true to ourselves and our mission. Everything else will take care of itself."

Bowing, Ari lifted his head to capture Fia's gaze, on level with hers since they were the same height.

"Forgive me. I am still adjusting to being away from my home. Without my brothers and sisters, and my community, I feel lost here."

Placing a hand on each of Ari's shoulders, Fia moved closer. "For all purposes, *we* are family too. We are your community by order of the universe. We share the same power and air of the living world, so don't feel lonely. Embrace the differences and just enjoy Paris and the interesting life you'll have here. I promise. You'll come to love us."

"Namasté, Fia. I think I can see that. You are a lovely, gracious, generous woman. I am honored to be welcomed into your world. It may take me some time longer, but I will adjust. We Totems have a long history of adaption, as you are aware."

"Namasté, brother. Let's go find some germs."

Ari stopped in his tracks, grimaced, then followed Fia into the level 5 biohazard containment module.

IN AUSTRALIA

"You are lazy as hell tonight, mate!"

Eras rolled over and grabbed the beautiful blonde before she could get out of bed.

"I'm lazy as hell every night, because bed is my favorite place to be. If I could, I'd never get up. Got an idea. You could bring me first meal and then stay here *with* me."

Beanie pulled loose and stood, her hands cupping her full breasts, the fingers moving over the nipples. "You are gonna wear these out."

One hand wandered down to press between her legs.

"Not to mention my supergirl here. I gotta go to work. Tio doesn't hold his jobs when a girl comes in late too often."

"You could quit."

"We've had this conversation, Eras. I like my job. I'm fucking good at it. When you move on and dump my sweet ass someday, I'll still be able to make a living."

Eras groaned and rolled back over to stare at the ceiling. "Bean, I am *not* going to move on and dump you."

She leaned down and kissed him hard on the lips, tugged on his cock, and walked to the door.

"Sweets, *everyone* moves on. It's the way of the world. See you later tonight, vampire."

For half an hour after the door closed, Eras lay spread-eagle on the giant mattress that filled most of the room. He'd rested well, he always did, but he just couldn't convince himself to rouse. He had rounds to make, the damn inventory needed constant monitoring, but his body was in a state of rest and the laws of inertia, being what they were, unless an outside force acted on him, he was pretty sure he was going to remain at rest.

Another hour passed as he dozed again, awakened sharply by his chiming fone.

"Shit!" *The outside force...*

He reached for his fone on the shelf near his bed, but once he touched it, he had full voice command and pitched it onto the adjacent pillow. Dropping his head back down, his eyes closed again, he bellowed, "What?"

Bura's deep graveled voice floated from wall-suspended speakers.

"You still with Beanie?"

"She's gone. What is it?"

"That blight that started in Sector 10 has spread. I need you to come assess the damage and decide on the action to protect the rest of the crop."

"Where's Nur?"

"She's at HQ. They want reports, specifics on produce health, quality, and max capacity. There's a small area in southern Africa that claims to have starvers."

"No way. Our yields feed two hundred times what they did just four years ago. If someone is starving in Africa, they aren't too interested in eating."

"Eras, I really need you, buddy."

"Yeah, I know, I'll be there. It's just lack of motivation, I'll be fine."

Using air displacement, Eras was showered, dressed, and out the door within fifteen minutes. He did the job he was assigned to do, and he did it well.

Australia had become one of the world's biggest produce hubs. Ninety percent of the continent was now an enormous farm that produced twenty-two varieties of vegetables. The country fed the eastern half of the globe. All Eras had to do was protect it from every threat. Most of the time, it was easy.

Thousands of rows spread over most of the landscape that spanned into the sky, each thirty-eight vertical rows high. Irrigation required only five percent of the water that would have been needed to grow crops the old traditional way in soil on the ground. Yields were higher, pests rarely a problem, and successful harvests approached one hundred percent. On occasion, where a problem did occur, it was critical to find it and contain it instantly. The loss of a significant percentage of Australian produce would create serious consequences for the global food market. Feeding the 60 billion people on Planet Earth took constant effort.

Eras got that his job was vital, he was just bored with it. Bored with being isolated to a country that literally did nothing but grow plants.

"Time to call Chione," he whispered as he stepped into his lift-car and took it up.

What might have been beautiful scenery at one time in history was now just row after row after row into infinity of growth containers suspended from the one above in vertical columns at least forty feet high. In the distance, long rectangular buildings lit by solar lights housed the more fragile varieties as well as genetically modified hybrids designed for extreme growth or size.

Before heading to Sector 10 to meet Bura, Eras took the lift-car to its maximum safe elevation...and then flew beyond it. On a steady climb past safe operation, the lift-car handled the push until the engine began to lug down.

Eras rose another one hundred feet before he caved to the inevitability of engine failure and eased back on the throttle. He allowed the computer to guide it safely back to cruising altitude and to adjust the trajectory to its intended destination.

Daredevil moments made his heart beat faster, something he needed desperately. Last year, he'd joined Caed and Mac for high-altitude ballooning, the first really good time he'd had in many years. Other than sex, which was frequent and satisfying, life here at the bottom of the world that was now just one enormous farm project, wasn't keeping him happy or fulfilled. His unalterable opinion? *His life sucked*.

As the lift-car dropped into his space outside the door of Building 24 in Sector 10, Eras blew out of his seat and managed a sheepish smile to the enormous Totem waiting at the entrance with his arms folded.

"Sorry, buddy." Eras clipped Bura on a thickly muscled shoulder.

Bura kept his stance, feet wide, arms held tight in the unyielding pose. "You said you were coming straight here an hour ago."

Yeah, Eras figured the big bear was pissed. And since, as Totem, Bura's spirit animal actually *was* a bear, he really didn't want to piss him off.

"Yeah, I know. Complications, my friend. Again, I'm sorry."

Bura shrugged and finally dropped his arms to his side.

"I know what your complications are. You need a change. This provincial life is killing your indomitable spirit. You miss the world, Eras."

"This is my place, big bear. Chione and Donovan say this is where I'm meant to be."

"To learn something, yes. I think that the lesson has been taught. All you need to discover now is what you have learned."

Eras stared at Bura. They'd worked together for two decades, with great success, trapped here on this big piece of farmland floating near the bottom of the planet. In that time, they'd become close. He admitted that if anyone knew what kind of man he was now, it was Bura.

"Fuck. Buddy, I have no idea what you're talking about. This has been four decades of dull, mundane, nocturnal hell babysitting freaking sprouts. You know I understand the importance of protecting what we do here, but where's the lesson in that? I'm heading home to a shit apartment at the end of my boring-ass night to my boring-ass life."

Disgusted, Eras pushed past Bura. "Let's go look at this blight. It's the most exciting thing in my life right now."

As he followed Eras into the blue light emitted by crystal diode bulbs that ensured all the tender plants received the right amount of light, Bura watched the tight set of his friend's shoulders, his back ramrod straight. They'd had some rip-roaring, wonderful times over the years, a shared fate in being assigned to the bottom of the world, but lately, Eras's needs had changed. He thought that it might be the first time in history that a vampire was clinically depressed.

He loved the man, he admitted it. He'd never had a brother, but Eras had become one to him. As Totem, emotional connections built into his race, he felt it *his* responsibility to help Eras find his balance again. Eras would not be happy again until he took a spiritual journey to find what was missing.

"Fuck me," Eras whispered as they reached the center of the building and it became apparent that the problem was greater than he realized.

"Yeah. It started out two days ago in the top three pantries, but I noticed this morning that it had spread too quickly. It's aggressive, so I think we need some earth magic here."

"Lucky for you, I'm feeling quite destructive tonight."

"You okay with taking the merge? You feel balanced enough to do it?"

"Bura, you know me better than anybody. I might be a dick sometimes, but I always do my job."

"You do. Get to it, buddy. Let me know what you need from me."

Eras shook his head and grinned. "Just stand back."

An hour later, crunched into the backseat of his lift-car, Eras struggled to keep from throwing up. Pulling in magic from the earth kept him humble; it tore the shit out of him. First blood DNA didn't protect him from severe burnout when he shared the magic he borrowed from the living planet so that he was powerful enough to perform miracles. The food source was safe, thanks to the combination of Mother Earth and Eras. He'd be down for 24 to 48 hours, his own energy zapped, but it would return with enough rest.

Bura gratefully flew him home, tucked him in, and called Beanie at the bar.

"He's spent tonight. Magic merge."

"Aw." Beanies voice, soft, her Australian accent charming to Bura, travelled through the fone. "Thanks for the heads-up, mate. I'll head home soon and take care of him. Cheers."

IN THE COLORADO ROCKIES

Outside her apartment door, Cairine held tight to Otto, a final hug before he left.

"It is so hard to say goodbye to you when it will be another four weeks before I see you again."

"I know. I wish you could come with me."

"Yeah..." Cairine drew out the comment. "Direct UV would really be exciting for us, for about thirty seconds until I went up in flames."

His hands wrapped around her face, Otto stared into her ocean green eyes as he memorized them. "Never. I wouldn't let anything hurt you."

"You wouldn't, I know that. So, no other choice, you go do your job, bring your clients home safe, and we'll take a few weeks soon and spend every minute in our bed. Sound good?"

"Sounds like heaven. Until then, miss me sometimes."

"Miss me too."

Otto disappeared down the hall as Cairine closed her door. *Miss me sometimes, miss me too.* It had become their standard farewell before he left for a mission. Space travel was much safer now than it had ever been, accidents fairly rare, but it was still a dangerous job. They lingered on each goodbye, just in case it might be the last.

Her fingers to her lips, caressing where Otto had touched, she looked up to see Talib smiling at her.

"You love him."

Passing by him, she led him onto the cantilevered balcony where two doves waited. Her eyes on his, she leaned against the railing. "I do. Otto is one of the finest men I've ever known. We see each other for a few weeks every time he's earthside. But he's gone for two or three months at a time."

"Might be the perfect relationship. Always saying hello or goodbye. Tender moments."

"Sad, sometimes. But in this case, you're right. It's perfect for us. He's a skypilot, he loves what he does. He belongs above the blue line. I have a destiny that requires most of my time and attention, so a full-time committed relationship would be difficult at best, perhaps impossible."

Nodding, Talib joined her at the edge of the balcony and lifted one of the doves on a finger. "It's indescribably beautiful up here."

"Mmm. Nowhere else feels more like home to me."

Scanning the environmentally lit landscape, amazed how no light beams escaped up into the sky, where nothing interfered with the natural boundaries, Talib glanced back to Cairine.

"So you and Eras are finished?"

Moments passed before she answered. "We never really had much of a beginning. That first year we left our homes, he came to me. We had ten months of passionate lovemaking. It was glorious. I'd had a crush on him for years. I still remember the feeling in my belly when he showed up that night."

After several more moments of silence, she sighed.

"It was beautiful. He told me that he wanted to be my first, and he was. But I'd already known that after that year, we wouldn't see each other for a long time."

"How?"

"A vision. Something like what you get. Fractured, strange, but the message was clear. We weren't meant to be, Talib. For whatever reason, we were never expected to be together for the long haul. I'll never forget how we felt that summer, though. It was pure, unadulterated human love, sex, and joy."

"You really haven't seen him since?"

Cairine shook her head and reached for the second dove, which came to her without hesitation. "No. He's in Australia, isn't he?"

"Chione sent him there several decades ago. He's channeling earth magic."

Her head swiveling to Talib, Cairine turned away from the view. "He is? That's unexpected."

"Everyone thought so at the time, but he's good at it. The power-merge puts him down for a few days, I hear, but he recovers quite quickly."

"Is he..." Cairine slid her hand over the satiny feathers of the dove. "Is he mated?"

"I do not think so. At least, the last I heard, he was not."

Shaking her head, Cairine watched the other two doves circling above them, finding their place on the air. Lost in thought, she didn't move until she felt Talib's fingers on her cheek.

"I'm sorry to make you sad, Cari."

"Sad? No, I'm not sad. Reflective, perhaps. Revisiting might-have-beens, but that never does anyone any good. Talib, I'm happy with my life, I love Otto, and while he isn't a mate for me, I think we have many years of love ahead."

"He's committed to you."

"He is. Come, first meal waits, and I plan to fly you to Denver for an amazing classic American meal of hamburgers, French fries, and apple pie."

IN ZAMBIA

Daylight waned, and Chione lingered in the bed she'd shared with Donovan for over a century. It still felt new, waking next to him, his even breathing always the first thing she heard when she opened her eyes. Rolling onto her side, she watched him in the pale light that illuminated their bed chamber. How was it possible to love him more with each passing year? She would have sworn she loved him with all her heart and soul the moment she realized that he was her mate all those years ago.

But each day brought a fresh understanding of how incredible it was that she'd found the one person meant to be her mate, and having the chance to make a life with him. Her hand moved down his back and she felt him arch toward her.

"Are you looking for something, lady? 'Cause, I have something that you might like."

Donovan turned over and showed her what he held in his hand.

"Ah, yes, I *would* like that, but I have to tell you something first. A vision came tonight."

Pushing upright, Donovan pulled his pillow up to lean against it. "The missing warriors?"

"Finally. I was beginning to think that we were done, but this vision revealed the remaining five."

"Okay. Nothing like waiting until the eleventh hour. So, who are the lucky humans who will never be the same again?"

"Amazingly, four are in the U.S. One, a woman, is in India."

"Unexpected. Okay. Did you get names or just random clues that we get to unravel?"

"A bit of both. Baby, let's get first meal and then I'll lay out the information."

"I'm good with that. Only…"

Donovan's eyes moved down Chione's body, from her full breasts to long slim legs tucked beneath her. "First…"

Three hours later, seated beneath a flowering tree transplanted from Park's garden in France, Chione touched her mate on the knee. "You will not believe who one of the human warriors is."

Waiting for long moments for her to continue, Donovan tilted his head.

"You've watched too many televids. You have the dramatic *expectant pause* down. Tell me."

"One of the revealed is a young woman in New York City. She is Rodney's daughter."

"Koen's Rodney?"

"Yes. It was a bit of a surprise."

"But I'm fairly certain that Rodney can't have children."

"The universe doesn't get this wrong. She's waitressing in a restaurant on the privileged side of the city. Her name is Scottie."

"Huh. Rodney is going to be shocked. So who are the other four?"

"Twins, in the southern state of Louisiana. I was thinking about sending Jackson and Sally to introduce them to their unknown destiny."

"Perfect choice."

"Another woman resides in India. I believe she is a physician. This will come as a fascinating surprise to her."

Chione paused again, her expression puzzled. "The last one is shadowed. Although I felt him, I could not see him. Chaos and sorrow surrounds him, but I saw nothing beyond that. No sense of who he is or what he may bring to the team, just a very specific location in Arizona and a name that is not a name."

"Like a nickname?"

"Yes. Yes, that is it."

"So we need to contact each and let them know their place in this battle. It's going to be interesting. We should have them all brought here at the same time to indoctrinate them. It will be easier for them as well as us."

"Agreed. Olivia is somewhat empathic and as first blood, able to control unusual situations. We should send her to the mystery man in the Arizona desert. For Rodney's daughter, I like Tam and Koen. What do you think?"

"Good choice. Rodney has become a son to Koen, so this young woman, she'll be family too. So, the woman in India?"

"Her name is Antoinette. I have chosen Park to go for her, physician to physician."

"I'll get our fones."

Three

IN LOUISIANA

"Hotter than a beach in hell again, 'bro!" Dani pushed her long spiral curls off her forehead. "Why can't we do this after dark?"

Dylan chuffed as he pushed the heavy barrier in place, aware that his twin sister only marginally helped. "Because it isn't safe around here at night."

"I can take any comers, Brace, you know that."

"Yeah, but they'll tear the shit out of me before you're finished with them. Look, we all know I'm the pussy here."

Dani laughed. "My six foot three pussy brother. You do not need to worry your soft little head. I'll always take care of you."

Dylan "Brace" Milliér stopped long enough to catch his breath. Dani might be a third smaller than he was but he admitted freely to anyone that she was better trained and significantly stronger than he was. He'd never understood how his tiny sister could out-bench him, outrun him, and outperform him on nearly any physical event. Thing was, it wasn't just him. No one in the parish could outperform her.

He wasn't jealous, he was proud of her. Nearly everything seemed to come easily for both of them. Now finishing their doctorates in multi-disciplinary sciences, they were excited to see what else they could accomplish to help fix this ailing world.

Dragging in a big gulp of the hot air, he pushed against the concrete slab. "Dani, please, you've ten times my power. Help here. Please?"

"Okay, but you owe me. I have the first date tonight that I've had in six months and I'm going to smell like rotting fish!"

Relieved, Dylan joined Dani, now fully engaged, and they pushed the concrete barrier in place along the seawall. There. This would offer some protection to the declining sea-life that came here to spawn.

"Victory! I appreciate your sacrifice. If you want my advice, don't offer to hand-wrestle him on the dinner table. Men prefer to wait until later in the relationship to be emasculated."

Dani punched Dylan in the arm without holding back much, the explosion against his heavy bicep forcing him backward so hard, he fell over the three foot high barrier.

"Shit, Brace, I'm sorry! I really do need to remember to pull my punches. The world isn't ready for me, is it?"

Dylan pulled himself up to rest his arms on the top of the concrete, one hand massaging the damaged shoulder.

"No, it isn't, but you're coming out into it anyway. Go, get cleaned up, have a successful date that results in a stay-over."

"Ugh! Advice on getting laid from my brother. Cool, that ain't, *cher*."

"Hey, you deserve a good night."

"I do. This guy…he's different. Came out of nowhere last night when I finished my shift. Handsome, smart, dressed nice, not from around here. I liked him right away, and you know our instincts are never wrong."

"They never are. I wouldn't have to worry about you anyway. If he tries anything, *he'll* be the one hurting. Have a great night."

Dani nearly skipped away to slide into the little sports car they'd both saved to buy for her, and disappeared down the lonely access road to this abandoned beach.

Dylan turned around and rested his back against the wall they had erected. It was so beautiful here. Trying to save this beach and those who depended on it to survive had been a long-term battle.

Erosion was playing its part destroying this fragile habitat, but the rising sea level was mostly to blame. He figured that he was fighting a losing battle, but fight he must. This was home. Or at least, the home he'd known as he grew up next to the encroaching ocean.

Soon, he'd be gone forever, and he knew that this beach would be too. Most of New Orleans was underwater now, and if things continued as they had been for the past eighty years, then yes, his home would become only a memory by the time he came back.

"Time to let go," he whispered. Like Dani's, his own coiled hair lay heavily against his brown skin, slick now from exertion in temperatures that could have fried an egg on the hood of his car. His white muscle shirt was soaked too, and although he did *not* have a date tonight like his sister, he wanted to get home to a cool shower and down a Snowball. New Orleans famous sweet ice-drink would hit the spot more than anything else right now.

Since this was the first of their last two nights here in the parish, tonight would include the cool down, then a visit to meet his friends down at the *Salty Dawg* for drinks and goodbyes.

He half hoped that Dani would meet him there later, and half hoped that her date would go well and she would have a romantic night. She could use it.

He sighed as he pushed off the sand. So could he.

As she drove toward downtown Metairie, just north of the partially submerged New Orleans, Dani thought about how long it had been since her last "hook up." It had been two years since she'd had sex, and now, in her mid-twenties, she was ready to make a connection again. This man she was meeting had charmed her from the first smile. There was something about him that seemed different. What it was, she couldn't put her finger on, but whatever strange talent she had to "read" people, had led her to him when he'd walked into the café where she worked.

Entering the restaurant she had chosen, she scanned the low-lit room and found her date leaning against the bar. Unexpectedly feeling apprehensive, Dani approached, hoping that she'd chosen the right dress for a first date; this socializing thing wasn't in either her or Dylan's skill set.

Her eyes moved over his well-built, comfortably lounging body.

"Hi, Jackson." She hoped her greeting sounded casual and not full of the excited expectation she felt.

He gave her the same warm smile that had enchanted her when she first saw him earlier in the day.

"Dani, you look lovely. I've already secured a table by the window."

He left her dumbfounded. Since childhood, she and Dylan had been able to tell the measure of a person almost immediately. Was this person honest? Generous, truthful, deceitful? Kind or cruel? People's true natures could not hide from the precocious toddlers. The skill had developed with the years so that now, at 26, she and her brother could guide their relationships appropriately.

But this man...

She didn't know what to think of him.

That he was honest and gentle, she had no doubt. But there was something...some aspect of who or what he was that she could feel, but not define. She planned to find out.

Tonight would be illuminating.

Jackson led the unexpectedly attractive young woman he'd been sent to meet to the table he'd chosen. Because of his lengthy blood-bond to Cairine, he had the ability to *sway* people's behavior in his direction. He couldn't compel them like a vampire could, and sometimes it didn't work at all, but he could often gain an outcome he desired. Using his skill, he'd procured this private table even though it had been reserved for some local celebrity. The prime spot was perfect to assess the right way to approach this new warrior and her brother.

Sally waited at the bar for his signal to join them.

He watched Dani take her seat, her carriage regal, her movements elegant. He meant it when he told her that she looked lovely. Long spirals of pitch-black hair coiled on top of her head as several curls escaped to lay against naked caramel-colored shoulders. She wore a simple sundress with spaghetti straps, and he sent a thank-you to whoever designed the barely-there straps. She'd make an interesting addition to their small group of earth guardians.

Tonight would be illuminating.

Jackson picked up a menu. "Shall we order, and then get to know each other while we wait for our meal to arrive?"

"Sure. I've eaten here before and I already know what I want. It's a local Cajun meal, spiced to the heavens, but if you like heat, you won't forget this dish very soon."

Nodding, Jackson laid the menu back on the table.

"I will take your advice and go for it. I *do* like spicy."

Aware of the double-entendre, Dani tilted her head.

"Then you just might enjoy this date."

Promises, she thought. Let's see how he does with that tidbit. If he jumped on it, he might not be who she hoped he was.

Jackson didn't say anything, he just watched her for a few moments. Suddenly, he leaned closer. "Dani, I think I just realized how to handle this situation. You're an honest and direct woman. No games here tonight."

No games? What games did he mean? Suspicious, Dani stilled. "Um, what do you mean?"

"I brought you here to assess how to tell you something that will change your life. I've decided that I'm going to come straight out with it. I came to Louisiana for you and your brother. You two have a destiny far grander than either of you know. You're human, like me, but I know already, neither one of you are normal."

Spooked, Dani nearly stood and walked out of the restaurant. The only thing that kept her in her seat was her ability to know that this strange man across from her meant everything he said, and there was no malice.

"I don't understand."

A soft voice behind her said, "We're here to explain."

Dani looked up at a tall slender woman with long blonde hair pulled back in a loose ponytail. She was beautiful, confident, and a complete stranger.

Now, this was all too much. Pushing her chair back, Dani laid her napkin on the table. "You don't need to. Whatever this is, I'm not interested."

As she turned to go, Jackson slid his fingers loosely around her upper arm. "Dani, you will be. You will be fascinated and grateful for what we have to reveal to you. Please, half an hour, that's all we ask."

Moving her gaze from Jackson's earnest dark eyes to the blonde woman's soft blue eyes, she used her skill and reached for each of these two odd people. What she read was complete openness and honorable intentions. Whatever they wanted with her, they were excited about it. Seconds passed before she could bring herself to listen to her instincts. Finally, Dani lowered herself back into the seat and picked up her water glass. "Thirty minutes."

AT *THE SALTY DAWG*

"Play that funky music, white boy!"

Dylan swirled the local craft beer he would miss a lot, and lifted it up after taking a long sip. "Whoo!"

His closest buddy Kev was up on the small stage, strumming out some gawd-awful crap that only passed for music amongst friends. Luckily, in the small neighborhood bar, nearly everyone was, so when Kev insisted on playing some of his own compositions, no one booed his attempts.

Everyone has a dream, Dylan thought. He hoped that once he was gone, the locals would continue this tradition of welcoming everyone's art, no matter how good or bad. Kev didn't have a lot of good things in his life, but this place was one of them.

Kev came off the stage grinning, his guitar slung over his back. "Whew. I'm beat. We brought out three tons of waste today."

For the past four years, Kev had been working with a group that was trying to salvage some of the city of New Orleans from where the sea had claimed it. It was dirty, dangerous work, but paid better than a lot of jobs in this depressed area. No one wanted to hang around a seaside city that was on the brink of submersion.

"Here. Have a beer on me."

"Thanks, 'bro." Kev dropped down onto his chair after leaning his guitar against the tabletop. "That's good, Brace. Man, I'm fuckin' gonna miss you!"

"Me too, bud. But you're going to come out and visit me. A bunch, okay?"

"Sure." Kev's eyes wandered to the stage. He knew he wouldn't. His friend was going to a job in a big corporation in Chicago. Not only did he figure his buddy would never be back, Kev felt certain that he'd never see Dylan again. *Yeah. It was how life rolled.*

"So, Dani must be really excited."

"Can a fish swim?"

"Figured. I'll miss you both as I slide into the sea, never to see the sun again."

"Kev, I'm serious, why don't you come and stay with me and Dani? We're getting a big apartment in the city center with plenty of room."

Kev polished off his can of beer. After a big belch, he slid his eyes toward Dylan. "Naw. I don't belong in the big city, 'bro. I don't fit. Naw, I'll just visit ya there. Hey, I'm fixin' to order the biggest pizza pie they have in celebration. You hungry?"

Hoping to return to their lighter mood, Dylan grinned. "Always!"

With an obnoxious yell, Kev called for their server.

Dylan lifted his beer to take a long draw when he noticed Dani coming through the door. "Hey, Kev, Dan's here. Now the party can really get started."

Dani stopped suddenly inside the entrance and turned to a tall man who entered behind her, the stranger followed closely by a very pretty blonde woman. Dani spoke with them and gestured toward his table. He didn't recognize either of them, and if that man was Dani's date, why the hell was she *here*?

He kept his eyes on her as she advanced toward him, and he could read almost at once that something was off. His eyes shot to the man and woman. Had they done something to her?

Dylan pushed his seat back as he stood, ready to confront them, to protect his sister at any cost.

"Dani," he said cautiously. "Is everything all right?"

Her smile was tentative, strange, but genuine. Neither of them had ever been successful at lying to the other.

"It's fine. It's just." She stopped there and looked back to the couple she'd brought with her. "Dylan, I need you to come with us. Now."

His immediate reaction was confrontation. Curious but suspicious, he folded his arms across his chest and stared at the man behind his sister, then at the woman. "Why? Who are these people?"

"That…" Dani hesitated, her eyes following her brother's to the couple close behind her. "That is a big story. Why don't we go back out to the Point where we added the concrete barriers this afternoon?"

Kev hadn't taken his eyes off Sally. "Dude, you should go."

While all this seemed janky, Dylan trusted his sister without question, so he picked up his beer, killed it, scanned his K-card to pay for everything, including the pizza Kev had ordered, and stood. "Kev, I'll try to get back tonight. If I don't see you before we leave, don't worry. We'll meet up again soon. Take care, *cher*."

Out on the Point, no outside lights anywhere near, the sky was black and filled with stars. Only a glow at the horizon line gave relief.

Sally lit a couple of transportable lanterns, placed them on the hood of their cars, and turned to face Dylan.

"So, big guy, ready to find out that the world is so much bigger than you could ever have conceived it to be? I'm Sally, this is Jackson, and we've got quite a lot to tell you."

"I can't even imagine what this is about."

Dani pulled herself up onto one of the concrete barriers. "No, you can't. It's life-altering, *cher*. I'm still reeling some myself. Just listen with an open mind."

"Do I want to hear it?"

Jackson dropped to the sand to lean against the same barrier Dani perched on, swinging her legs past his head.

"Yes, you do, although, honestly, it isn't exactly *your* choice to make. This is all from powers much greater than ourselves."

"Greater? Like the leader of the nation?"

Sally looked up into the star-blanketed sky. "Higher."

Dylan's gaze followed hers. "God?"

"Of a nature. Jackson took point and clued Dani into your destiny, so, for *you*, I'll start."

"Destiny," Dylan repeated, as if he didn't hear her right.

"Destiny. Get comfortable."

Uneasy, Dylan rested his weight against his own car, half certain that this had to be some kind of lame gag from Dani, who he admitted had a wacky sense of humor. Her accomplices were good, though, he'd also admit *that*. His ability to read people wasn't as effective as Dani's, but he still could, and there really *was* something strange about these two that he couldn't put his finger on. It was why he waited patiently for whatever this gorgeous blonde had to say.

"Dylan, you and your sister have always had odd abilities that no one else has, am I right?"

His eyes shooting to Dani, Dylan's unasked question hung in the air. What the hell? They'd long ago realized and agreed that they tell no one what they could do. As children, they'd discovered that people either thought they were crazy or were freaked out by them. But she had told these two about their unnatural skills? He wasn't about to admit to anything.

"Huh. Don't know what you mean."

Sally laughed. "I understand. Okay, here's the gist. Jackson and I are from California. We went to college together to discover, unexpectedly, that we'd been *brought* together by the greater powers of the universe to be a part of an incredible team to protect this world. Over a hundred years ago."

A laugh escaped Dylan's tight lips. "Okay, *now* who's the crazy one?"

"Yep. We sound crazy. Except that everything I'm going to tell you here tonight is true. Although we are completely human, just like you and Dani, we are, technically, over a hundred and twenty years old. You're going to like this part."

IN ARIZONA

Olivia's lift-car flew so low, it left whirlwinds of crushed dust in its wake. Normally, the cars never hovered or flew so low to the surface, but here in this endless desert, with nothing but cactus, and lightning in the distance, keeping near the ground was the easiest way to find her target.

She choked out a laugh, aware that only an occasional prairie dog might hear her. *Like she really knew who or what her target actually was.*

Chione hadn't had much information. Go to the tiny desert town of Tequila Flats and find a man who is destined to become one of the final humans to join the guardians. "I have only a nickname for the man," Chione had told her. "It's *Biker*."

"You don't know his real name or what he looks like?" Olivia had asked.

"No. All I received in the vision was that nickname, the location, the name of a bar, and that he had a traumatic past. I'm sorry, my dear, but that's what we have to work with."

Accustomed to the weird capriciousness of this mission her new family was involved with over the past century, Olivia accepted her challenge and headed to the U.S. to *find* a man with that limited information.

The terrain was rough and unfriendly, mostly harsh scrub and sand, a true desert in appearance and environment. The air was thick and hotter than Hades, even at night. Luckily, she could engage the forceshield and keep the air cool surrounding the open top of the car.

With the car moving across the land at a height of only thirty feet, her view was exceptional. Scanning to the horizon, she admitted that, while rough and uninviting, it was breathtaking here in the desert southwest. Lightning continued to play along the distant perimeter, the harsh brush and cactus almost elegant in the frequent electric illumination. She'd never spent time in a desert before, so this unexpected appreciation surprised her.

"So where are you, biker boy?" she said aloud, as she followed the rarely used highway that cut an endless line through the beige ground beneath her.

Eventually the car approached an area to her right with several buildings and low lights that barely escaped into the dark. As the car flew closer, ancient blue tube lighting identified the bar she sought, *The Crazy Stallion*.

As Olivia lowered the car, she noticed the small unpaved parking area held several lift-cars like hers, several ground vehicles, both cars and modern jet-bikes, and a few old-style gasoline powered motorcycles.

Pushing back her long curly hair, she glanced down at the low-cut vest she'd worn with a short skirt and mid-calf high boots. Pushing her breasts higher, the nipples close to exposure, she grinned.

"Well this ought to get his attention."

Centuries of attention to her considerable feminine attributes had trained Olivia, even before she was vampire, to use them whenever she could. With men, she believed nothing worked better. *Sex sells*, a phrase popular for decades, was quite true.

Slipping from the car, which went into secure mode immediately, she walked past the old-style motorcycles, sliding her fingertips along the smooth curves of a black Harley-Davidson. She remembered some wild sex on one of those back in the 1970's. The long leather seat had supported her ass while a well-endowed young human male had done his best to satisfy her. She couldn't remember if he had.

As she opened the door to enter, hard-driven guitar riffs blasted out, as well as a lot of voices and laughter. A little oasis in the middle of a largely empty desert, the place had more patrons than she expected. Most of the heads turned toward the door as it slammed closed behind her, and kept their attention on her. First blood genetics made her nearly irresistible. She wasn't vain about it, it was just a fact.

Smiling, Olivia headed to the bar, where a bar stool became available immediately as a tall, rough-looking dark-skinned man stood. He might have been handsome some thirty years ago, but life's troubles and human aging had taken their toll on him. He had a lovely smile.

"I appreciate the seat, young man," she commented, her British accent uncommon in this area, and watched the smile widen. It was true, compared to *her* lifespan, he was a child.

"Could I get a whisky sour, heavy on the whisky?"

Several men scrambled to place the order for her, but her new friend had claimed the right. "Love exotic women. I can't imagine why a vision such as you would visit this hole in the universe, and that's *not* a complaint."

"Sweet." Olivia spun in the seat and let her eyes roam over the group of mostly men. Only two women were present in the smoky din. Very few people smoked cigarettes or cigars anymore, but it seemed popular here. Turning back, she leaned in. "Do you know a man who goes by the name of *Biker*?"

The tall man leaned against the counter and gingerly touched Olivia's hand with his index finger. "I can go by any name you want."

Sighing, Olivia leaned into him, curled her hands around his collar and pulled him closer. "Look into my eyes."

He didn't hesitate.

"Now. Tell me, do you know a man called Biker?"

His manner stiff, it took a second for him to respond to her compulsion. "Uh...yeah. Yeah, he was here earlier. Ain't seen him around for an hour or so. He might be at the waterin' hole."

"And where is this waterin' hole?"

"Out back. It gets mighty hot around here. It's the desert, you know."

"I gathered. Thank you."

Although she was petite, she had no trouble sliding off the too-high bar stool. Running a long fingernail over the thickened bulge in the man's jeans, she smiled up at him.

"You should get that looked after. Sorry I can't help you tonight."

Breezing out the back of the bar into almost pitch blackness, Olivia slowed her speed that was still slightly faster than a human could move. After a few moments, her eyes adjusted, and when they did, she noticed dim candlelight some distance from the noisy bar.

"The waterin' hole, I presume." Drawing another long breath, she told herself that she deserved a nice night on the town in either Los Angeles or New York City for taking care of Chione's little human project. The way Chione had described him, the little she knew about him, he was likely to be as uninspiring as this backwater dive. Besides, she'd been in Brazil with her family for the past year, hidden away in Dez's fortress, so she was ready to break out and party.

"Find this guy, get him clued in, get him to Chione and Donovan in Zambia, and head somewhere civilized," she murmured as she approached a strange pool dug into the sandy ground. Flickering candles created a weird strobe-like effect, but, this close, they were bright enough to show a single man at the other end of the pool. Leaning against the edge, his head laid back on the stones that lined the crude pool, his face was turned away from her.

"Hey, buddy. Are you Biker?"

Several seconds passed before he roused and rolled his head toward her. From that distance, she couldn't see his features clearly.

"I might be. I might not. Who are you?"

His voice was graveled, deep, as if he hadn't spoken in a while.

Frustrated, Olivia didn't like his attempt to control this situation. "Could you come out here and look at me? I'll identify myself then."

"It's pretty cool in here. You better start talking if you want to convince me to do it."

"Oh, for fuck's sake, come out of there."

That demand got his attention. As if in slow motion, he rose from the water, which couldn't have been more than three feet deep, rivulets pouring from him. Unbidden, Olivia found herself mesmerized by his movement, her eyes locked on him as he stood, tall, a body as ripped as any man she'd ever seen, pushing back long hair as it dripped over his face. He was naked, and she thought that he should always be.

This man Chione had dreamed of was magnificent. Olivia held her breath as he cleared the pool and walked to her, every muscle gleaming in the limited light as the water continued to slide over his skin. Once her eyes moved to the oversized organ hanging between his legs, she didn't lift them again until he cleared his throat.

Her gaze went straight to his face, which she admitted was every bit as sexy as his cock. Square jaw, long dark hair that hadn't obeyed him when he pushed it back dripped over pale blue eyes. His cheeks were covered by thick stubble which did not hide an old scar that ran from below his left eye to his mouth. It did not detract at all from the overt masculine sex appeal of this man. Big muscled arms crossed over his chest as he spread his legs and watched her. She recognized the symbol tattooed in dark ink that covered his right shoulder, then brought her eyes back to his.

They stared at each other for over sixty seconds before he cleared his throat again. "Look, whatever you're sellin', I'm not buyin'." His voice deepened as he looked

Olivia over from her full black hair to stiletto-heeled boots inappropriate for the desert. "Not that you aren't hotter than hell. Fuck, whoever sent you tore you from my dreams. But I'm not in the market or mood. Go find another customer. You won't have any trouble with that."

Olivia's eyes dropped back between his legs, where his left hand cupped the expanding cock. His eyes followed hers.

"Yeah, well, it has a mind of its own. I meant it, you could turn on any man on the planet, but this one isn't interested. Go back inside, gorgeous."

He turned away and started across the trail behind the pool.

"Biker," Olivia called out. "This isn't something you can choose. You must come with me."

Will had been at least thirty feet from the striking woman and yet suddenly there she was, in front of him.

How could she be so fast?

She reached up to capture his face, and pulled it down to her, a hard reach for one so much shorter, his nose now only a few inches from her. His eyes went to hers, and his head swam. Damn, he'd been drinking, but had never experienced this kind of dizziness, even after the accident.

He struggled to speak and failed. "Umm..."

"You must come with me. We have much to discuss."

Shaking his head in hopes that the motion would clear the fuzziness, Will looked back into those mesmerizing eyes. Finally, his mind cleared and he could utter an understandable word again. "No offense, lady, but you're not my type."

"I'm everyone's type."

"Not mine."

"How so?"

Will paused, his eyes moving over a face he thought he might never forget. "Because you're the type a man falls in love with. That isn't me. I don't do emotional entanglements."

"Really? You never have?"

He shifted his gaze to the horizon behind her as it lit up with multiple horizontal bolts of lightning. "Not recently. Look, I don't share. Go back to the bar. I guarantee you'll have your pick of *dates*."

Olivia pushed the compulsion to force his compliance to her will. Locked on, she watched him close his eyes and shake his head again. He was locked in to *her* now, too.

"Biker, what is your real name?"

"I was born Willoughby Jasper Collins."

"Why do they call you Biker?"

"I'm the last dinosaur. I ride an old gas-powered bike that will hit 150 years old in a few months."

"I saw it in the parking area. It's a sexy machine."

"Yeah. I like how it feels between my legs."

Olivia had been fighting her sexual reaction to this warrior she'd been sent to initiate, but that comment sent her eyes to his now filled cock. Oh, *powers-that-be*, if she wasn't careful, she'd be naked and on top of this man riding him hard…without sanction or permission. He was under compulsion, and she'd never had sex with anyone under forced influence. It would never be necessary, and she never would.

But, fuck's sake, she wanted him! Likely without even knowing it, he was sending out sexual pheromones that nearly sent her to her knees to take him.

Turning her back on him, she took the moments necessary to pull herself back together.

"Get dressed."

He hesitated, then shocked her by stepping toward her. That shouldn't have been possible. With that specific command, he should have immediately reached for his clothing and dressed quickly.

"Put your clothes on. Now," she pushed.

He did not move. Humans could be compelled. Period. No escape, no choice, no loopholes. *What in the hell was going on?*

"Biker." Perhaps physical contact would do it. Olivia moved to him, and placed a hand on a hard curved bicep.

"Go now and dress."

Stilled in place, Will took her hand and brought it to his lips. "And then, what? What do you want with me?"

"I'm taking you with me. We need to talk."

Will dropped her hand and stepped back. "Life hasn't been kind to me or those involved with me. I must be paying for some bad karma in a previous life. Run, gorgeous. Run fast and far, but leave this old broken down dog behind."

He reached for a bundle of clothes on a rough wood table and walked away from the woman who was the most attractive he'd ever seen. She made him uneasy. Many years ago he'd stopped getting involved with anyone he might ever think he could feel any attachment to. Safer for all.

Frozen in place by the incongruity of events tonight, Olivia watched Will disappear into the darkness beyond the pool. It didn't matter where he went, she could outrun him now that she'd found him, but his ability to defy her compulsion gave her pause. Chione was right, this *normal* human man was anything *but* normal.

"Biker." As she moved toward him, her voice loud enough to pierce the distance, her vampire vision efficient even with little light, she finally found him heading around the edge of the building toward the parking area where that Harley Davidson she had admired earlier waited for him. His dark outline against the navy sky continued away from her. He had dressed.

"Biker, you must wait for me. Stop." Then, smiling, wondering if it would work, she said, "Will."

It worked, making her think that people around here didn't use or even *know* his real name. He stopped at that moment but didn't turn toward her. "I think we finished our business."

"You may think so, but we haven't." Olivia walked around his body, as immoveable as a mountain.

"Let me explain something to you. I have some special skills, and one of them is a method of compulsion where I can make someone like you do anything and everything I want by simply asking. It works on everyone. Oddly, it didn't work on you. You understand my confusion in this circumstance then, yes?"

"Sure." She could hear the amusement in his voice. He didn't believe her, of course he didn't, but at least she got his attention.

"Anyway, you're something different. What, I don't know, but since my usual tactics didn't work to get you where I need you, I guess I'll have to use my considerable charms and powers of persuasion on you."

"Lady, truth-be-told, I'd love to have you *persuade* me all night, but I meant what I said. People get hurt around me. If you're wise, you'll go inside the bar and pick out a nice big cowboy and fuck *him* all night."

"Will, I'm here for you. You need to come with me. There are greater things in this world than you or I. And you don't have to worry about me, Biker, I'm quite unbreakable."

Both his hands moved toward Olivia, and slid along her chin until he cupped her face in them. "Right at this moment, I wish more than anything that was true."

"Would you like me to prove it to you?"

"Waste of time. A china doll in the arms of a bulldozer."

"Hardly. Show and tell time."

Although Will easily weighed twice what Olivia did, she lifted him over her shoulder and transported him the hundred feet from where they'd been to where her lift-car waited. As she lowered his body to the ground, she could feel the incredulous inertia when she dropped him and he didn't move.

Seconds passed before he sought her eyes. "What was that?"

"Magic. Something that proves to you that your concerns for my well-being are unfounded. I'm unbreakable, Biker. Please allow me to show you why."

He was hooked. Whatever this woman needed to tell him, he *needed* to know. An irresistible woman, he might be able to resist, but one who could do impossible things, a mystery he must know the answer to, he couldn't. He glanced at the waiting lift-car. Only *that*, he couldn't do.

"Whatever you're selling, I'm buying now. But I can't go up in that."

"It's just a lift-car. The safest way to travel in this world. What, you can drive that land-beast a hundred miles an hour, but you can't ride in a lift-car?" *Oh, she really needed to find a way to compel this guy!*

"No. Bad history." Quiet for a few moments, Will uttered, "Fuck," hoping she didn't hear him. "We'll take my bike."

"Where?"

Again he hesitated because he hadn't taken anyone to his home since he'd lived in the desert. "My place."

Olivia nodded. "Okay. We can do what I need to do there."

In the long centuries of her life, Olivia had never rode on the back of a motorcycle. The experience was illuminating: her arms around this man's warm body, his heat infusing her with sensual energy, the wind ripping at her hair, the speed of driving through it so openly, the sky around them lighting up. *God, she needed sex!*

She wanted to stop this machine, use her speed to remove his clothes, and impale herself on him. At the same time, there was something deeply visceral and exciting in this moment, both of them trapped in this column of air, speeding into the darkness, her body pressed to his.

One thing often missing from a long life? New experiences that redefine joy, and this moment qualified, so she laid her head against Biker's strong back, her fingers sliding low to bury themselves into the waistband of jeans that had to have been manufactured decades ago. Olivia let herself *feel* every second of being here with him, now, on this archaic machine, heading somewhere that did not matter at all.

All too soon, she heard the engine wind down, the Harley-Davidson slowed, and Will turned off the lone highway onto a dirt path carved out only by the use of tires.

"We're here."

Rolling up on what looked like a tin shed surrounded by dim solar landscaping lights, the bike slowed and stopped.

Olivia had to slide her fingers out of the waistband of his pants to let him swing a leg over, simultaneously reaching for her and lifting her from the long seat.

"Don't expect much." Leading her to the rough-hewn wood door, Will pushed it open. "No need to lock out here. Prairie dogs and rattlesnakes don't bother anything."

Entering ahead of Will, Olivia let her eyes slide over the single room, surprised to see low-level blue solar lights that he must have brought inside before he left for the night. They formed the only light in the room, which was sparsely furnished with a pallet in the corner made of layers of blankets, an old-fashioned reclining chair, and a small vidscreen set in front of a computer keyboard. Beside the chair, a large cabinet backed up to the wall, which she assumed held most of this man's possessions, and a beautiful handmade rug covered the entire floor. The building had been covered by metal siding on the outside, but various colors and types of fabrics were affixed to the center and tied to the sides of the walls to mimic a circus tent.

"This is actually quite charming," she said, turning to face him as he followed her inside.

"It's all a man needs. That, a grill outside to cook on, a place to shit, and…" Will's eyes went to her breasts, then slid lower. "Never mind."

"It's quite warm, though. You don't have any environmentals? A big man like you could sweat gallons in this heat."

"It's…uh…not necessary."

That was quite evasive, Olivia thought. There was so much more to this man than human. It was time to get down to her mission. "So, Biker, what can you do?"

Will had set a kettle on an f-plate to heat and turned sharply at that question. "What?"

"Listen. I'm here because I know that you are something other than just ordinary. I was sent by some pretty remarkable people to tell you some things you need to know. Here." Olivia perched on the recliner, the heat getting to her. "Let me tell you about myself and then you'll understand what I mean."

She had his attention now, as he leaned his weight against the cabinet. "Biker, I am a first blood vampire. That doesn't mean anything to you until I tell you that I am many hundreds of years old, I live at night only, intake blood to maintain my health, and have powers that will amaze and perhaps concern you. I can show you my power to prove my claim, but that can wait. You are the one that matters here. This world is in rough shape, I think you'll agree."

Will stayed immovable, still leaning back, arms folded, expressionless, which didn't surprise Olivia.

"Okay. That's one hurdle. One of my skills is the ability to use forced compulsion to get a human to do anything I want them to do. All I have to do is capture your gaze." Taking a beat to do so, she smiled. "Remove your pants."

Although he lifted his eyebrows, otherwise, Will did not move.

"You see, that shouldn't be possible. If I tell you to remove your pants, you should immediately do exactly that. I should be looking at your impressive penis right now, yet you haven't complied. So, again, what can you do? You must have some skills beyond normal humans. Obviously, you can't be compelled. What else?"

He watched a thin layer of sweat cover smooth skin that his fingers twitched to touch. While he'd sensed something in her that he'd never sensed before, her claim to be something supernatural, a vampire, was ridiculous. And yet it struck him at the same moment that the things he had always been able to do were ridiculous too. How could it be impossible that other people existed with strange abilities if *he* had them?

Sliding the twitching fingers forward, he fell to his knees and curled his hands around one of her boots.

"You really want to know?"

Olivia nodded.

"Okay then." Will slipped the boot off, then the other.

Laying his hands on the top of her shins, he moved them slowly up each leg until they stopped just under the hem of her short skirt. "You're hot."

Smiling, her breath coming hard, Olivia nodded again. "I'm glad you think so."

"No. I mean you're warm to the touch. Let me cool you off."

"I think you're more likely to heat me up. Besides, you have no environmentals here."

"I don't need them." Circling her thigh with his hands, Will closed his eyes. Cool air began to rise from the ground and move like smoke around Olivia's bare legs. It rose and twisted around her face, caressed her skin like cold satin.

Breath held, her eyes sought his, and he seemed to know that because he lifted his lids and looked into hers.

"You can command the air," she whispered, awed.

Shaking his head, Will licked his lips. "No. But I have a connection to the ground, to the earth, and when I touch her, whatever she is, I seem to be able to touch it too. This air comes up from beneath us at my will. I don't know how I do it, or why, but I can."

"Always?"

After a great sigh, Will lowered his head, disconnecting from Olivia. Moments passed, then he nodded his bowed head. "Yes. I didn't know what it was at first, and I…"

He stopped speaking, and when he began again, his voice was thick with emotion. "I made, uh…some mistakes. People I loved died."

Immediately, Olivia understood, and her hand went to his head, pushing *impression* on him in an attempt to help with his pain. It didn't work, any more than the compulsion had. "I can feel your heart, Biker. You could not have been blamed for what happened."

He lifted his head abruptly, his eyes awash in tears. "I was completely responsible. It was this thing, this connection, that caused the accident, and I will never forgive myself."

Sliding off the recliner, Olivia pulled him into her arms, surprised that he let her. "Rest, Willoughby Collins. We will revisit this tomorrow night."

Moving back, she looked around at the tin walls. This wasn't a safe place for a vampire. "I cannot stay here. I would ask that you come with me. My lift-car can get us to a safe room in less than an hour."

"You don't understand. I can't get into a lift-car. My connection to the ground…it's unbreakable. If I leave the ground, it pulls me back."

"You can't fly?"

"Never."

Olivia considered what he was saying, realized what it meant, and asked anyway. "Will, the accident you mentioned, was it because of this connection to the earth? Is that why you feel it was your fault?"

"It *was* my fault. I bought a lift-car because it seemed the more practical conveyance. My fiancée was carrying our baby, and I wanted her to have quick, safe transport when I wasn't home. My job as a materials engineer sometimes kept me away from home for as long as four weeks at a time. I took her up, and while we flew over the city, I couldn't control the thing. I could feel it, this power, this attachment, pulling at me. It made no sense, but when I tried to land the car, I felt a yank so hard, the engine couldn't overcome it, and we fell from the sky. She was killed instantly. The baby was too young to survive. So, yes, it was *all* my fault."

"You obviously couldn't have known."

"Doesn't matter. She died, my child died, and it was because of me. Okay, the subject is done."

"Understood. Then we take your bike."

"Where?"

"Somewhere safe."

"We're safe here."

"*I'm* not. Vampires and daylight do not mix. This shack cannot be secure against the chance of daylight exposure."

"That's true. I'll take you back to your car."

"I'm not leaving without you."

"If you want to avoid daylight, you'll have to. I think you're a little mad, lady. I'm something strange, yeah, but vampires are a storyteller's perfect monster. They don't exist."

After pushing off the floor, she watched Will stand and reach for the whistling kettle. This hadn't gone well at all.

"Ugh! A stubborn human that can't be compelled. Chione, you really owe me!" The option of using her skills to put him out and hauling him with her wasn't good. If he was right, the lift-car would be drawn back to the ground.

"Then I'm going to tell you what I came to tell you, and let you decide what you want to do once I have. It is life-changing. And Biker, I think it is exactly what you need."

"Right now, that's a bottle Cilio's whisky. Do you want to share?"

Olivia grinned. "I do."

Abandoning the tea he had prepared for them, Will pulled a large bottle from a shelf inside the cabinet and poured a generous amount into two juice-size glasses.

Dropping onto the rug, he leaned against the cabinet again and caught Olivia's attention. "Okay, tell me what you've come to tell me. I admit I'm curious."

A few long draws later, Olivia, sitting on the floor in front of Will, her head lying back against the seat of the recliner, her eyes closed, she began her story.

"Biker, with these unusual talents you have, have you ever wondered if there were others out there like you?"

"Yeah. I mean, I don't understand what I can do, I know it isn't normal, but I also thought that surely I can't be the only one. I've never met anyone else who could do anything like this. In my life, I've only told three people about these strange abilities, and all of them were weirded out, including my fiancée. None of them had ever seen or heard of anyone who could…" He stopped for a healthy swig of the whisky. "After the accident, I didn't care, I just got rid of everything in my life except that Harley and came to the most inhospitable place I could think of."

"Well you are not alone. The talents are rare, but they happen. You can't deny them, it isn't healthy."

"Weren't you listening? I don't give a fuck."

"Yes, you've made that abundantly clear, but after I tell you what you must know, you will. So, let's begin as I said, with my own nature. I am not normal. I am vampire, a creature brought to this world many millennia ago to protect this living planet when the time came. Biker, the time has come. There are many of us, but a little over a century ago, a special group of vampire children were born as warriors, guardians, for when they would be needed. They are trained and tasked toward a destiny to stop certain catastrophic events that could destroy much of the life on this little world."

During a pause, Olivia watched Will's face. Quietly reflective, he gave her his full attention. "Here's where you come in. The ten vampires will be paired with ten supernatural beings, and ten humans. Until recently, only five of the humans had been known to the guardians of the guardians. I have been asked to let one of them know of their great destiny. You, Willoughby *Biker* Collins, are meant for something much more than you can even imagine."

"You're smoking something ancient lady. Peyote?"

"Peyote? I wish, but no. It's a little thing called magics. They infuse the earth, the sky, the universe, and they're inside every first blood vampire. And, apparently, sometimes, those magics are in humans too."

After hesitating, Olivia moved closer. "May I touch you? I have an empathic ability and it will help me *read* you and your talent."

"You've already touched me."

"Not like this. Please, Biker, it is important."

Rolling his eyes, he raised his arms to spread them wide. "Why not? After you're finished, we might as well fuck."

Olivia didn't tell him that she was of the same opinion. Touching him again might be necessary to gain the information Chione and Donovan needed to verify that he was the one, but it wasn't wise. She couldn't count how many years it had been since someone had revved her motor like this.

"Appropriate analogy," she murmured as she prepared.

"I'm going to have to touch you directly on the skin. Near the heart is the most effective place. So, if you wouldn't mind?"

Will pulled his tee shirt over his head and pitched it over near the pallet. "I won't be responsible for anything you think you see. It's been a rough life."

"Don't worry, I won't see details exactly. Just impressions of who you are, your talent, integrity, honor, spirit."

"Shit," he groaned. "All right. Do it."

"Just close your eyes and breathe evenly. You might feel my presence, so don't be alarmed. I'll be brief."

His eyes closed, Will did all he could to meet her orders.

Her gaze on the hard muscles of his chest, the carved columns of his abdominals, the thick, well-defined arms, Olivia placed her right hand over his heart. Her fingers had a will of their own and moved back and forth lightly over the moist, smooth skin. She could feel the steady beats, and to help her own mind focus, she closed her eyes too.

And reached inside…

It was there, riding on the surface and buried deep…this man was tethered to the earth so inextricably, a merge so pure, she was shocked that he hadn't always been known to Chione and Donovan, who carried a deep connection to the living planet as well. Their connection had been granted by the universe, but Willoughby had been born to his. He was right…any distance from the ground would pull at him and force his return. He was as bound to it as a tree that depended on roots dug deep into the earth for life.

Before she could slip away from this spiritual link, Olivia glimpsed the depth of love and passion that rode within Will. It was a mistake, and she yanked herself out. Already, she had felt something with him. Now, she understood why. He was Shoazan, and a mate for a first blood vampire. And that made him dangerous to her.

Breathing too fast, Olivia pushed up and crossed the room, leaving Will to gain his feet alone after the dizzying spiritual event. She should have stayed and supported him, but she needed the distance.

"You're earthbound, Biker, there is no doubt. Your power, it's enormous. You haven't even begun to understand what you can do. There are people in Africa who are waiting to guide you, to *teach* you, how to touch it. Will, you need to come with me."

"Look, this has been interesting, but I'm fine right where I am. Here, I can't hurt anyone. I have no illusions of my own importance or value in the world. I'm a simple man who likes to ride through the wind at breakneck speeds across the vacant lands of the desert. That's all I am. If you need to get somewhere before daylight, you might want to see to that."

Will paused, reached for his whisky, drained it, and looked back into Olivia's eyes, keeping his gaze on her for several long moments. "Unless you want to stick around. I…um…I've changed my mind about, uh, being with you."

Oliva shook her head. She couldn't take him up on that even though she could barely refuse.

"You need to understand me. One last thing, then, that should convince you. I'm going to show you my nature."

Surging forward, she planted her hand on his chest again, and blasted into him. He grabbed her, which was wise, because they both fell to the ground, wrapped together, as Olivia entered his mind and showed him the proof that what she told him was true. All that made her vampire, that made her first blood, revealed to this unique man who held her tight. His world had just changed forever.

Removing herself from his mind, Olivia needed several moments to recover, aware that he had to be even more disoriented. He still held her, her head dropped onto his chest. Pushing away, she supported herself and reached a hand out for him.

Furrowed brows showed he didn't think such a small female could help him gain his feet, but then it struck him that if what she showed him was real, she was much more powerful than he was. Will lifted a hand to her and she pulled him up.

"I'm sorry. That was a bit sudden. It can be a little invasive, but you need to know the truth, and I can't do it properly with compulsion, so this was what I had left. Are you all right?"

"Yeah. I think so. I still think you're crazy, but…"

He shook his head again. "You're a vampire? And I'm supposed to go with you to fight a war for this planet because I am connected to it by birth?"

"Give the man a prize. Yes, Biker, all of the above."

Olivia moved close enough to lift up on her toes, her lips brushing his cheek with the next words. There was no reason to fight this attraction; it hit her hard in the belly and below. She wanted him, knew he wanted her, so she didn't need to see a vision of the future to know that they would be together. *Someday.* Not today.

"You will love this life I take you to."

Viscerally aware of every element of this woman's presence, her beauty, her scent, her presence, the intense sexuality, Will had no idea where she wanted to take him or what she really wanted from him. The sensations and visions that she'd fed to him had seemed real, but it was all too fantastic to actually believe. He only knew with certainty that whatever she wanted from him, he wanted to be there with her. This woman took his breath away, and he hadn't thought anything could ever do that in this miserable life he'd led from birth to now.

"Yes, I will come."

He watched her eyes widen in surprise and gratitude before a slow smile showed perfect white teeth that he wanted to slip his tongue past.

Heading to the door, she turned back. "Take anything you want to keep. You won't be coming back anytime soon."

Four

IN JAKARTA, INDONESIA

Naked, lying on her belly, face buried in a thick towel, her low groan filled the tent. "I think I'm in love, Natal."

"You always say that, mistress."

"Ummm." Shani glanced up at her masseuse. "It's because I think I really am. Natal, please, I am *not* your mistress."

"I work for you, and I like to call you mistress."

She didn't tell him that for the past six months, his hands were the only ones touching her, and she was needy as hell. His fingers expertly slid over smooth skin that were meant to relax her, and they did. Only she had been so horny lately, even this light pressure, or the hard kneading, made her wet and ready for a more *sensual* massage.

"Perhaps I should reconsider Dean's offer," she whispered to herself, her face back on the table once again, committing all her attention to Natal's incredible ministrations.

She was exhausted, but that wasn't unusual. Between Dean, Pilar, and herself, they managed every species of animal on Africa, Indonesia, the entire Middle East, Russia, and China. Just making sure that not one more went extinct was a 24/7 commitment by her team of 100 humans, supernaturals and vampires.

Sleeping came easily because of the vampire imperative to rest after daylight arrived, but anything else, like a social life, took planning that she admitted, frankly, she hadn't given enough attention lately.

"Gotta see to that," she murmured as Natal moved down her body to expertly work her glutes and the back of her thighs. The moisture and heat between her legs increased.

"Shani!"

Dean. The handsome human she'd worked with for two decades burst into the room, his eyes moving over Shani's nude body stretched out on the massage table. He whistled. "Timing is everything. And mine couldn't be better."

"Ugh! Dean, no sexual innuendo while I'm lying here naked."

He moved to the table, leaned down to lift up the lush dark hair that covered her left ear, and whispered. "I can help you with that."

Releasing her hair, he stepped back and munched on some of the berries she kept in the room. "Hey, I've got as much pent-up energy as you do, Boss."

"You're horny, Dean, and I can think of at least five women right now who would throw you down and get on top of you if you asked."

"Yeah, but..." His voice trailed off.

She knew what his "but" meant. It wasn't just sex that he missed. He was lonely. They had worked together almost every night for the past twenty years and had become close. Even though she had complete control over her empathic skills now, sometimes she dropped her shields and reached out to him. He was still in love and couldn't move forward.

Finishing with a thorough foot massage, Natal pulled Shani's robe over her.

"You are perfect again, mistress."

"Now *that* I'll agree to. I feel remade after your wonderful hands do their magic. Thank you, Natal, I'll see you tomorrow."

Lately, daily massages helped her to cope.

Dean waited while Shani slipped off the table, tying the satin robe around her waist as she reached for a bottle of ice-cold water.

"Have you heard from her?" she asked.

"No. I blew in here because Jackson messaged ten minutes ago with a semi-urgent 411. He said that the geologic activity is increasing in both power and frequency. Cairine wants everyone on alert and ready to fly in on a moment's notice." He let his eyes wander over Shani, elegant as usual even in the thin white robe, her bare feet still shiny from the massage oils.

"Sally won't call. She made that clear last year when she told me that she was committing to the asshole."

"Rick isn't an asshole."

"In *this* case, he is. I can't compete with a vampire and he knows it."

"Rick has always done exactly what he wants. He doesn't pay attention to how his actions affect others, he just lives his life by his own terms."

"Yeah. Asshole."

Walking over to a wide raised beach chair near the balcony, Shani pulled her feet beneath her. "To be fair, you and Sally broke up ten years before they got together."

"Yeah…" Dean followed her and kissed her on the forehead. "I know I'm being a jerk. The truth doesn't make any of this better. I often wish we were still in California."

"You've lived long enough to know better than to wish for impossible things or live with regret. You're a beautiful man, Dean. Go get one of those girls who want you and fuck her properly."

"You're one to talk. How long has it been since you've had a good fuck?"

Shani lifted a foot and shoved him back with it. "Get out of here. I need to dress and get in touch with Cari. *My* sex life is not the question here."

Grinning, Dean held Shani's water bottle to his crotch and squeezed out a long stream. "You've motivated me. Off I go to get that tension release."

"Good. Come back to work in a better mood."

The door slammed closed as he left, and a sad smile came. This conversation had led her mind somewhere she rarely went…into the past to what she'd just told him not to do. To lives taking a right instead of a left. To lost possibilities. To regrets. *To might-have-beens.*

"No." She pushed off the chair and went out onto the balcony to look over the estate she managed with Dean and Pilar. "Nope. I just need a blood meal, and, like Dean, some good sex, and I'll be fine. Better than."

In spite of the promise to herself not to revisit paths not taken, the face of a large man with smoldering eyes, long dark hair worn in braids, and a body that made hers react, even after all these decades, filled her mind's eye.

Rodney. Shit! When his name surfaced, her gut always clenched and so did her chest. The area between her legs had apparently never learned to move on either, since the mere thought of him brought heat and moisture and she nearly always found herself in her room, alone, where she would bring herself to orgasm.

Of course, there was a reason for her uncontrollable reaction. He was the one that got away. The one she had never been with, so he remained the untouchable dream, even though long ago she'd convinced herself that he was nothing more than a youthful crush and that it would never have worked.

Shani hadn't seen him again after that first summer when she'd come home paralyzed from their journey to help the Totem's in Patagonia. Her mother had convinced her to join her sisters and their new friend Crezia in America, where they'd traveled and enjoyed their human lives for the next several years.

Later, after they had all converted to their first blood natures, Rodney had committed to raising and protecting two more of Koen's grandchildren, so he'd never come to her.

At the time, she remembered that he told her he wouldn't.

I wish I were your destiny, but you were never meant for one as unremarkable as I, he'd said to her then. He'd told her he wasn't worthy of her, that she was meant for someone much greater than he.

So as the years moved on, and she met a quiet, kind man in Australia that following summer, he introduced her to the sweetness of love-making. He hadn't brought the almost destructive intense heat she'd felt when she was trying to force Rodney to take her, but it had been a beautiful introduction to sex. They'd stayed together for the next twelve years, but at that point, she'd sensed he was ready to move forward with her, and she'd already known he wasn't the man she would spend her life with. He most certainly wasn't a *mate*.

Head back, she closed her eyes to force herself to stop thinking about Rodney. "Stop it. He's just a man you never really knew. You were never his and he *definitely* was never yours. Odds are, you will never meet him again."

As far as she knew, he was still human. Once in a great while someone would mention him, and, feigning disinterest, Shani never asked further. There were moments when all she wanted to do was grab that person and ask a million questions, like…*how is he…is he happy….does he have a lover…did he ever ask about her?*

She had always been able to stop herself. It didn't mean that the unanswered questions went away, it just meant that she never got satisfaction.

"Maybe I need to heed my own advice. It's been a long, long time since I had that childish obsession."

Picking up her fone, she waited for Dean's face to appear and when it did, she paused. He really was a wonderful man. *Maybe…?*

"We're going out tonight, you and I, and getting stinking drunk. After, we'll just see what the night brings. Invite anyone else you want."

"What changed your mind?"

"The excellent advice I gave *you*. It's past time for me to move on, too."

"Together, we ride. Okay, I'll pick you up in a few hours."

Ringing off, Shani dropped her robe and glanced in a mirrored wall across from the balcony. "That's better, vampire. And don't forget it's past time for a blood meal."

There was work to be done. If Cairine's warning had teeth, they would all be busy for a long time to come. Little time to worry about lost loves. So, tonight, drinks and a good fuck. She was still uncomfortable with turning her close friendship with Dean into a sexual one. No, a good fuck tonight, yes, but not with Dean.

He'd be so disappointed.

IN NEW YORK CITY

God, why was the traffic always so bad here? With lift-cars, which gave commuters lots of options, it should have been possible to get from one side of the city to the other in a reasonable amount of time.

Scottie, pissed and in her usual hurry, used her jetbike to cross Times Square against traffic. It was illegal, and if they caught her, again, she'd have to pay another fine that she did not have the money for. But the tube was on the other side of the street and she was more than late; she was probably fired.

As if that wasn't unusual in her life. It had been one long series of missteps, jobs that sucked just to make a meager living, and bad relationships that ended in violent altercations that more often than not brought the cops.

"Fuck, someday I'm going to get out of this city," she murmured aloud as she punched the bike stand to get her claim ticket. She'd leave her one valuable possession here to ride to the Ta District for a job that was above her station in life. Which is why she figured she'd lose it soon. Everyone there knew that she wasn't from *their* class, although wasn't completely uncommon with many of the staff and servers. Still, serving gourmet meals in one of the finest restaurants in the city would bring tips like she'd never seen. *If she could just keep the job.*

When she arrived to the base of *The Loft*, a towering building that included expensive homes, shopping, and high-end services, she proceeded to the back of the building to a secure service elevator. The silent mag-levs released a small hiss as it stopped at ground level in response to her call. Her eyes went to the tall burly man who provided security and operated the elevator.

"Hey, Yakib."

"Your shift started half an hour ago."

"I know. Transportation trouble. You understand."

"Yeah, but Darling won't."

Scottie rolled her eyes and sighed. "Yeah, yeah, I know. There's every likelihood you'll be bringing me right back down."

After she stepped out onto the prep room of *The Loft* restaurant on the top floor of the 130 floor building, Scottie pulled her long black hair back and secured it to the nape of her neck with a sparkly clip provided by her boss. Her two-piece uniform, a tight-fitting halter top with an even tighter-fitting skirt, needed a lot of smoothing out to control the wrinkles.

Just as she reached the kitchen, where she'd find her assignment, a high-pitched voice blasted her.

"Baradiso! Come with me!"

Pissed at her supervisor, who'd caught her arriving late, and more pissed at herself for it, Scottie turned and faced the woman with hair bleached brighter than the face of the sun.

Ms. Darling's high-heeled stilettos tick-ticked against the Italian tile floor as she walked briskly toward a series of office doors that lined the hall.

Fuck, fuck, fuck! This was the highest paying job she'd ever had and she had to go and *fuck* it up! Without it, she'd be back down on Darby Street selling beer and illegal drugs to the lowest common denominator of human existence. It was ugly, dangerous work that she'd finally crawled out from under, and now she had fucked herself and would be back by the weekend.

Pushing the door to her office open, Ms. Darling stepped in and turned to face Scottie.

"Ma'am, I am so sorry I'm late. I come from the Pier District and it's hard to get across the city this time of day. I know that's a lame excuse, but…"

"Shut. Up."

Her arms folded across a shiny red dress that Scottie thought was one of the tackiest things she'd ever seen, well aware that it cost more than she made in a year, Ms. Darling's overbright pink lips were pursed.

"I don't want to hear it. If I had my way, you'd be fired and never seen here again. Unfortunately, Mr. Bellamy likes you. He sees something in you that I certainly don't. Either way, he owns the club, so you get to work tonight. But understand me. If you keep disrespecting this job, I'll get rid of you. Ultimately, it's the restaurant Bellamy protects. Tell me that you understand."

I understand I want to punch you in those plastic-coated lips, Scottie thought, but said, "I won't. I mean, I will *be* an exemplary waitress."

"Huh. I'll believe that when I see it. Okay, get out there. Chelsea has been handling your tables. Remember. One more chance."

It took everything she had to go on out to the dining room instead of quitting this job and telling little Miss *I've been privileged all my life* to go fuck herself. Self-preservation and the fact that she wasn't an idiot kept her from making that bad move.

Scanning the busy dining room clad in pale champagne and ice-blue, Scottie saw that the entire rotating restaurant with 360 degree views was nearly full tonight. She'd work her ass off, but she'd have a nice payday for it.

Across the room, Chelsea was returning with an empty tray.

"Chelse, hey, sorry I'm late."

Chelsea, obviously upset, shrugged her shoulders.

"That's what they get for hiring from the wrong side of the city."

"Bitchy, although probably accurate. Give me my tablet and let me do my job."

Chelsea threw the crystal clear tablet at Scottie, who barely caught it. "Next time, I don't help you."

"Like you had a choice. You got the same boss I do, but hey, thanks anyway."

Glancing at the tablet, Scottie easily determined where she was needed. Table 16 had just been seated, the order needed to be picked up for Table 8, and Table 12 needed to be checked on.

"Go to work, girl," Scottie barked to herself.

An hour later, on point, all guests well-serviced, her feet aching in the high heels the establishment insisted the servers wear, Scottie thought she'd take a moment's break when she saw the hostess seat a couple at her one vacant table.

"Shit," she whispered, plastered on her signature smile, and approached the table.

Glancing at the couple, her usual greeting stalled as she scanned them. The blonde woman was remarkably gorgeous, probably the most beautiful women she'd ever seen. The enormous man across from her, equally as handsome, had a smile that crushed.

She realized that she was staring. Recovering, she apologized. "I'm sorry, cat got my tongue. Welcome to *The Loft*. May I bring each of you one of our signature drinks to begin?"

Oddly, Scottie, suddenly aware that they were staring at *her* too, felt a weird vibe. Something was off about these two. She took a second glance as she went to get the large order of drinks the sexy man requested.

Koen couldn't take his eyes from the young waitress. He'd been shocked when Chione called and told him about Rodney's daughter. He'd questioned her about the accuracy of her vision, but sitting here in front of her, there was no doubt. This girl was Rodney's child.

He could see his adopted son in this lovely young woman. Her hair and face were almost identical to her father's. Big pale blue eyes, hair the color of the darkest part of the night, a hard jaw line and full lips, long legs, a fit tight body. And the attitude. It came through even her polite words.

"Aye, lass, why don't you bring both of us two of each of your signature drinks? We can handle anything you can throw at us."

The waitress nodded, smiled, and after leaving a menu, she told them she'd be right back.

Tamesine nibbled on a bowl of chocolates in the center of the table. "Wow. He can't possibly unclaim her. She's definitely Rodney's."

"No doubt at all, even if Chione hadn't confirmed it in her vision. The spittin' image, isn't she?"

"You two didn't think about this?"

"We were on our first U.S. trip in decades, I certainly never thought about it, and if I remember correctly, I don't think Rodney came up long enough to do it either. It was right after Bas and I put up the forceshield barriers around our villas. We're so isolated, and Rodney never got out much. The boy went through several pretty lasses that weekend. Obviously, one became pregnant."

"You would have been long gone by the time she found out, and she would never have had any way to contact him. Well, it's done. This is the girl."

"Aye. So, let's get her to Zambia. Chione feels that something is coming, and soon."

"Compulsion, it is."

The waitress returned to place eight uniquely shaped glasses on the table. Koen squinted up at her.

"Lass, you don't mean to tell me that these tiny glasses are meant to be a full serving."

"I'm afraid so, sir. I can bring you as many as you'd like, of course. All are considered to be the finest in the states."

"You better bring the bottle that each is poured from."

Waiting before she spoke, the lovely girl nodded. "You realize that each serving is thirty dollars."

"It matters not. Go ahead and bring the bottles. And while you're at it, we'll each have the top three meals listed on this menu."

Koen smiled at the confused expression on Rodney's daughter's face. Suddenly, she grinned. "Anything you want. I look forward to watching both of you enjoy the meals. All three choices are outstanding."

Once she left again, Tamesine downed two of her small glasses. "Ummm. She's right, these are wonderful. The flavors are different than anything I've had before. I look forward to the dinners."

"I figured that we're both hungry, so we may as well eat before we get in the sky again."

"That's why we've remained partners and friends for over a century. We do think alike."

Koen lifted a glass in toast. "Who'd have thought?"

After the two voracious guests had torn into the three meals, Scottie stood, amazed, almost afraid to ask her next question. "May I bring you anything else?"

The man laid a huge hand heavily on the table and stared up into her eyes. "Your name is Scottie, aye?"

She usually introduced herself when she arrived at a table, but she knew she hadn't done so tonight. Why did the fact that he knew her name spook her?

"Uh, yes, it is. I apologize, I usually explain that before I begin caring for my guests. I hope you were pleased with the service."

"Outstanding!" He called out. "Scottie, we need to talk."

Automatically, Scottie stepped back, because anything that began with that phrase was never good.

The man stared directly into her eyes. "Stop," he commanded.

More concerned now, she backed further, unsure of what was going on.

"What the hell, Tam?" the man asked his companion. Scottie switched her gaze to the blonde woman and saw her shrug.

"I didn't expect this, but there's precedence. Olivia said that compulsion wouldn't work on her human in Arizona.

For whatever reason, this girl apparently can't be compelled."

"This is bullshit." Koen stood. "Young lady, my name is Koen. You might as well know that we came here for you. I know you grew up without a father, and if you have any interest in finding out who he is, you will come with us. I can tell you that he is a magnificent man, and had he any idea that you existed, he would have been father to you every moment. You can stay here and dredge out this meager existence, or you can come with us and find your destiny. Which is spectacular, by the way."

Scottie didn't move. She'd known from the beginning that these two were different. Now, she was worried and fascinated all at once. They knew her father? *How?* Even her mother didn't know who he was. It didn't seem likely.

"I can't imagine how you would know that. My mother has almost no memory of him. How would *you*?"

"There are more mysteries in this world than you could ever know. But if you come with us, we'll introduce you to a lot of them, as well as the man who made you. You strike me as inquisitive and adventurous. Much like your father Rodney."

Rodney. *A name...more than she'd ever had.*

"What the hell is going on here?"

Scottie twirled to face Ms. Darling. "Uh, just a discussion with a guest. It's nothing."

"It doesn't *seem* like nothing. I knew this would happen as soon as I let you take your place here again. Mr. Bellamy won't be able to save you." Ms. Darling faced Koen.

"Sir, has your server been inappropriate? I apologize..."

Koen caught Ms. Darling's narrow-eyed gaze. "Stop. This young woman is too good for the likes of this job, and you will respect her and honor her from here forward. Now go away."

Without another word, Ms. Darling turned and hurried from the dining room.

Scottie looked around at the other diners, stopped mid-meal, as they watched the odd events at Scottie's table.

Her eyes moved to the kitchen door where Ms. Darling had exited, then back to the impressive man standing too near to her now. She stepped back and looked at the woman.

"Is this true?" She asked, as if she had any reason to trust his companion.

Tamesine nodded. "It's true. Your father is a wonderful man who has lived with us for...well, a very long time. He doesn't know about you yet, but I guarantee you, he'll be overjoyed to meet you. I expect it will be awkward at first, but this will change your life. Please, come with us."

"What did he do to Ms. Darling?"

"Nothing, much, just sent her away. There is an explanation, but this isn't the time or place. Please, Scottie, you are meant for so much more than food service."

She was done here. This was the job of a lifetime for someone with Scottie's background, but not only was it apparent it wasn't working out, she admitted that she hadn't really *wanted* it to work out. Years of searching for her place in the world, for a way to feel relevant, like she was accomplishing something, had led her here. This was the moment. These two strange individuals who might lead her to her father, to the one person she realized she needed to know more than anyone. To find out who or what she was.

Only *he* might be able to help her understand the *weird* thing that she could do.

"Yes, I'll come. I wasn't cut out for this waitressing thing anyway."

"Lass, I can say with all accuracy that you could do anything you set your heart to. But it was never something as insignificant as serving meals to people."

Scottie searched the deep green eyes. "You don't know me. You have no idea what I'm capable of."

"You'd be surprised about what I know. Do you have anything you need to attend to before we go? You may be gone for some time."

"Yeah. I want to secure my jetbike and see if my landlord will keep my apartment for me."

"You've no problem, we can fix everything. Come, we'll take you where you need to go."

As she followed Koen to the guest entrance and elevator, Scottie suddenly had a strong sense that this was indeed a life-changing moment and that she would never return to her life in New York City again.

IN BOMBAY, INDIA

Park stood on the corner of the building named after one of her mentors. Dr. Sharif had built a medical empire over the past forty years, his brilliant vision to create a research facility with no limits had culminated in this 43 floor building called *R-Cubed*. The name meant *Repair, Replace, and Recovery Research Center.*

It was a work of architectural magic. Lit with low-emission crystal lanterns, the unusually shaped structure looked like it was made of glass and light. Dr. Sharif had wanted the space *inviting*, a promise of the best care possible in medical science, but more than that, it promised passionate dedication. While she was here, she wanted to see him, but if she did, she would have to use compulsion to make him forget that his beautiful friend still looked exactly the same as she had four decades ago when they'd worked together.

On the point of compulsion, Olivia and Koen had both contacted her last night to let her know that neither of their targets could be compelled. That alone proved how special they were. Humans were not immune to that vampire skill.

This building housed most of the Earth's recent medical advances, its brightest doctors and scientists, and the last best hope for many terminal patients. While most of humanity's illnesses had been eradicated or managed, there was always a new virus or challenge. Life on all levels, including microscopic, was hardly static.

Inside this remarkable place, according to Chione's vision, she would find the last human soldier, a young physician named Antoinette.

Coming into the center after dark, Park knew the staff would be at a minimum, but it was her starting point of contact for the newly-discovered human earth warrior. She still thought it bizarre that the powers-that-be had not revealed these final five humans long before now. The first five had been indoctrinated and blood-bonded over a hundred years ago.

This sudden revelation left everyone in the community concerned that it showed an imminent timeline…the warriors would be needed soon. As the mother of two of the warriors and several young vampires, she couldn't help but be concerned. God, she hoped that the universe had gotten everything right.

But now was not the time to dwell.

As Park cleared the entrance, pausing to appreciate the clean lines of the building, it struck her how incredible it would have been to work here. No time for that now, though; tonight was about finding Antoinette.

A quiet young man sat at his station behind a crystal clear reception desk as Park approached. For quickest results, she smiled into his eyes and engaged her compulsion skills. "Hi, I'm looking for a doctor. The only name I have is Antoinette."

"Her name is Rachmat. Dr. Antoinette Rachmat. She's in the lab and not available at this time."

"That's okay. Tell me where this lab is located."

He did so, he had no choice, as Park instructed him to relax, removed any memory of her presence, then proceeded to the elevator to travel to the 18th floor where her target was working late. The receptionist had revealed that the young doctor was monitoring results from a series of tests on an unknown bacterium found in the seas off the coast of one of the most northern islands of Scotland.

The door to the level 2 research lab opened easily, and Park entered, her eyes adjusting from the soft light of the corridor to the harsher white light in the lab's anteroom. A lone dark head was bent over a microscope on a counter near the back of the room adjacent to a heavy door that would lead into the full research cube. The head lifted as the *swish* of the entry door closed behind Park.

"Yes?" the woman inquired.

Park smiled as she moved toward a striking woman she guessed to be about thirty years old. Her black satin hair, waist length and pulled back into a single clip, framed classic Indonesian features. Huge shining liquid black eyes were wide and unguarded.

She already knew she was her target. The woman's aura was filled with latent power. "Antoinette?"

A bright smile burst forth immediately. "Yes, yes I am! Are you from Kareen's department? I have his results ready." Her soft voice was accented, not Indonesian, but British.

"No. I'm here to see you."

The smile dropped, and the young doctor stood. Her eyes closed for several long moments, then she moved forward to place a hand on each of Park's forearms. Lifting her eyes to look into Park's, Antoinette's slow smile returned and her gaze softened. "Yes, I can feel that."

Paused, her fingers dug lightly into Park's flesh, her eyes widened again. "You are not…I can *feel* you. Your energy, your spirit, your chi."

She moved closer. "The magics that swirl in you."

Stunned into silence, Park locked on her. "Tell me how you know this."

Eyes glittering now with moisture, Antoinette answered her, but Park knew at once that it was not under compulsion. Like the other new warriors, this woman could not be compelled, but she openly and freely told Park what she needed to know.

"Your nature screams to me. In the beginning, I feel a tingle. I know then that you are something different, just as I have always known. You are not the first special person that I have met."

Careful, Park asked, "You have met others like me?"

"Oh, yes. How I know this, I have no clue. But those, like you, who are beyond human, have a glow around you, an unseen signal you boost out into the cosmos. No other people seem to see this; to know it is there, that you are different. Powerful." Antoinette shrugged. "Except for me."

"And you have always been able to do this?"

"As long as I can remember, yes. And I feel…"

She stopped again, her eyebrows drawn together. "I feel as if your presence here tonight is a harbinger of something that changes the course of my life. Am I right? You are here for me?"

So much for figuring out how to convince this woman to come with her. "I am, actually. Dr. Rachmat, are you telling me that you *knew* I was coming?"

"No, no. I am saying that I knew when I saw you that this moment had weight. I knew that you were not just a visitor to my life. The aura that surrounds you? It's like it is filled with glitter and that you are here for a great purpose."

"Okay. I expected to have to figure out how to convince you that I needed to you come with me, but I guess I don't. Right? You will come without a full explanation?"

"I trust you on the faith of my ability. Yes, I will come."

Antoinette turned to her computer and engaged the coms. "Roberto, please let Director Thorsen know that something has come up that will take me from my duties for an unspecified period of time. This project has finished anyway. Let him know I will contact him soon with more details. Thank you, Roberto."

She began to gather up her belongings. "I trust you, but it doesn't mean that I don't want an explanation. You will tell me on the way, yes?"

THE NEXT NIGHT IN ZAMBIA

Chione checked the gardens to ensure everything was ready. Within half an hour, the remaining warriors would arrive. She'd taken to thinking of them as the Final Five, all human and so unprepared for this transformative path on their journeys. Anticipation bubbled in her belly at the thought of meeting the last warriors that the universe had selected to contribute to the grand destiny.

It was all overwhelming, daunting, frightening, and impossible to predict or control. As a possible extinction-level event, or events, the idea of what this grand destiny would involve was too big an idea to contain. That is why the warriors were placed in threes, all with life-sustaining connections to the living planet. Vampires first brought from other worlds, humans born of this world, and supernaturals which bridged all forms of life, would stand together and merge their power when the time came. With those connections, they would make it through it all.

Something big was coming soon, so there was little time to prepare and make sure that everyone was ready and in place. Chione had no worries. They *would* be.

Donovan had gone to meet the groups as they arrived at the barrier protected by first blood magics; only a first blood vampire, or a vampire with a magic-infused talisman, could find and enter the community. The children of the moon had lived here near Victoria Falls for several millennia, safe, largely untouched by the outside world. Here, then, they would welcome the Final Five.

"My mate, they are here." Donovan's deep voice cut through Chione's reverie as she lifted her eyes to the rag-tag group that had just arrived on the continent to come straight to them. Immediately, she recognized all five from her visions. They stood in a line, the escorts she'd sent to bring them in lined up behind them.

"I am Chione. My mate, Donovan, and I are your hosts. Welcome my friends. Your journeys were long, so please, sit and enjoy an excellent meal prepared just for you. So not to overwhelm you, the rest of our community is staying away from these gardens tonight. This night is all about you. We want you to be relaxed and satiated before we discuss why you are here."

Her eyes moved to the twins from Louisiana.

"Genetics were kind to you. It created beauty and then doubled it. I am pleased to meet you, Dani and Dylan."

Moving linearly down the line-up, Chione held out a hand to Scottie, who looked her up and down suspiciously.

Chione could see Rodney's calm fire in his daughter, and bowed her head to her. "Young woman, your journey promises to be the most fulfilling of all. You will discover your heritage."

Scottie rolled her eyes. "Yeah, well, we'll see. Most men aren't a bargain, not in my life, and definitely *not* my missing pop who's been absent for every second of it."

"You will find that you may have to reconsider that idea. Rodney is an honorable man."

Next, the difficult one in her visions, the one that revealed so little, the one that intrigued her, was the man from the desert. "So you are Biker. Olivia tells me you had to come by water. I wasn't sure we'd find you."

Sexy, rough, big, the man stood before her, legs set wide, arms folded, confrontational. Several days of beard growth covered a vampire-handsome face. His body tense, the muscles were on full display. She noticed that Olivia avoided looking at him. *Interesting*.

Finally, he answered. "If I hadn't wanted you to, you wouldn't have. Your soldier is just *that* good."

Olivia lifted her gaze from the ground she had been studying to Chione. "I *am* that good. *He* is too. You'll see."

"Perfect. We *need* good." Her eyes moved to the woman beside Will. "So, our Dr. Rachmat, it seems you have an interesting life."

Antoinette stood back a little, next to Park. The smile that Park was already accustomed to was broad. Park had already discovered that Antoinette was a completely engaging, happy soul. Of all of them, it was apparent that it was the young doctor who embraced and accepted this sudden destiny the easiest.

Chione lifted her eyes to Park. "You are right, this is a truly remarkable woman."

Everyone watched as Chione reached out to Antoinette at the same time Antoinette reached for her. Hands clasped, eyes closed, a bond formed instantly. When Chione opened her eyes moments later, she tilted her head forward, a gesture of respect.

"Madame Doctor, you grace us all with your presence. The universe has *truly* smiled on you."

Stepping back, Chione scanned the group. "I do not mean to imply that any of you are lesser. Your talents and gifts are critical to the success of our mission."

"Which is what, exactly? I really have no clue." Scottie's impatience permeated the calm air.

"That is what we shall learn after you eat and settle in. There is *much* to discuss. Please, my new friends, the plates are large and you are expected to fill them with whatever you'd like and as much as you'd like. I recommend trying anything that looks interesting. The food here is always exceptional. Please, go ahead and dine."

For the next hour, food and drink flowed, new relationships cautiously begun, and the human guests got their first glimpse of a world that they never knew existed.

Silent, keeping separate at the other end of a long table, Will watched everyone and everything. Listening, and recording to his mind, he was awed beyond measure that this hidden community and power lie so near to people and yet remained unknown and unattainable for so long. He wondered if he would finally know who and what he was and how he could do the things he could.

In spite of his fascination with this unique world, his eyes still returned often to the woman who brought him here. Even with so many beautiful people all around this garden, he couldn't stop looking for her. *Damn*. He'd let her in.

Scottie watched from where she sat only slightly displaced from the group. So these were the other four in the *warrior* team of humans that the massive man Koen had told her about.

The black couple, twins, Tamesine had told her, looked nothing alike. The male was tall, built well, handsome as hell. His sister, small, but apparently really strong physically, had a Dresden-doll delicacy about her, but with dark caramel skin instead of the paper white. The gorgeous Indonesian woman, holy fuck, she was annoyingly cheerful. In Scottie's current mood, that endless smiling was too much to handle. She decided to keep her distance from the overly *pleasant* woman.

Now, the last guy, big, quiet, rough, brooding...*he*, she could relate to. A man who live alone by choice. No way he couldn't have had any woman he wanted; he exuded dangerous sex-appeal and women ate that up.

So this was the lot. *Huh, just have to see how things play out*, she mused silently.

Most of all, she wondered when she would get to meet her father. Her gut tightened at the thought. Was she excited at the prospect? No. Anxious, uncertain, aggravated, *yeah*. Hopeful? Perhaps. She expected nothing from him, and hoped she was wrong.

THREE HOURS LATER

"Let me get this straight for clarity. We are to help avert geological, meteorological, and ecological damage to this world...and whatever else may come? Possibly on a massive scale such as earthquakes, nuclear events or pandemics?"

After Chione revealed the mission of the earth warriors, Antoinette's persistent smile had finally faded.

Donovan spoke now that Chione had addressed the Final Five and their sponsors who had stayed with them for this introduction to the mission they were to become part of.

"Whatever may come, Dr. Rachmat, yes," he responded, for clarity. "We don't know what the future holds, but, from a scientist's perspective, we have been able to determine a great deal. Sixty years ago, our ten vampires gathered their powers together and eliminated the threat of nuclear weapons. The devastation would be catastrophic and probably ultimately un-survivable. All life on this world might have perished if the crazy people who had access to those nuclear bombs had used any or all of them."

He paused before he continued. "We're working to restore the Amazonian basin. It has been destroyed, the ground cleared many decades ago with tragic consequences. The life that survived is sheltered deeper in South America until we can re-seed and restore their habitat. It's a task of unimaginable proportions that *we have* to imagine."

Chione continued. "Air quality is managed artificially for most of us in the civilized world because of high populations and extreme demands. In many places, it is toxic or at the very least unhealthy. People sometimes wonder why many of the huge buildings in cities have homes, businesses, and facilities within the same building. Practicality. Many of those buildings are basically vertical neighborhoods. The design is efficient, safe, and easier to provide services for the millions of people who live in them. The air quality is self-regulated to each building, a far easier task than trying to clean the air outside the tower neighborhoods. Our engineers and scientists are responsible for these cities."

"They need that magical barrier you guys have around this village," Dylan threw out.

"It would be great, but even first blood vampires cannot maintain a shield of that magnitude. We are powerful, but we *do* have limitations. This is where you will make a difference. As we mentioned earlier tonight, the universe has put into place ten vampires, ten supernaturals, and now ten humans, all gifted specifically with earth talents that will be combined to meet this challenge. When you are called to serve, the power of thirty strong will be beyond anything ever known on any world. Does that help you to understand your importance to this calling?"

The silence was thick enough to measure.

For the first time since they'd arrived in the first blood community, Will stood and cleared his throat. "You've explained to us about vampires and supernaturals and this crazy-ass team supposedly built and sanctioned by a universal power or consciousness or whatever the hell it is. What I want to know is, what is everyone bringing to the dance? What I *mean* is, what kind of weapons do we really have to accomplish this? What can these five people do?"

Will paused, still for a moment, his hands crossed in front of him. "I'll go first. I didn't know I could do this when I was a kid, but I realize now that it was always there. I just hadn't learned how it worked or how to use it. Apparently, according to my sponsor there, Olivia, I am bonded to what she calls the living planet. If I concentrate and reach inside myself, I can touch the ground with a hand and draw power directly from the earth. Heat, cold, electricity, I can power my own world without any outside source."

Fascinated, Chione asked, "Can you illustrate?"

At first Will didn't respond. Seconds passed before he lowered himself into a crouch and placed his open palm against the soft grass. About ten seconds later, he stood and held out the hand, his fingers spread. Electrical currents cracked and sparked from one finger to the next, reaching into the air.

Donovan whistled. "Wow. And you are just human?"

"Boggles the mind, don't it?"

"Yes, Willoughby, it does." Chione looked around. "We are not accustomed to humans with gifts, but we're getting there. Thank you, and I agree, it's beneficial for all of us to see what each can do. Dylan, Dani, would you like to go next?"

Dylan shrugged. "Our talent isn't quite so active. Well, mine isn't. My sister has something else going on that has always freaked me out, and kind of pissed me off because it's *so* unfair. We both have the ability to read a person's nature. Like we can tell a lot about a person, their past, and who they are almost on contact. Let me demonstrate."

He faced Olivia. "Would you mind letting me touch you?" Dylan grinned and looked at his audience. "What? I'm not gonna pick one of the prettiest girls in the group? Which, by the way, is a freaking tough call. Gorgeous isn't in short supply around here." He turned back to Olivia, who nodded agreement.

All Dylan did then was slide his fingers along Olivia's bare arm, then he stepped back.

"Wow. You're…wow. The most complicated person I've ever touched. Do you object if I…"

"Go ahead, I have nothing to hide," Olivia agreed.

"The power that moves through you is so huge, I can't even define it. I saw that you didn't always know that you were this special vampire. When you found out, it changed your life. You found a family." He smiled again. "You like dangerous adventures. You once robbed a jewelry store. Not to steal the merchandise, but to see if you could do it without your vampire skills. You couldn't."

Olivia laughed. "No, I couldn't. But it took my vampire skills to get me out of it."

"And not just adventures, but sex. A long time ago you made a pledge to yourself to, and this isn't *my* language, but to fuck your way through every country on earth. You're only 8 countries short of that goal."

Olivia cocked her head. "I'd forgotten about that pledge. Holy shit, you really can read a person's background."

"We have been able to since we were very young. And there's one other thing."

"Dylan, no," Dani interrupted. "We agreed to never tell anyone."

"This is different, Dani. These people are like us, they'll understand."

He wasn't sure he convinced her, but he continued.

"We found out that if we combined our talents, we could actually push thoughts into people. It sounds bad, and it is, if abused, but we never did. We used the merge only two times. Once to get out of chores at home when we were seventeen so we could go to a party. The second and last time was to punish a man who tried to rape Dani. We had no evidence but her word, so he would never have been held accountable for his actions. And he would have hurt someone else eventually."

"I hated it," Dani whispered.

"He deserved it. After we pushed a behavior into his mind, he was trapped with it."

"What the fuck did you two do to the creep?" Scottie asked.

"We pushed the thought that he hated sex. That he found it dirty and perverse and would never again have interest in it with anyone. Including himself."

Scottie nodded. "Poetic. I approve."

"We're still not proud we did it, but it was necessary."

Koen weighed in. "No, lad. What you did was very like vampire justice. You made the punishment fit the crime and in doing so, protected others. Do not be ashamed. Your action was just."

Dani put a hand on her brother's arm, but spoke to Koen. "Perhaps, sir. But my brother and I are kind people. I've had to fight to protect us since we were children, and because I am uncommonly strong, I always win. Still, we try to leave no lasting harm."

"That, too, is the vampire way. You will like it here, lovely girl." Koen bowed and noticed that Dani was shy about the attention.

Chione drew everyone back to her to break the distraction. "We have a pair of powerful allies with you two. I look forward to showing you what you can do with your skills. Antoinette, please tell your team about your special gift."

Antoinette stood straight and tall, her hands automatically sliding against her dress to ensure she was tidy. "I, too, have a passive talent. Upon meeting someone, I seem to be able to know the immediate future as it relates to an individual. For instance, when Park entered my lab, I knew right away that she would take me from my life and that it would begin a terrifying, yet beautiful journey. Like the twins, I can read someone's nature, and while I could not put a name to it, such as vampire, Park's spirit and powers were stronger than anything I had ever known, and they were clear to me instantly. I have no ability, that I am aware of anyway, to affect someone else's thoughts or behavior. It is merely imminent visions that I carry."

"Paired with someone who has the same talent, you may be surprised at what you can do," Donovan explained.

Antoinette inclined her head in another bow. "I look forward to testing that theory."

Donovan looked at Scottie. "So, young lady, what hidden power lurks behind that thoughtful expression?"

Scottie looked at all the expectant faces. "It's show and tell, and now it's my turn? Okay, yeah, I've got a crazy skill too, but it isn't going to be of any use in any battle. It's stupid, really. When I showed it to my mother for the first time, she told me to keep the damn secret to myself. I always have."

"Not here. Everything you are is a great treasure to us," Chione reminded her.

"All right. It's more of a parlor trick that a supernatural talent."

Searching the garden, Scottie stepped away from the group. Finally she walked up to vining clematis reaching up a high trellis, covered with unopened buds. Curling her fingers around several of the soft willowy stems, the group behind her watched, amazed, as all the buds quivered, then began to open so quickly, they looked like a time-lapse video. From a promise of blooms to full-out huge flowers that covered the plant in less than one minute.

Awed murmurs brought Chione close. "Scottie…"

Shrugging, Scottie dropped her hands. "I told you it was stupid."

"Hardly. Scottie, you are a nurturer, and that is a rare skill indeed. You bring life. Your spirit is capable of infusing any living thing on earth. You are *exactly* what this battle needs."

"You guys might be delusional."

"Scottie, all of you have been chosen, do you understand that? This is your destiny, the place you have in history, and it is critical to saving this world. Starting right now, you must all accept your value to this planet. I know that I will love you all, and that we will succeed. So, how about it? We shall rest tonight, and then tomorrow, your training begins."

After uneasy rest during daytime, the next night all five new warriors sat at first meal with their hosts, who were leaving to return to their lives right after they ate.

Will still felt uncomfortable with so many people, so he chose a distant table again. Olivia approached, uncertain if she'd be welcome, since he'd become so quiet after they arrived.

"Care to share your table with a vampire?"

Will looked up and shocked her by smiling.

"I guess I'd better get used to that."

"I guess you had." Olivia dropped down, probably too close, but she couldn't help herself. Stealing a slice of his bacon, she nibbled on it, then cleared her throat.

"So, Biker, I just wanted to tell you it's been interesting, and although I'm leaving, perhaps I'll see you again one day. You never know."

"Yeah, maybe." *God, he wanted her! It had to be those irresistible vampire genes.*

"May I ask you…the tattoo on your arm, a triquetra, do you know what it means?"

"I'd be a stupid shit to put it on my arm if I didn't. Yeah, it stands for past, present, future. My fiancée and I both got one when she told me she was pregnant. Now, it's just an ugly reminder of…" He stopped and dropped his eyes.

"I'm sorry. The past creates who you become, now, in your present, and the future is where you take yourself. Will, I think you have an extraordinary future. That tattoo might mean something else one day."

Olivia bent closer, unbuttoned her shirt, and pulled it aside to reveal the exact same symbol permanently inked near her right breast just above a dusty rose nipple.

Standing, she closed her shirt. "I'll see you again."

Five

IN PARIS

"Damn it, Pirot, didn't we get those results in time?"

Fia was in a mood. Although her job was to manage the European WHO facility, sometimes she felt like all she did was stand over the labs to make sure the work got done.

"They were outsourced to *R-Cubed* three weeks ago."

"And that is relevant because?"

"Um, they haven't sent the final panel to us yet?"

"Oh. So we just wait until they get around to it?"

Sighing, beyond frustrated, Fia reached for inner calmness. Her own desire for unyielding perfection could be an issue. Part of the problem was that she'd blown off first meal tonight, hadn't bothered to see to a blood meal in over a week, and hadn't had sex in six months. On every front, she was starved.

After using a breathing technique that Cairine had taught her, Fia looked at her assistant and smiled.

"I'm sorry, Pirot. Would you kindly contact *R-Cubed*, get the panel over to my neo-virology department, and tell them I want the final from the series by tomorrow night?"

"Yes, ma'am."

"Thank you. I'm leaving now. See you in 24 hours."

Her body thrummed with exhaustion. She needed food, yes, but desperately needed her blood meal.

"First," she whispered as she headed toward her office.

Still upset and inattentive, she barreled through the corridor and slammed into someone.

"Whoa, little doggie." Taylor's rough voice penetrated the foggy state of her mind, his hands tight on Fia's arms.

"Are you okay?"

"I'm beat. And I need blood."

"Now, from what I can see."

The word, *"yeah,"* came out on a deep sigh.

With a groan, Taylor clasped her hand and pulled her toward his office.

"Where are you…"

"Shut up. You need blood, I have hi-test stuff, you're going to feed."

"Taylor, you know I don't…"

"Yeah, yeah, you don't eat where you shit. But look, it's 3 a.m., everyone's gone, and I'm your best option. Whether you like to feed off people you know or not, you need blood, and *I* have it."

He was right. If she was going to be functional at all the rest of the night, she needed this.

Taylor led her into his office and closed the door behind him, his eyes on Fia as she leaned against his hardwood desk.

"So. Are we going to do this?" he asked. A catch in his voice made Fia pause. Helpless to stop herself, she let her gaze wander over his body.

He'd been on her blood for decades, and now the blood cocktails, and his size had increased. The dark hair he wore long had a tendency to curl around his face, drawing attention to deep blue eyes that Fia had always found hypnotic.

She didn't want to feed from him. In her current state, she wasn't just hungry, she was horny, and a feeding could get out of hand. Sex with Taylor was a complication she'd always avoided in spite of his frequent sexual jokes and innuendo. It had not been a secret that he was attracted to her.

But sex...it complicated things, and she wouldn't risk ruining the incredible closeness and friendship they'd developed through years of working together. Sex was recreation for her, and because of that, she wanted and needed variety. Her sex partners were lucky if they kept her interest past a few months.

No. Not Taylor. He was sacred *because* she really cared about him.

But tonight...the blood craving...the need...

Her eyes went to his face, and she shook her head because he wore his trademark smirk. It always made her smile.

"Come on blood-sucker, live up to your legend," he taunted as he stepped around to the other side of his desk.

"I wonder if this works?" Before she saw what he planned, he picked up a letter opener and plunged it into his wrist, careful to miss the artery. Blood surged from the wound, the scent striking Fia at once.

"Taylor! What the fuck!"

"Just helping you make the right decision. Feed, Fia, you need this."

He held up his arm to show her the wound as blood slowly slid into his palm.

It was impossible now for Fia to refuse. The scent too intoxicating, she *needed* to taste it. Had she ever been this desperate? Never.

"You asked for this!" Using air displacement, she shoved Taylor onto a reclining bench near a wide window along the back of his office.

Now on top of him, she moved her body against his. God, he felt incredible beneath her. She scanned the bleeding wrist and bent over to lick it clean, then licked the wound to seal it.

"I don't feed from there." Sliding forward across his lap, grinding herself against his cock as she leaned in, she lifted the strands of satin hair from the side of his neck.

"This is my second favorite place," she whispered, and buried her teeth into him. Fia felt the first few seconds of his reaction to the punctures before his body succumbed to the euphoria common in a vampire feeding. His body relaxed and his arms went around her, pulling her closer to his neck and tighter to the swelling organ trapped in his pants.

Sucking, curling her tongue along his skin, drawing his blood in so fast, too fast, Fia didn't realize what it meant. All she knew was that his blood was like none she'd ever tasted before...*and it was addictive!*

As she drew longer, fear coiled in her belly. It was too much, she had to pull back. Blood thralls were rare, and she'd never even come close, but now, she had to drink.

Stop! her mind called to her. No, it wasn't her mind, it was Taylor and he pushed her back. He was human and shouldn't have been able to overpower her, but thankfully, he had. *The blood cocktail, thank you universe.*

He held her from him, fingers gripping her wrists.

She shook her head. *What...?*

Full memory struck hard. "Taylor, oh God! I'm so sorry! Are you okay?"

"Fine. Yeah, good." He stared into her eyes, reading her confusion. "I'm hard, Fia. Really hard. You're right, this blood-feeding thing is a sexual act."

"It doesn't have to be. I mean, it can be, but it is usually just a feed."

"Not with me."

"No." Still on his lap, Fia fully aware that he was hard, her own wetness pressed against his. "Not with you."

She started to slide off him when his hands moved to her thighs, wrapped around them, his thumbs caressing her through her skirt, moving toward the inside.

"We should finish this." His voice was now so raspy, she barely understood him.

"Taylor, no. I don't want this. Not with you."

His hands dropped away as she pushed against him and stood up.

"Wow. Way to make a guy feel special."

Fia dropped back onto her knees and put her arms on *his* thighs. "You *are* special to me, Taylor. I keep trying to tell you that. Sex is temporary. *You* are permanent to me. I can't take the risk."

"How do you know it won't work out? I might rock your world."

"You *do* rock my world. But sex is just a fuck, thanks, and goodbye to me. I was never the clingy type."

"What am I going to do with this?" Taylor cupped the thick mound between his legs.

Fia almost went to one of her old jabs, *go find one of the thousands of girls in Paris who'd love to fuck you*, but the thought stabbed her in the gut. That wasn't...oh, it couldn't be, could it? Jealousy? *Envy?*

"Cold shower, my friend. Every guy knows how to take care of that."

She needed to get out of there, so she lifted back off the floor. "And for the blood, you were right, I needed it badly. Thank you."

"Anytime," he said.

Never again, she thought.

IN COLORADO

Cool air coursed over Cairine's bare skin. Minutes earlier, Otto's big hairy body had covered hers, but after aggressive sex play, he was already in the shower.

Tomorrow morning, he'd be back on the launch deck and off to Moonbase 6 to shuttle guests to and from the other 3 facilities available to civilians.

She would rise shortly to join Jackson at the station while Otto returned to the bed to get a good night's rest to prepare for his offworld flight.

This was a shorter run, he'd only be gone for two weeks, but she'd still miss his electric personality. Rolling over to stretch out and fill the bed, Cairine let herself linger. In quiet moments like this, her mind would wander.

Talib had returned to Patagonia six weeks ago, but he'd left her pining for contact with her family and friends. Eyes wide open, she stared at her softly illuminated ceiling.

What was on her mind tonight, even after the passionate lovemaking with Otto, was Eras, brought on by her discussion with Talib about him.

Cairine usually didn't let herself think about that year they'd spent together. Eras had told her that he wanted to be her first lover, and oh hell, had he been! For three months, they only left her mountain hideaway to restock supplies. They had hiked and made love, talked for endless hours about life and love, hopes and dreams, the futures they wanted to build.

For the ten months that they were together, she thought that he was all of that for her. *He* was her life, love, hope, and every dream that she could ever dream.

It was love in its purest form, the childish belief that they would be together until they drew their last breaths.

Innocence, joy, ignorance…bliss. She had adored that man with every human cell in her body.

Now, a century later, if she closed her eyes and calmed her mind, she could touch those ecstatic feelings once again. If she let herself truly remember those days, the depth of their feelings, pain surged in. *That last day…*

It was why she tried to never think about that year.

"Babe." Otto's voice cut through her absent attention.

"I'm sorry, love, I've been daydreaming. What is it?"

He lingered against the door to the lavatory. "I know I just showered, but I can't stop myself. Once more?"

Otto had towel-dried his hair and pushed it back, which she found irresistibly sexy, standing naked on powerful legs, his cock already full, as he asked to get inside the woman he loved one more time before he had to leave.

Cairine pulled back the slick sheet as an easy smile lit her face. She'd never turn him away. "Come to me, spaceman. And I mean that literally. Come."

He launched into the bed.

Twenty minutes later, Otto collapsed. "I'll just take a really quick shower before I go in the morning. Wake me at 5?"

"Done. Get your sleep. I have to go to the station. Jackson sent a 911 text that he really needs to see me tonight as soon as I rise."

Already losing consciousness, Otto rubbed his furred chest, his eyes closed. "Okay, babe. Go see your *other* love."

As she closed the sliding door to seal Otto in the room, Cairine trekked slowly toward the galley after pulling back her UV blocking panels, opening the balcony doors, and glancing out to see the doves perched on the railing. They waited there most nights for her. She hated to think of the day when she opened the panel, and they wouldn't be waiting for her. She'd come to adore them.

A nesting pair had laid eggs two weeks ago, which thrilled both her and Talib.

Lifting her coffee cup, she smiled. Otto was right. Jackson was like a brother to her, and they *did* love each other. She couldn't imagine a day when he wouldn't be there either.

After this grand destiny stuff played out, someday in the future, she expected to make him vampire.

A quick meal later, Cairine entered the western geo-station, only twenty minutes by lift-car.

"Hey, Jax, what's so urgent?"

"New readings. They show the increasing activity we've been watching for and several spikes that are drawing a lot of concern along the epicenter. Have you felt any movement in the towers?"

"No, nothing. And you know I'm sensitive to it."

She sighed. "Okay, let's go over the numbers. It's going to be an all-nighter."

LATER IN ZAMBIA

The past two months had flown by, in which the Final Five's talents had continued to grow along with their friendships. Chione had been pleased to see the special group of humans bond on a level closer than she knew any of them had ever felt before.

"Take on one of them, fight all five," she commented to herself as she watched Donovan put them through their last paces of the night.

Shortly, she and the other vampires would go to safe places to rest for the coming day. While most of the time, the group matched their guide's schedule, she knew that sometimes they liked to stay up and enjoy the day. All five were now blood-bonded, but still fully human.

Oh, God, she understood. More than once, Chione had lingered at dawn to feel the warm rays of heat and light from the rising sun. As a child of the moon, she could tolerate direct ultraviolet for several seconds before it would begin to burn. It was worth the risk.

Right now, her eyes were on Scottie. Shortly after arrival, she'd told Chione that she didn't want to meet her father yet.

"It's too much. Until I'm ready, would you tell him not to come? I *will* meet him, I want to, but not until I adjust to all this freaky vampire, destiny, battle shit. Okay?"

Chione had nodded compliance. She *did* understand.

When she had left this community to go out into the world to find her *own* path, Chione had felt alone and lost.

Tonight, on rising, Scottie had come to her. All she'd said as she approached Chione was one word. Looking into Chione's eyes, she'd said, "Now."

Bowing her head, Chione responded. "I will make the arrangements."

Scottie had nodded and walked away. Rodney would arrive tomorrow night.

Her breathing even, at the edge of the gardens she'd come to love, she let her mind wander. This new life, this father she was expected to adore, this world that no one else knew existed…it was a lot to take. Lifting her head to the sky, she admitted, she was adjusting pretty nicely. After tomorrow, though, she might have to reassess.

IN SOUTHERN FRANCE

He sat watching the silent sunrise as he had so many times since he came to this country. And even though the sun rose over the same ocean as it always had, today it seemed different. Rodney was going to meet a young woman that Koen told him had been born from him thirty years ago.

Sadness and exhilaration spiraled in his heart and mind. A daughter to a man who had never expected to have a long life, let alone a deeply fulfilling one. That he had never known, had never been there to watch her grow and change, to be her protector and home whenever she needed one, broke his heart.

There'd been a lot of heartache over the past many years. Much joy, yes, and finally the family he'd never had, but this, after all he'd endured, to find a daughter he knew must feel as if he'd abandoned her in the world, tore him up. Pain twisted around love seemed to define the way his life began and followed him through his journey.

After a century of life, he found that he was tired, and that made him sad too.

When Koen and Tamesine had come to him several weeks ago, he'd grinned when they asked him what he'd do if he found out he had a daughter.

"After what we've been through with all these wild kids, I should prove to be a stern disciplinarian."

Koen had clasped him on the shoulder. "Lad, ya might want to sit down."

And there, in a life that had changed on epic scales more than once, the most unforeseen event of all…Koen told him he had a child. He had been disbelieving.

"Koen, Park told me that I was sterile from the infusion of vampire blood. She checked."

"Aye, she did. But son, I have discovered that if a child need be born, nothing in this world or beyond it will stop it. Your daughter, Scottie, was meant to be born."

So. He was a father without ever having been one. After nearly two months, he still had no idea what to say to her. Tamesine had hugged him and told him that when the moment came, he would.

Taking a sip of his over-sweet coffee, he chuckled and spoke aloud. Only the rising sun and rolling sea heard; the vampires were already in bed.

"Tam, my dear, you have more faith in me, lovely lady, than I deserve. But rise to the moment, I shall. Could there be anyone else on earth better suited to be a shadow parent?"

He would have to travel to Zambia this day to arrive as the vampires rose.

Africa. He tried to never think of the country, let alone to travel there. The reminder of the greatest sorrow of his life lay in the heart of the continent.

No matter his wish, no matter his intention, it didn't really take a reminder to push his mind back to the all-too-brief days when he was with Shani. He had a long history of sexual conquests before he became blood-bonded to Koen, and many notable women afterward, but only one had touched his heart, entered his soul, and remained. It wasn't even accurate to think of her in sexual terms, he'd never actually *been* with her, and yet she was the sexual fulcrum of his life. *She* was the one he would always want, always need…and would never have.

He couldn't ask about her. The other children he protected for all those years, yes, he loved to hear about their lives and loves. That they were happy and doing well.

But never the stunning empath. He'd always known that *he* wasn't good enough for her, but he couldn't hear of, think of, *imagine* her, with another man. Even now, a hundred years later, the thought ripped him up inside.

While he knew she wasn't in Zambia now, everything else would remind him of her.

"Just think about your daughter." Rodney stood and leaned over the railing to catch the stiff breeze.

"Scottie. *My* daughter, Scottie."

Fuck, it sounded weird to say those words. He had no memory of her mother, but assumed the woman had been kind and attractive and that they'd enjoyed each other. It still blew his mind that not only did he have a daughter that he should not have been able to create, but that she was one of the warriors meant to protect this planet.

Gods, it struck him...she would work alongside Shani!

"Oh, fickle fates, you must be laughing your asses off!"

IN ZAMBIA

She was nervous. It wasn't something she ever was, and she sure the fuck wouldn't admit it to anyone, but her stomach was doing fucking flip-flops. The only thing going through her mind when she woke up tonight was what she would call him. *Father? Pops? Dad? Dadio? Hey you?*

He'd be here any minute now. Scottie looked down at her attire. She'd determined that she wouldn't do anything special. Her hair was yanked back in its usual plain clip, her jeans too tight, her shirt too loose, long leather straps tied up her arms with silver beads threaded through them, earrings that looked like daggers. Yep, just normal Scottie.

"He's coming around the hedge," Chione said, and Scottie's head rose to search. Yes, she saw him. Tall, black hair, long braids tied together, and a neatly trimmed beard. She squinted. *What the hell was that?* Fuck, he wore a strapped leather wristwrap with silver beads on his right arm, similar to hers.

He was handsome. Ridiculously so. She tried to imagine what a man like this would have seen in her plain, unexciting mother. She couldn't, not at all.

The first thing she noticed when he was near enough was that he looked uneasy too. Good, great. *Two losers in a meet and greet.*

Her eyes locked on him, she had to admit that he *was* kind of elegant, in an ancient *gothy* sort of way.

"Scottie." His greeting by just saying her name took her attention, the voice deep and engaging.

She found herself trying to memorize every nuance of this first meeting. He lifted her hand and placed a brief kiss in the palm.

"We are far past the day when this introduction should have taken place. It seems it took a perfect storm to bring us together, but now that we have, I anticipate an interesting bond. I am assured that we are blood kin. Please let me tell you that you are precious to me. We shall trod this rocky new path side by side. Welcome, Scottie. I am Rodney, and I am your father."

What could she say to that? His declaration of devotion to her seemed impossible, and she was not inclined to believe him. But she wanted to. His speech was odd, and she decided to focus on that.

"Sure, Shakespeare, we'll just be all cozy." Bitchy, she knew, but dismissive attitude was her go-to when life got out of hand. This magnificent man from this incredible race, was her father? She felt small and petty next to him, certain she would be a disappointment.

Scottie watched Rodney's jaw tighten, his bright smile slip. Her gut clinched. She'd been rude and knew it.

This man was her father! She held out her left hand.

"Sorry. I can be a bitch, but you'll get used to it. Shouldn't have barked at you. I *have* been promised that none of this is your fault, so I guess I'm inclined to give you the benefit of the doubt. So, uh, yeah, I'd like to get to know you, but, uh, let's just take this slow, okay?"

Bowing low over her hand, Rodney took it, and instead of shaking it, he pressed his forehead to it. "I meet your terms."

Geez, what was this guy, a medieval knight?

Yeah, she knew she was being a flippant asshole, but, inexplicably, she felt the tightness in her gut calm. There was a possibility that this would go well and the idea that she had a father, and would get a chance to know him, brought a tickle of joy that she wasn't sure she knew what to do with. Letting herself believe that this was happening was the hardest part.

IN COLORADO

"Oh, fuck, Jax, it's here. What we've been dreading."

"We're not wrong this time, Cari. It's really coming."

"I think so, and it looks to be as terrifying as we could have imagined. Jackson, how the hell are we going to manage something of *this* magnitude? I'm not convinced that our powers are great enough to stop this."

"My dear Cari, only one way to find out. Call them. Call *all* of them here. I don't know how much time we have to prepare, but I expect we'll need all we can get."

"Any guess?"

Jackson stared at the series of screens surrounding him, each monitor showing, in real time, seismographic readings, tremors, quakes, and s-ratings. He began to shake his head from side to side and couldn't stop.

"Cari, we've discussed this at length, and I have no more answer now than ever. All I know is that it appears to be sometime soon."

She leaned over his back and put her arms around him. "I know, Jax. God, I know. It's one thing to be watching for it, but it's another to know it really may happen."

A chime brought Cairine back to attention and she moved away, reached for her fone, glanced at the face, and nodded. "No surprise with his premonitory talent. *Accept call*. Hi, Talib."

"Cari, do you see it? Do you feel it?" His voice came through the speaker, the concern obvious.

"We know about it, yes. You've had a vision?"

"Catastrophic. Initial devastation of nearly the entire continent."

"Talib, tell Jackson exactly what you've seen and particularly anything about when the eruptions may begin."

"I can't tell you when, that wasn't in the vision, but I have a strong sense of imminence. My geological frame of reference isn't scientific, but I assume you have monitors where you need them. One thing that I can tell you is that eruptions split the earth at several different sites, but the major site blows its top early in the morning. I could tell by the position of the sun. Cari, it's awful."

"It is. Ash and rock as fine as dust will cover everything for thousands of miles and won't stop there."

"I saw it shoot up into the sky hundreds of feet up and into strong wind. It moves around the nation in record time. A lot of people will die."

"I'm sorry, Talib, you're right and unless we can control it, we can't stop that outcome."

"I am sorry to be so vague, but I'm just an observer in these visions, and all I could do was stand there horrified at what I saw. We have to stop this!"

"That's the plan. We're calling the entire team here, so get Su'ad and come to my apartment. Prepare to stay a while. Jackson and Sally will get you two settled in a nice room. And let your community know that they should go into survival preparedness, just in case we can't stop this."

After ringing off, Cairine watched Jackson pressing multiple commands at his computer keyboard, sending multiple reports to his home station. "Cari, is there anything else you need me to do?"

"I'll contact Koen and Chione, but, yeah, if you'll have Sally fly in right away to help with room prep and make arrangements for food, that would be great."

"Done."

"Thanks. Koen will contact Fia and Bryson, Mac and Caed, and the human and supernatural companions posted with them."

"Hey, good, I look forward to seeing my boy Taylor. I wonder if he's still addicted to beer."

"I don't know. Last time I spoke with Fia, she said he was a brilliant pain in her ass."

"Yep, that's Taylor, all right. Genius with a side of crazy."

"That may be exactly what we need to pull this off. Chione will reach everyone else for us."

As he packed up, Jackson suddenly stopped, his eyes on Cairine's. "There's no reason to call for an evacuation, is there?"

"How do you displace millions of people on an uncertainty? How do you warn them that if the worst-case scenario happens, they can't run far enough or fast enough? What we need to do, if this turns out to be what we're afraid it will be, is to find a way to restrain it, or redirect it. If we can *stop* it, we'll party for a week. If we can't, we protect all that we can. I'm already heart-sick and bone-deep weary, so let's jump out of the frying pan, shall we?"

"By your side, Cari, always, you know that. If *you* go down, *I* go down."

"Jax, I've told you how much I love you, haven't I?"

"Never need to. I can practically *hear* you thinking sometimes."

"God, I'm predictable."

"No." Jackson pushed a long strand of copper hair back. "We've been together so long, I'm just part of you."

She slid her hand into his. "I'm so happy Chione gave you to me. I mean, *assigned* you to me."

"You got it right the first time. Go. Let your peeps know that it might be showtime."

Her fingers lingering on Jackson's, Cairine reached for her fone as she moved back through the concrete corridor that led to their field station.

"Chione, hi. It's time. We need to put some safeguards into place. I need everyone here."

Chione's voice traveled through the crystal clear lines.

"I've felt a disturbance in the ground, in the air, with the earth. I truly believe this eruption is ready to fire up."

"We will be there then."

"Do you have accommodations for all of us?"

"Of course. My mother taught me to be the perfect host."

"We will swarm in from all over the globe, my dear. I will be bringing the new warriors."

"Oh, yes, that's right. Jackson told me about them."

"It seems Mother Earth likes the element of surprise. They've only been a part of our world for a few months and now it seems we'll throw them into the fire."

"True, but Chione, *none* of us are prepared for what is to come. We're all elated and terrified at the same time."

"As it should be. Darling, know that Donovan and I have all the faith in the universe in all of you."

"Namasté, dear guardian."

"Namasté. We'll see you soon."

IN PATAGONIA

Talib hugged Kalia and stepped back to watch the tight embrace when Su'ad moved forward to hold her mother. He dropped his head so he couldn't see her tears.

"You two come back," Kalia whispered.

Unable to speak, Su'ad nodded into Kalia's neck, where she'd buried her face.

Talib spoke. "My mate, we need to go if we are to be settled in Colorado by daylight."

Su'ad lifted her head, her face transformed to its feline state. Soft black fur covered her cheekline and fine whiskers moved delicately when she spoke. "I know. Goodnight, my mother, not goodbye."

"Goodnight, my children. Travel safely." Kalia touched both Talib and Su'ad's hands before they disappeared into the brush.

Several minutes later, still standing exactly where she had been all that time, Kalia looked up as Luka entered.

"Did I miss them?"

"They're gone."

Luka perused his mate's wet face, now furred from deep emotion, and reached for her. "My love, we've seen what these first bloods can do. They'll be back, safe and sound, I promise."

Both her daughters were going to be in Colorado after tomorrow night. Nothing was going to reassure Kalia when she knew that it was the most dangerous place on earth to be.

IN ZAMBIA

"Well, pops, I guess this is goodbye for now." Scottie put out a hand to clasp her father's, largely because she wanted to touch him. No one knew what to expect from this journey.

Rodney didn't take her hand, but turned to his side to pick up the pack he'd brought from France.

"No, it's not. I'm coming with you."

"What? Why? Donovan says it's going to be dangerous."

"Which is the reason why nothing could keep me away. I've been a soldier almost all my life; always protecting someone or something. The people that I've protected all those years, and now you, will be in danger. I need to be there."

"Wow. Noble, like a knight of the round table."

"The comparison has been made."

"I can see it. This week has shown me that you're a good guy. Maybe when this is over, we can see how this goes. I'd like to come back to France with you, if that's okay. There's never really been anything for me in New York."

"Your mother isn't still there?"

"No. She died six years ago. I guess you wouldn't remember anything about her."

"Scottie, you know how different our lives are. I never had a long term, normal relationship. Whatever I had with your mother was a lovely time, but I never had the option of building a life with anyone. I didn't abandon you, I hope you understand that. I've already explained that I was not supposed to be able to father a child."

"Yeah, I get it."

"And yes, I would be disappointed if you didn't come to France with me. First, we have to get through this mission, and it's likely to bring the fires of hell."

"Yeah," she sighed. Swinging her bag over her shoulder, Scottie followed Rodney across the gardens to where everyone else waited.

Dani and Dylan were perched on a tabletop, their travel packs on the bench at their feet. Antoinette sat at the same table, but on the bench, her eyes on a tablet computer she rarely laid aside.

In the corner of the garden, Scottie watched the guy they called Biker crouched down, playing with a pair of Chione's kittens.

She looked from one to the next. So this is part of the team that's gonna save the world.

Yeah. Heaven help us all.

"Are we going to let Koen or the others in France know about the mission? Shani's parents?" Rodney asked Donovan.

"The kids don't want us to. Since they aren't part of the guardians, and they'll want to come to help, the kids have asked we keep them out of this. To protect them."

"It's probably wise." He would have his hands full just trying to make sure the first blood children were safe, Rodney didn't feature having to look after the rest of his beloved adopted family too. It was the best plan.

IN PARIS

"Got everything? Taylor, what the fuck are you doing?"

Fia waited at the door to his apartment, wondering why it took him three times longer to pack than she had. "*I'm* the girl, *I'm* supposed to take too long to pack. *You're* the guy. All you need are two pair of briefs, a toothbrush, and a pack of condoms. And the briefs are optional."

Taylor finally came from his bedroom. "Ha, ha. I'm packing up some gifts I picked up for my posse. Damn, it's been a long time since I've seen them."

Grabbing the collar of his shirt, Fia yanked him out the door and flung his three satchels into the lift-car where Ari waited.

Taylor faked brushing off his shirt. "By the way, doll, no one uses condoms anymore."

"I know that, but you're such a Neanderthal throwback, I thought *you* might."

"Someday you're going to eat those words."

"Uh, huh, won't lose any sleep over it. Here we go."

Taylor closed his eyes and curled his fingers over the edge of his seat as Fia brought the flying car up far more steeply than it was meant to. She scared the shit out of him.

IN AUSTRALIA

Colorado. Cairine. End of the world. The Big Destiny arrives.

Out of everything, it was Cairine that scared him the most.

Eras lay on his bed, his mind racing. A lot of lovers had come and gone since he'd been with Cari. A lot of years had.

What was she like now? She wouldn't have aged much, physically, but in the past century of life, she would have matured and grown. He wanted to see who she was now, but he was afraid to, because he feared he had fared so much worse.

"I'm still the overbearing lame asshole who thinks he knows it all. And I'm still as unaccomplished."

Was talking to yourself out loud a sign you were losing it?

He sighed and rolled over onto his stomach. Everyone together again. Thirty-one people meant to fix this mess of a world. Eras didn't have a lot of faith in their chance of success, but then, he didn't have a lot of faith in *anything*.

Bura's booming voice sliced through his stream-of-consciousness ramblings.

"Eras, Shani texted me and said that she and her crew are coming to pick us up, then on to Bahrain to pick up Brigitte. I've cancelled your jet."

Groaning, Eras shot up his right hand with the OK symbol and stayed still. He heard Bura grumble and the door swish closed behind him.

He should treat Bura better. Lately, Eras admitted he'd been more detached than ever; even rude to the big bear. Bura didn't deserve that. The kindest man Eras had ever known, Bura took care of him. Honestly, vampire or no, Eras wasn't sure he'd be here right now without his right hand man. Without his *brother*, for that was what Bura had become.

He shoved himself off the bed and bellowed. "Bura! Bura, get your giant ass in here!"

Moments passed before Bura walked back through the door. "What?"

Eras crashed into him and hugged Bura hard enough to crack ribs, had Bura not been a super-sized supernatural.

"I just wanted to give you a hug, buddy."

"Uh, huh. Thanks. Pants would have been appreciated."

Eras looked down. Yeah, he was naked.

"Sorry, 'bro. Just went with the moment. But you get it, right? I depend on you and I know I don't treat you with respect all the time, and I apologize for that, but I do respect the hell out of you."

"Fine. I get it, thanks. Get dressed. Your sister's plane is 30 minutes out."

With a pat on Bura's back, Eras added. "Then I'd better hurry."

Bura turned to go, but he was smiling.

At least he wasn't going to have to throw Eras in the shower. It had been a possibility.

IN SIBERIA

Bodies wrapped tight enough to squeeze the air between them, Crezia and Caedmon finished so hard, they nearly fell off their mattress. It wasn't a long fall, the mattress was on the floor, and piled high with plush blankets, and it wouldn't have been the first time.

Struggling to breathe and laugh at the same time, Crezia held onto Caedmon to keep from keeling over backward. "It's a good thing we're so good at this. Whew! Cari better give us a private room."

"I've warned her."

"What? You did *not* tell her about our acrobatics!"

Caedmon pulled Crezia close and nuzzled into her neck to bite, then licked along the edges of her breasts before he returned to draw blood. "Ummm. No details, just the simple facts. We fuck like rabbits three or four times a night and we can make no promises for propriety."

"Great. Everyone will think I'm your slut!"

"You *are* my slut," Caedmon said before he continued his blood meal. "And *I'm* yours."

"We need to get moving. I've ordered the jet for immediate prep."

Caedmon groaned and pulled Crezia against his chest. "No…" he whined. "I don't want to go."

"That's because we've gotten used to being naked and lazy."

"Nothing else to do in Siberia. And then there's the fact that there's nothing else I want to do *anywhere*."

"It's been a nice vacation for three decades, but fun and games have to give way to big destiny moments. We're needed, my love."

"I know. It will be great to reconnect, but I'm not changing the tradition we've built. We meet at least thrice each night to fuck."

"Try to stop me. Get up, Caed. I want to walk the lake once more before we go. I've noticed some odd bloom on the northeast edge."

"Shit. We've worked so tirelessly to keep this water clean."

"We've achieved a lot. Baikal is still one of the cleanest lakes on earth. Contaminated at times in its history, yes, but we've managed to protect it from complete destruction, and I'm proud of what we've accomplished."

"So let's go do some more." Caedmon watched Crezia slide off the mattress and walk to the bathroom, shaking out her hair, which had grown long enough that her curls brushed her perfect buttocks he wanted to bite. He would, too, and soon.

IN BAHRAIN, SAUDI ARABIA

Eras and Bura leaned against the plane, waiting for Shani and Brigitte to greet each other. Her greeting for Eras had been slightly less exuberant, and a whole lot less shrieking. He understood. His sisters had been placed side-by-side in the same cradle when Brigitte came to live with them, and they'd been inseparable since. Even when assigned to their guardian locations, they'd often sneaked off to visit the other in *her* assigned location. No one could keep them apart, or ever should.

"Are you finished?" Eras asked after five long minutes of grating greetings.

Brigitte flew across the tarmac and jumped at her brother, giving him a hearty hug and then a take-down. Sweeping a leg out from under Eras, she dropped him.

"Man, you went down like ultra-dense deuterium." Sitting on Eras on the hard pavement, she grinned up at Bura.

"How's my big fluffy?"

Bura's face reddened. It was embarrassing when Brigitte called him that. He'd never admit to anyone that he loved it. The nickname meant that she noticed him, and considering that he thought she was the most beautiful, smartest, and funniest woman he'd ever known, it pleased him.

"I'm well, Brigitte."

Her eyes moved over the Totem whose body was as powerful as his spirit animal. Clad in loose-fitting khakis and a tight tee shirt that showed his strong body, she felt the familiar tweak she usually did when she saw him. She'd never done him, mostly because he was one of the warriors. Too bad, his scent was intoxicating and she rather liked *big* men.

"I'd say you are," she whispered, and felt Eras push up, dislodge her and dump her carelessly onto the ground.

Bura hurried to Brigitte and lifted her in his arms. "Are you okay?" His eyes went to Eras. "Asshole."

"She isn't hurt, are you, Bridge?" Eras looked hard at his sister, concerned when he saw her pout and put her arms around Bura. Aw, hell, she was going to fuck with his friend. Bura didn't need that, he already had an unrequited crush on her.

"I hurt my ass," Brigitte complained, glancing with a sweet smile up into Bura's eyes. "Can you carry me onto the plane?"

Eras rolled his eyes as he joined Shani. "She shouldn't mess with him like that. Bura is crazy about her and he has a sensitive nature. She's going to hurt him."

"I know. You're right, but I will tell you that Brigitte, and she's unaware of this, is pretty crazy about him too. She might treat him like a big dope sometimes, but watch what happens in the future with them."

"Ugh. Now I'm going to be sick. Can we go?"

"Yup. Dean, Pilar, go get Nur and we'll board."

Shani followed everyone into the plane, her eyes lingering on the glowing skyline of Bahrain Bay. It had been a city in ruin when Brigitte and her crew arrived forty years ago. Now, it sparkled in the night, the ocean blowing in warm breezes over clean beaches. She loved this city and hoped that all went well in America so they could come home soon.

IN BRAZIL

Ife slammed the door and pushed her satchel to the front room with her right foot.

Abasi grimaced and grabbed it to lift it to the table.

"Sally flew out yesterday."

Lifting her head from her computer, Ife nodded. "I know. I understand this urgency, but we have a pretty urgent matter here too. We can't get anything to grow in the pitch valley. If we can't accomplish that, it will stunt our efforts to reintroduce wildlife to the region next year. We just don't have this kind of time to spare."

"Ife, if we do not stop Cairine's caldera from exploding, there may not be a reason to reseed life in the Amazonian basin. It could destroy everything."

"I get that. I'm sorry, it's just bad timing. And I've had another one of those horrible visions. I thought after we finished in Patagonia, and I didn't have them for decades, they were just a weird construct caused by my connection with Talib in that instance. Now, it's happening again."

"Another one? You did not tell me. What did it show you?"

Defeated, Ife scooted up on top of the table. "This basin, burning. All going up in flames; everything we've accomplished, wiped out. I guess that's why I'm so upset. I don't know if the disaster happens because we leave, or because of the volcano. We've made such progress, Abasi, I can't let anything hurt this land."

She pitched a glass vase across the room to shatter into the wall. "Why are these fucking visions so vague? If they're meant to guide, to help us, why aren't they clear? And if I'm meant to have them, why so infrequently?"

"The universe does not answer to us."

"And why is that? We are their *chosen* warriors. Why do they tie our hands and hearts?"

Abasi, slim, but strong, reached for Ife. "We are all in this together, and together we shall prevail. Trust in this, in your talents, in your friends. But get off your pretty ass and let's fly. We do not want to be late for the apocalypse."

Ife shook her head and slid her arms around Abasi's neck. "Your spirit animal may be a snake, but you have the soul of a vampire. You are right, my dear companion, we must believe. Off we go, then."

IN ANTARCTICA

"Women, again! No offense, Ban, but you are not my type and I'm pretty sick of looking at *your* naked ass."

"Mac, you are very far from my idea of sexy, too. Right now, all I'm looking forward to is eating something palatable again."

Banyu shoved his underwear into his bag, aware that they probably could use a good wash. *Everything* in there could. With just the two of them in camp most of the time, hygiene had become a luxury. Now they were on their way back to civilization.

"I hope we don't stink too much."

Maccabee sniffed under his arm. "Whew! You aren't wrong! Wonder why I didn't notice before."

"Because you didn't have a reason to care. Thankfully, that'll change by tonight."

"Hope that tin can stays tight."

"It will. Mac, you know how uncomfortable I am around crowds. I'm a little freaked out about being in the company of over thirty people."

"Buddy, I've got your back. Plus, nine other Totems will be there, all childhood friends of yours. If you need someone to pull you off the ledge, I'm your man. I would never let you fall."

"Thank you, my friend."

"Always. So, let's get out into that sub-zero shit and see how well our thermogenesis works!"

QAANAAQ, GREENLAND

Bryson poked Jessie in the side, rewarded with her usual giggle.

"Stop, I'm trying to focus on this. Indah, do you have your reports?"

Indah held up a hand. "Over there. Bry, would you fetch them for Jess?"

"Girls, we have to fly. This needs to wait until we get back."

Pushing from her seat, Jessie slid between Bryson's legs. "Sweetie, can you go get me some *kalaallit*? I'm going to miss it so much if we have to stay in the U.S. too long."

"All right, but you gals need to be ready by the time I get back." Groaning, Bryson took off using a controlled version of his vampire speed.

While she tried to choke back her laugh, Indah walked over to secure the project reports Jessie had wanted printouts of. "You have that man by his balls."

"I know. Who would have thought? He's an alpha male, sexy, huge, powerful, and I'm still the same little geeky computer hacker I was when we met. I could never have guessed."

"Jess, you always underestimate yourself. After living so long, I'm surprised you haven't cast off all those old confidence issues. He loves you, Jessie, for everything you are. You're beautiful."

As she gathered up her own reports, Jessie shrugged and leaned against the desk. "He makes me *feel* beautiful. That's the thing I love about him. He's never judged, and when we're alone together, he makes sure that I feel like the only woman in the world."

"I wish I could find a mate like that."

"We're not mated. Bryson is vampire and I'm not, so I don't know exactly how that works. Does he just ask, like humans do? I need to call my best girl and see if she has any advice."

"It's deeper than just a connection. Soul deep, my friend. One must feel it in the heart, mind, and spirit."

Indah paused and laid a hand on Jessie's arm. "Do you?"

Watching Indah's pale green eyes, Jessie raised her shoulders in a dramatic shrug. "I don't know. Honestly, I know he adores me, but I can't tell if he *loves* me. I love him, but, *soul deep*? I don't think I know what that means."

"My Jessie, when you do, you will *know* that you do. Just let life take you where it must. Do not fret over anything. Love will come, in its own way, in its own time, and you do not need to do anything when it does."

"Ugh. I liked when things were simpler. We better get back to it. I want to take print copies of all the readouts on the new geothermal systems we've supervised for the past six months. All schematics and efficacy reports, any complications, as well as new proposals. I can get a lot of work done in the waiting time between finding out what's actually happening in Yellowstone, and the time when we have to act. You know me. Can't stand to be idle even for a moment."

Indah knew. She lifted a webfiber bag that would support the weight of the files without adding even more and began to organize Jessie's information so that everything would be easy to find. While the work here at the top of the world was satisfying, she missed her brothers and sisters from the bottom of the world and couldn't wait to hold them all in her arms again.

ON A FLIGHT TO THE U.S.

"Shhh…they can still hear us."

"Then we'll just have to cuddle." Chione curled against Donovan, eyes closed, relaxed. Several moments later, she sighed and opened them to stare at the heavily shielded metal walls to protect the interior of the jet from sunlight.

"It's happening. They're coming together for their first big trial. Do you think they're ready?"

"We've spent a hundred years putting everyone where they needed to be. For a century, we've averted every financial disaster, eliminated the threat of nuclear destruction of the world, kept over 75 billion people fed. We're repairing the damage to the earth's natural spaces, recovering habitats, and stopping pandemics. Chione, we've done all we can to protect both our world and our charges. I hope there will be a time to rest soon. These warriors deserve a normal life."

"They never *had* normal. I'm not sure they'd know what to do with it."

"We've been busy. I'm ready to rest for a little while, too. At least we get to see Talib again. It's been far too long since we've seen our son."

"True. Although he's in the right place with Su'ad in South America."

Chione glanced above her head. "You know, with the sound of the engines, and the new human warriors distracted by all the crazy new stuff on their minds, I bet we can…"

Donovan rolled his mate over and stopped her with a kiss on her ass. "You know, I think you're right. Ma'am, prepare to be boarded."

IN COLORADO

Jackson and Sally dropped onto the soft lounges on Cairine's balcony.

"Thank God that's done! Jax, I'm glad you were able to hire that hospitality team to help us. Preparing all those rooms is ridiculous. And I can't even imagine making arrangements to feed that many people, nearly half of which are vampire."

"You can see why Cairine asked if you could come immediately to help me. Thanks, bud, I can always count on you."

Sally nodded, and glanced up at a dove that had taken a perch just above her head. "Shoo. Shoo I say!"

Eyes closed, Jax moaned, fatigue obvious. "Sally, I thought you *liked* birds."

"Love them. Not above my head where they can drop squishy white shit in my hair." This time she stood and waved her hand. "Shoo!"

When the bird didn't move, she dropped back and mirrored Jax, closing her eyes with a moan. "I give up. Shit away, my friend. I'm going to be in a shower and then a bed soon anyway."

They lay still for another ten minutes before Jackson cleared his throat. "You know Dean is coming in with Shani."

Silent at first, Sally finally responded. "I know."

"Where are you guys?"

"Um, not bad, not good. He tried to keep in touch, but after I got serious with Rick, he finally backed off."

"So you think it's really over this time?"

"Yeah. We tried, Jax, you know that. I loved that man from the first moment I saw him. God, even all these years later, I can remember exactly what he looked like walking across campus. I think I used to drool when he walked by. Muscles, that long sexy hair, that bad-boy attitude. It still gives me shivers when I visualize those days. And the first ten years we were together we were pretty perfect too. But, time changes people, things that happen, things that don't."

"It wasn't his fault."

"No. He wanted kids and I couldn't give them to him. That was a deal-breaker. He never agreed, but it began to fall apart about that time and we never got it back together. You know we tried, Jax."

"Yeah, I do. I always hoped you could pull it off. Dean's a good man, and you're my best friend. I always wanted you two to be happy. Together, if you could."

"I wanted it too. Maybe if we hadn't…"

Sally stopped. Maybe if they hadn't lived for a century, if this whole vampire, destiny thing hadn't happened, they would have made it. *But it did and you couldn't go backward, only forward.*

"Anyway, I'm okay. Seeing him again will sting, but I have pretty high pain tolerance."

"So you're not in love with Rick?"

"No. It's playtime, plain and simple. He knows it."

"Aren't you interested in happily ever after?"

"Nah. It's kind of impossible when you've been alive for so many years. I think happily ever after is just a children's fairy tale."

"Woo, look at you, living on the dark side."

Popping her lids open, Sally turned to face Jackson and saw him staring back. "Look who's talking! How many serious relationships have *you* had in a hundred years?"

"It's time for a shower. See ya."

Jackson hopped up and felt the brush of Sally's hand as she grabbed for him.

"Coward!"

Six

IN COLORADO

Squeals filled the large banquet room where the new arrivals from all over the world converged to meet with Cairine and find out about their accommodations. More than that, it was old friends and family meeting, many after decades apart. Their duties demanded attention, the earth and her children came first, but now, at a time when they must all come together to protect the world, they could take a few moments to hug and be with those they loved.

Cairine couldn't stop touching each and every traveler. The women she loved like sisters, Shani and Brigitte, arrived first, and she threw herself at them, all three crying as they held each other.

"Shani, my God, your hair is gorgeous! Look at you, my sweet sisters, how much more lovely you've gotten, and you were obscenely beautiful before!"

"It's a reflection of our company, Cari. Oh, this is heaven!"

Jackson and Sally stood back and watched the reunion, tears flowing too. They may not have been vampire and had the history these women had with each other, but they'd been with them for a century and felt a connection that went beyond friendship.

Jackson glanced at the door because he knew that Dean would have come in with Shani, and Eras would be here too. Those two men would bring strong reactions from Sally and Cairine, the women he loved more than anything else in his life.

As he watched the vampire ladies reunion, the door opened, and he saw Dean skirting it, lingering, as he glanced in and saw Sally watching the vampires. His eyes went to Jackson and he backed out, the door closing silently again.

"Sal, I'll be right back." Jackson laid a hand on her arm and walked out to see Dean in the corridor.

"Hey, buddy." Dean's quiet voice greeted Jackson as he walked up and pulled him into a tight embrace. They stayed like that until it felt awkward, and Jackson stepped back.

"Nice to see you again. Whoa. Looks like you've been working out." Dean's observation that his computer nerd friend looked buff made Jackson grin.

"Knew I had to compete with my old friend with the super-hero body. Not bad, huh?" Jackson punched himself in the gut to show his hard, and hard-won, abdominals.

"You look good." They both knew that Dean wasn't talking about Jackson's muscled body. "Missed ya. Missed the whole gang since we got split up. I cannot believe how many years it's been since we were together."

"Time has a different feel now that we're kind of immortal."

"Temporarily. Once this whole thing is done, we'll probably be put back on the street."

"Yeah…" But Jackson knew better. The humans were a part of their vampire families now. "I don't know how we'd readjust after all we've been through."

"Nah. So, uh, how's Sally?"

"She's great. You might as well come on in and say hi. You can't avoid her this whole time."

"No. Is she still with, uh…"

"Yes. But you got this. Come on."

Dean nodded and followed his old friend into the large room to see the one, the only, woman in all these years that he truly loved. Life, even a long one, didn't always work out the way you wanted it to, and his relationship with Sally was the thing that he wanted to work out and wasn't going to. His chest felt tight as he lock-stepped Jackson up to where she stood.

When she turned around and saw him, he watched her eyes, her lips, to see how she reacted. Controlled response, eyes on him the whole way, lips still, jaw set. Did that mean that she was as apprehensive as he was? Or that seeing him for the first time in so long meant nothing to her? He couldn't tell, and that made this much harder.

"Dean."

"Sal."

She was a vision of yesterday and tomorrow wrapped in a tight-fitting sundress. He almost went on his knees and begged her to let him have another chance. Pride wasn't what kept him from doing it. The fact that she was with someone else, and apparently happy, did.

"You look lovely, Sally," was what he said instead.

Sally watched Dean approach and all the old feelings swept in. He had been her dream once, and she realized that nothing had changed. What she wanted to do was throw him down and lick him from top to bottom. The college girl she'd been when they first got together might have pitched all their bad history into the wind and done precisely that. Instead, the confident pragmatic woman she'd become made her nod when he complimented her and answer casually.

"So do you. It appears that the tropical environment is good for you."

"Oh, yeah. We drink fancy cocktail drinks with umbrellas around the clock."

What an odd thing to say, Sally thought. Then it struck her, he was nervous. Wow, Dean...*nervous*. That certainly didn't fit in with her vibrant memories of the cocky Dean telling her what it was he needed and explaining that life gave you one chance and you needed to live it to the fullest. Right before she knew that he was right, and that he wasn't fulfilled in the life that they'd built. That she had to let him go.

No ruminating in lost dreams or possibilities. Sally gave Dean a nice smile and walked over to greet the ladies who had just arrived.

It was all she wanted to deal with right now.

Two hours later, settling in, Shani released a happy sigh as she lifted one of Cairine's local drinks to her lips.

She used her tongue to move the viscous fluid around her mouth until it slid down her throat, an exquisite flavor like nothing she'd ever tasted before. "What did you call this again? This is spectacular!"

"It's called *giera*. A local food chemist created it. I knew you ladies would love it." Cairine topped Shani's glass off.

"Love it?" Brigitte stuck her tongue into the glass and licked at the surface of the drink. "I want to *make love* to it."

Shani glanced at her sister. "Bridge! I see you haven't lost your penchant for making everything about sex."

"Babe, everything *is* about sex. The question is, why haven't you discovered that by now?"

"I don't know. Maybe I need some true motivation. It's been a while since I had a good… No, I'm not going there; you'll find men and keep sending them my way. I know you, Bridge, you won't stop until…"

"Until you're good and fucked."

"Ugh! I can take care of that. I mean, I can find my own men. Lately, I've just been too busy."

"Dean seems to be interested."

"Dean's a darling, but we're friends and I'm not interested in him sexually."

"I'm still going to work on that for you while I'm here. Cari, how's the local talent?"

"Pretty nice."

Brigitte rolled to face Cairine. "Are you still with that space pilot?"

"Otto. Yes, I am, and it's going great."

"Yum." Silent suddenly, Brigitte scooted upright and reached for a plate of sweet breads. "Cari, you know that Eras came in with us."

It took a few moments before Cairine answered. "Yes, I know. I, um…haven't seen him yet."

"Jackson took him and Bura straight to their rooms. I guess he's trying to be sensitive."

"He needn't be. Eras and I were such a long time ago. I assume he's long moved on."

Shani glanced at her sister, then slid from her chair and walked over to land on Cairine's, straddling it, her hands on Cairine's thighs.

"Sweetie, Eras isn't trying to be sensitive. He honestly doesn't know how he himself will react when he sees you again. Cari, he's *never* moved on."

Cairine looked into Shani's earnest face, then to Brigitte's, then back to Shani. "I really don't know what to say. Should I go talk to him? Let him know it's all right and that he's welcome here? Remind him that we were over before this century even began?"

"I think you should talk to him, yes, but be gentle. I could feel his emotions as we traveled here and they're all over the place. For Eras, *you're* the one that got away. You're his perfect dream."

"No, I can't be."

"I think you are. So, maybe just tell him it's nice to see him again? Let him take it from there? Be honest, but remember that he's the type of uber-macho male that blusters his way through life thinking that it's all parties, and sex, and fun. It isn't, and he knows that, but he doesn't want to admit it. He's hurting, Cari."

"I never wanted that for him. Okay. Uh, why don't you two enjoy the evening and I'll go talk with him. I'll come back when we're finished. Thanks, Shani. I think you're right, I need to see him and get this over with."

Cairine left her drink behind and went through the apartment to the corridor beyond.

Brigitte closed her eyes and dropped back into her lounger. "That's messed up. Poor Eras, he won't know what hit him."

Sighing, Shani took her chair again and mirrored her sister by closing her eyes to block everything out. "Poor Cari, too, Bridge."

"Cari? She has her life made!"

"No. Cari doesn't realize it yet, but she's never *really* moved on either."

Past the corridor in front of her apartment, up to the floor where she'd put all her guests that had arrived or were yet to arrive, Cairine's heart pounded. This, of everything, was impossibly hard. She thought she could handle this catastrophic event better than having to stand face to face with Eras and make nice polite conversation.

And it shouldn't be this way. She loved Otto, they had a perfect life together. He made her laugh, he satisfied her in bed, and she knew that he loved her. Eras had been her first, yes, that made him special, but it was a hundred and seven years ago. She'd moved past that relationship. Hadn't she?

Of course she had.

She began to talk to herself out loud, aware that she was trying to convince herself this was okay. "He's just someone that I grew up with and fell for when I was young and ready to discover love and sex."

When she reached Room 5, assigned to Eras by Jackson, it took a full forty-five seconds before she hit the buzzer.

The door opened immediately and Bura stepped out to hug her.

"Big guy, hey. You look great. How is it down under?"

"Hot. A lot of work, but fulfilling." He paused only briefly before he continued. "Are you here for Eras?"

"Um, yeah. Is he inside?"

"No, he went up to the roof. It feels a lot more enclosed here than it does in Australia."

"I bet. Thanks. Uh, I guess I'll go look for him."

Bura didn't close the door and go back inside until he saw her disappear around the corner.

Might as well do this…she was going up to find Eras.

Once on the roof, Cairine let her eyes wander over the thick gardens, to the greenhouses, to the oversized coop she'd had built for the pigeons.

At first she didn't see him, then her eyes landed on a large figure on the other side of the rooftop, leaning dangerously far over the edge of the building.

"That won't kill you, but it will certainly mess you up."

The figure turned to face her as she advanced on him. The closer she moved, the more distinct the outline, and…*dear heavens, she'd forgotten his erotic scent!*

"Cari, Cari, quite contrary." The little jibe he used to say decades ago since even then they often butted heads on ideas and then made love to make up.

His deep voice filled the space between them, drawing her forward. She needed to see him, to be near, but she knew, especially now, this near to him, she'd better not *touch* him. Her fingers twitched and she balled them up.

She had to lick her lips so she could speak.

"Hello, old friend." *Old friend.* That was safe, wasn't it?

She watched him drop back against the stone wall that surrounded the rooftop, his body rigid.

"Old friend. Yeah, I guess that's right."

Near enough now, they could see each other clearly in the rose-colored string lights she'd hung all along the perimeter, giving the roof soft illumination and a festive atmosphere.

"Of course it is. We've known each other forever. I wanted to welcome you to Colorado."

"You mean *back* to Colorado."

"Yes, of course. Welcome back. It's changed a lot."

"Tower buildings, like everywhere else. Yeah, it's changed. I like how it was before."

"Well that was a long time ago, Eras."

"I remember every moment."

He was going there, he wasn't going to let this be easy. *He would break her heart again.*

Okay, fine, if that's how he wanted this to be. Shani had said he was hurting, had asked Cairine to be gentle with him, but she felt like she needed to be on the defensive to protect herself.

"Those memories are precious and mean the world to me, yes, but that's all this is. Remembrance, and perhaps regret for choices made that ended our time together. It's been decades now, and we both have lives away from each other, Eras. Respect that, please. I want to remain friends."

Before she could react, he was inches from her, his face so near, she could feel his breath, his fingers curving up her jawline and under her hair. "I could never be friends with you," he whispered.

Stunned at the direct admission and his sudden touch, Cairine didn't move, barely breathed, as Eras lowered his head and his lips touched hers. She wanted to bury herself in him, bury her tongue in his mouth. It took everything she had to keep from pulling him onto the rattan mats she had all over the floor of the rooftop, and rip his clothes off.

He *tasted* incredible, he looked *perfect*, he felt like he'd *never gone.* The young woman who had fallen in love with Eras before she'd become vampire stood in his arms again, in love with him again, like all those years just evaporated, like there hadn't been several lifetimes since they'd been together, and like they hadn't hurt each other so long ago.

Only, it wasn't true, was it?

"Eras, back away from me. We're not lovers, we shouldn't do this."

Eras stopped, but he didn't move. He dropped his head and buried it beneath Cairine's hair, his hands still curled around her face. She could feel as well as hear his sigh. "I can't, Cari. Don't make me."

Finally, she slid a hand up and buried it in *his* hair, which felt like smooth satin, and against her better judgement, weaved her fingers in. "Eras, I'm not *yours* anymore."

The statement slid between them and stung him. He knew that she was with someone else. *He knew it*, he just couldn't admit it.

Wordless, emotions raw for both of them, they stood entangled in each other, every touch magic and torture, until Cairine stepped back, pulled his arms from her, and pushed him away.

"Eras, you are a member of this team, and always a friend, family really, but you must understand that I cannot do this anymore. I am not only involved with another man, I have responsibilities that require most of my heart and mind. I hope you have a good time here with your fellow warriors, but what we had, what we *were*, is long over. Now, there will be a second meal in the dining room in one hour. I hope you'll join us."

Cairine turned and left so quickly, she thought she split the air a little. She couldn't look at him again; she didn't trust herself. It was clear to her now that she had lied to Eras. Their feelings for each other, *her* feelings for him, were far from over.

Just after everyone had been seated for second meal, a loud female voice bellowed from the doorway. "Is this the free community meal?"

The diners looked up to see a flood of people racing in. Fia, Taylor, and Ari had arrived from Paris, and just behind them, Ife and Abasi from Brazil. No sooner had they come into the room, welcomed with tight hugs and loud greetings than another group entered.

Bryson, with Jessie and Indah, blew past the others to grab Cairine. "Cari! Hostess with the mostest! God, it's great to see all of you again!" His eyes moved around the room. "Hey, where are my bro's?"

"Caed and Mac aren't here yet, and Eras must be in his room. He hasn't come down to eat tonight."

"What a pussy! Okay, I'll go get him in a minute, but first…look at all of you. Fuck, I missed you!"

After welcoming the new groups, conversations flourished, ceaselessly, along with generous mountains of food for the next several hours.

At one point, Cairine noticed that Bryson had disappeared, but neither he or Eras showed back up. She couldn't help but wonder what was going on, where they were, and what they would talk about. She hoped like hell it wasn't *her*.

Arrogant, she thought. *Bry and Eras are just old friends catching up. I'm sure you're the last thing on their minds!*

She admitted, however, that *Eras* wasn't the last thing on *hers* tonight.

Cairine turned to Shani. "So, four more groups will arrive tomorrow night. Mac and Banyu will be coming in from Antarctica, Talib and Su'ad from Patagonia, Caed and Crezia from Siberia. Chione and Donovan are bringing the new human recruits."

Brigitte snatched three macadamia nut cookies from Shani's plate, grinning as she chewed one. "I hear they're a unique group."

Fia nodded and grabbed one of the cookies back from Brigitte, who complained, "Hey! Those are the last of the macadamias!"

"Serves you right. They weren't yours to start with."

Shani put a hand out to each woman. "Children, do I have to get out a paddle?"

"No, Mother." Fia and Brigitte laughed as they answered together. Finishing off the cookie she stole, Fia wiped her mouth with the back of her hand. "Hey, I hear that one of the new recruits is Rodney's daughter."

Brigitte's eyes shot to Shani.

As if she hadn't heard anything Fia said, Shani focused carefully on swirling whipped cream onto a plate of strawberries. When she looked up at Brigitte seconds later, she smiled. "Rodney's daughter? That's interesting. He's with someone then?"

Brigitte placed a hand on Shani's, who pulled away as if she'd been burned. Almost instantly, Shani moved it back to intertwine her fingers with her sister's. "I'm fine."

With their shared empathic skill, Brigitte knew that wasn't true.

Shani looked back at Fia. "So, he has a mate?"

Re-occupied with the food on her plate, Fia spoke as she chewed on a fried cheese stick. "Um, no. I mean, I don't think so. Cari, do you know the details?"

Since Fia had brought the subject up, Cairine had been quiet, watching Shani deal with the news.

In Patagonia when they'd flown in to rescue the Totem children on their first mission together, most of the team had been completely oblivious to Shani and Rodney's involvement. Even if they hadn't been, so many years had passed, no one here would have thought anything was going on between them.

And it wasn't. Cairine knew it never had. Rodney had refused Shani's advances then, telling the sexually awakening young woman that she was meant for a better man than he.

Although decades had flown by, there had been a lot of living, a lot of loving, in between those days and this moment when the shocking news of Rodney's daughter had been delivered unsuspectingly by Fia.

Cairine could see Shani's stoic demeanor as she tried to hide her reaction. *Yes, she knew the details*. Now she needed to tell them carefully. Her eyes moved between Fia, who'd asked, and Shani, whose heart beat fast rhythms as she waited.

"I know that the young woman in question never knew that Rodney was her father. He didn't have any idea he had a daughter until Chione's vision that she was one of the final warriors."

"And the mother?" Shani asked, the words carefully enunciated.

"A random stranger. A single tryst one night decades ago when Rodney had accompanied Koen back to New York City for a simple errand."

Cairine captured Shani's misty gaze. "He doesn't even remember her."

Fia, thankfully, was unaware of the emotional trauma her seemingly innocuous bit of news had caused. Laughing, she tore into a deep-fried onion.

"I bet that was a shock after 30 years. Not only do you find out that you have a crazy world-saving destiny, but you meet your father, and he's not only hot, but he's the same age you are. Classic vampire-level drama. I remember Rodney well. As sexy as any vampire I've ever met."

Shani's chair screeched on the shiny tile as she pushed it away from the table. Standing abruptly, she smiled to all the ladies around her table. "Hmmm, this has been lovely tonight, but I've a headache. You know how my empathic talent works. Too many people, too many thoughts, can be overwhelming. I think I'll turn in. Cari, thank you for your hospitality, the room is beautiful. Bridge, Fee, I'll see you guys tomorrow night."

She couldn't get away fast enough. God in all the heavens, the last thing she expected to be confronted with here, in Colorado, reunited with her family and friends, was Rodney.

And the news that he had a child with some woman, random or not...hurt. Regardless of the years, the lovers that *she* herself had entertained over all that time, being presented with such obvious proof that he'd had sex with other women, made her stomach clench.

Standing in the center of her room, she assured herself that she was happy with her life, with the choices she'd made, but something like this forced her to face one inescapable truth...*no*, there was one choice she wished she *had* made. After her conversion, she had always wished she'd gone to France and thrown that big-ass wannabe vampire onto the sand. She would have ripped that damn sleeveless vest off over those huge arms, those too-tight leather pants, and...

Good God, the memories of him were too vivid, too raw.

She was ashamed of herself for not being honest with her sisters just now. She'd learned to control her empathic input from people many decades ago. Her sisters knew that. Well, Fia might not, but Cairine and Brigitte certainly did. Before she'd left the table, she had read their emotions...they were acutely aware and intensely concerned for her.

They needn't be; Shani would have these unwelcome feelings under control soon. Rodney was nothing to her but an overtly attractive man who had ignited a powerful crush for her emerging sexuality; a dream long dreamt and abandoned in her young girl's past.

So why did she ache so much?

"Sleep. Blessed rest and I'll be good as new tomorrow night. It's the unexpected shock that knocked me off balance, that's all."

Sliding her clothes off to drop abandoned onto the floor, Shani stopped in front of a mirrored wall, her attention on the naked woman who stared back. She was breathing too hard, a hand on her chest to control the tightness. The image faded and one of the memories from those days at Koen's villa when she met Rodney bloomed before her now closed eyes.

This…she couldn't deny. This…a memory so sharp, so real, she could *smell* his scent. *Waves crashed around them as he picked Shani up and her arms went around his neck. She remembered how good his skin felt, the smooth heat, and suddenly sliding her fingers upward until they weaved into his long hair. He smelled like sex, and her body reacted, deep longing struck her between the legs, and she wanted him.*

In the memory, their eyes met and Shani realized, *now*, and then, that this was the moment she'd fallen for him. This was the moment her heart told her that this hard-bodied, perfectly-made, noble man, was hers. All her efforts to forget him fell into an abyss. Rodney was still there, in her heart, her soul, and her body waited to feel him on her, in her, a part of her.

It had been one hundred and seven years since Shani had touched that man, and nothing had changed other than a failed attempt to forget him.

The memory of Rodney slipped away and Shani opened her eyes to see her own image again in the mirror, one hand curved over her breasts, another resting on her belly.

"Not tonight," she whispered. "Sleep, and then consider tomorrow how you will deal with meeting your lost lover's daughter."

The sheets felt sensuously cool against her skin. Sleep would be hard won this night.

On the rooftop of a building adjacent to Cairine's, Bryson and Eras sat on top of the stone wall that protected the edge.

"Fuck," Bryson murmured. "That is a long fucking drop, buddy. Even a vampire could get seriously banged up and die if he fell off here."

Eras nodded as he took a long drag on a lit, brown-paper wrapped weed. His eyes watering, he glanced at his friend. "Shit, Bry, this stuff is amazing. What is it?"

"We grow it in the interior. Since Greenland's ice shelf starting melting, we lost a lot of the coastline, but gained about thirty percent of the interior. You know I live on a fucking floating glacier, don't you? Anyway, this stuff was called marijuana in the old days, but we've reengineered this strain and it's powerful enough to get a vampire high. Cool, yeah?"

"Fucking yeah. I feel calmer than I have in a long time."

"Great, just don't get in the habit. They call this a *joint*, and we primarily produce it as a pain reliever, and to help some people cope with bad situations, but it can be addictive." Bryson paused before he continued. "And buddy, I can see you are troubled." He paused again. "It's Cari, isn't it?"

"Yeah…" Eras sighed and let his gaze wander out over the descending mountainside of tower buildings. "I hadn't realized until she walked up to me tonight that I've been hurting since we broke up."

"Dude, *you* were the one who chose to take off back then. You wanted to see the world and experience it wholesale as a human man. When you joined me and Mac, you partied harder than we did. I can't even remember how many women you fucked back then, but it was off the charts."

Smoke curled from the joint Eras held and he nodded.

"Yep. No one to blame but myself. I was young and stupid, and didn't think that I was ready to fall in love and stay with one woman forever. That seemed obscene to my raging libido at the time."

"Mac told me that five years later, you called Cairine and wanted to meet her again. She said no?"

"She said *drop dead.* She told me that she'd had several lovers since I'd left and that *all* of them were better than I was."

"She was hurt."

"I know that now. But way back then, I was an arrogant asshole. Fuck, *I* wouldn't have taken me back. Cairine has always been the smartest of us. I lost her, man, and my life just went to shit trying to rediscover that connection, that joy, that we had. I never have."

"I'm sorry, 'bro. Well, the good news is that we're immortal and you have plenty of time to woo her back."

After taking several long draws from Bryson's *miracle* weed, Eras smiled. "I am. I am going to win her back. She loves me, I know she does."

"You better be sure *you* love *her* this time."

Eras didn't answer Bryson at first. Suddenly he stood up on the narrow ledge. "She's my mate. I know that. I think I've always known. The stupid young man who left her has a lot to answer for."

"Good. To second chances. Fix it, my friend. For now, though, the sun isn't far from rising."

"I can feel it. Let's go in. Thank you, Bry, for providing clarity."

"I just provided a sounding board."

"Yeah, and this stuff helped. I want some more."

Bryson wasn't sure that was a good idea.

Seven

Rodney followed the group of warriors into the ridiculously high building. Although the Colorado Rockies were incredibly expansive, he felt claustrophobic the moment he stepped inside the towering building. Being so enclosed set him on edge.

It couldn't have anything to do with the fact that he knew Shani was here, could it?

The decades had flown by, and he'd been busy watching over Koen's next three grand-children. Park and Bas had continued to have the precious first blood children they desired, and although things had calmed down significantly, and no threats to the family had presented in all that time, Koen still liked that Rodney was there to protect them when the vampires couldn't.

But his conversion was coming soon. Park's last child had changed to vampire just two months ago, and now, for the first time in a hundred and thirty years, Rodney had no charges. Two weeks ago, Koen had told him that he wanted Rodney to do the final conversion to vampire.

Rodney was grateful. He was tired, and ready to accept the new life as an adopted member of Koen's family. He was already family, he knew that, but the conversion would make him stronger, and immortal. He'd need to seek blood meals, but he wouldn't have to drink the power cocktails of drops of blood from multiple vampires anymore. It was a change he welcomed. No one remained blood-bonded forever.

Now, here, within breathing distance of the only woman he'd ever loved, he found he could barely breathe. How had she changed? She would be as lovely as she ever was, he knew that, but he craved a moment to just sit and watch the woman she would have become from the sensual innocent she had been.

She would be magnificent, he had no doubt. His heart pounded in anticipation of just that moment when he first saw her after all this time.

Everyone was tired and hungry. The new recruits, excited and apprehensive, watched everything with fascination. Except, Rodney noticed, the sullen man from the desert. He'd signed on to this willingly, but he didn't seem to be open to the experience.

Donovan led them through the building to an elevator near the back of the first floor of the tower that led to the top floors owned and occupied privately by Cairine and her *special* group of friends.

As was typical for him, Rodney took the rear of the line, the best position from which to guard and protect. His daughter travelled in front of him, well within reach and line-of-sight, easy for him to get to in case of trouble. None was expected, but he still remained on guard.

The elevator was one of the new mag-lev systems and glided soundlessly, quickly, smoothly, up over fifty floors until it stopped with little discernable motion and the wide doors slid back to reveal a high-arched entryway and a big welcoming party.

The noise level shot up as effervescent greetings filled the acoustically efficient room. Rodney watched his daughter move into the fray along with the other recruits, Chione, and Donovan. He stayed back and just watched, his eyes seeking Shani. She dominated his mind right now, as his heartrate peaked and his breathing shallowed.

He needed to see her, and more than that, he wanted to touch her. It was crazy how he'd lived all these long decades without her, and now, so near, he was almost desperate for her.

"I'm losing it," he whispered. Eyes still searching, he caught a glimpse of a dark-haired woman behind his own group of new arrivals. Locked on, he watched the pale peach of her dress that he could only see glimpses of behind other guests. And then they parted and the woman turned around.

Shani. Luminous. Smiling, her genuine warmth radiating, beautiful in a dress that hugged her breasts and waist and flared out into a full skirt that flowed around long sexy legs. She was barefoot, like she had been the first time he saw her.

God... He was still in love with her, deeper than then, aware now that there was nothing to stand between them, nothing that would stop him from taking her...except her forgiveness.

That smile could melt him, it had before. Rodney watched every move, everything she did, as Shani reached out to take Dani's hand to welcome her to the mountains, when he saw her expression change and her head move up, her eyes searching the entrance of the room until they landed on him...shocked.

Her polite mask slipped, and he wanted to go to her to explain, to tell her he loved her, that he'd waited.

Rodney didn't move. Shani wasn't just shocked, *she was pissed*.

From across the room, she felt something hit her gut so hard, something she couldn't identify, a feeling, a sense of recognition, but she didn't know what. Seconds later she knew, it was a scent that assaulted her, one she *did* recognize, but thought how crazy she was...he couldn't be here.

The gut punch grew, so Shani looked up to scan the faces filing into this banquet room. She knew most of them, noticed those she didn't, and then her eyes landed on a face she hadn't thought to ever see again. Rodney, *here*, staring at her like he could eat her, the way she was afraid that she was looking at him. God, she'd just tried to purge him last night, and here he was, waiting for her. For a split-second, her heart reached for him, but the remaining split-second, pain and anger surged. How dare he show up in here without warning or explanation? At the very least, she should have been told he would be coming here.

Someone needed to answer to that!

Rodney, sudden, close enough to touch, to kiss, to slap, to strike, *to fuck!*

"I've got to get out of here." Shani was unaware she spoke out loud until Dani, waiting in front of her, responded.

"It's overwhelming, isn't it? I feel the same way."

"Yes, it can be. Dani, welcome to our team. Excuse me."

It took everything she had for Shani to walk out of the room instead of run. More than anything, she wanted to use air-displacement to blow out of there and get as far as possible from any chance of confrontation with Rodney. As she cleared the back entrance to the room, she grabbed her shoes, and did exactly that. Out of the building, moving across the curved landscape as she moved higher up the mountain, she didn't stop until she reached an undeveloped ridge that showed the expanse of mountaintops below. A nearly full moon illuminated an awesome landscape.

Dropping onto the edge of the ridge, her eyes moving over the beauty below, the sky filled with lingering white clouds, she realized that if he'd come to her, she might have hit him. Right now, her knee-jerk response was to punch him in the face for showing up and knocking her off balance.

After a deep cleansing breath, she spoke a mantra she'd used for years, never more needed than at this moment. "Peace within, peace without."

She could *do* this. "He really *is* nothing to me."

Why, then, had he wrecked her? Why, then, had she run away, so stung by his presence tonight, she thought that if she saw him again, she might throw up?

Everything felt tight. Shani pulled the band from her hair and let the wind take it. She slipped her shoes off and threw them behind her. *Better.*

Finally, her breathing slowed to a calm cadence as her mind cleared enough to reach for the reasonable woman she knew she was. She could do this. Co-exist with Rodney for the mission. When out of nowhere, his scent came back to her, strong and erotic, she smiled. *And maybe not.*

She laughed at herself. "Perhaps I should just leave."

"I wish you wouldn't."

For ten seconds, Shani looked over the mountainside, and wondered if a vampire could survive that jump.

He was behind her. He must have followed her from Cairine's building. Apparently he was still blood-bonded, carrying Koen's vampire talents, and it appeared they had continued to increase.

There was no option; she had to face him sometime.

Tamping down rising panic, Shani pushed off the ledge, stood, and turned.

"You know, coming to me on the edge of a mountain, alone, could be a bad tactical mistake."

"Yeah, I considered that. I came anyway. This moment was going to happen, and I thought that it would be better away from everyone else. It appears you haven't forgiven me."

"Hmmm."

He stood, legs wide, set hard, no more than ten feet from her, bigger than she remembered, raw sexuality pulsing from him. Or was that just *her* response?

His attire had changed, although he still wore the black leather pants and boots. The sleeveless vest that drove her mad back then had been replaced by a tight white shirt and a tailor-made full-length leather coat that fit his heavily muscled body perfectly.

"Why are you here?" Shani barked the question with more venom than she intended.

"All the people I've been responsible for since I joined the vampire community are here and in danger. I had to be here to fight alongside this team, to offer any assistance I could. "

He stepped closer, one step, two, three. "And then there's you."

Although his blue eyes that used to mesmerize her were lost in the darkness, Shani remembered every detail.

"And then there's me. Just another one of your charges."

"Never. You know that. Shani, we have to talk about us. I won't let this distance remain. When I knew I would see you tonight, part of me figured you would have long ago forgotten me, that I really *was* no one to you. But I had hope that perhaps you still cared. Even if only as friends."

Only as friends. *Only as friends?*

The phrase struck her like a dagger in the chest. Shani was on him before he saw her move. The ground flew out from under him as she shoved him to the ground viciously enough to knock the air out of him.

Straddling him, she leaned in until she was just inches from his face. "Friends? Friends, my ass! You have to know how much pain you caused me. How much I apparently still feel in spite of my desperate attempt *not* to."

Lying on hard ground, sore as hell, all Rodney could feel was Shani's body pressed against his. Her face, the most beautiful he'd ever seen, close enough to touch and kiss, her dark eyes glistening in the low light of moonshine. He wanted to roll her under him and bury himself in her to never come out again.

A smile came as he thought about how much damage he'd sustain if he tried that. She was shaking, fury and pain obvious, so at least he knew one thing now that he hadn't before…she had *not* forgotten him.

"Shani…"

"Don't. You may be right, but not now, and not soon. I need to process this situation. I don't want to see you around, so do me the favor of walking the other way if you see me first."

"We will not achieve…"

"Don't try to charm me. What I say goes, blood-bond."

Harsh. She was attempting to invalidate him, to forge an impersonal relationship.

That would never happen. Rodney's fingers lay on the ground near her thighs and he couldn't stop himself. They moved up to slide along the smooth warm skin above her knee, and when she didn't push him off, he continued to move up, and up, toward...

Shani exploded off him as if his hands burned her.

"I'm not yours. Don't touch me like that again."

Standing up, careful with a now injured right ankle, Rodney smiled and saw Shani flinch. No, the woman was not immune to him as she hoped.

It was at that moment that Rodney knew that he would move hell and earth to be with her, to see her happy for the rest of her life.

He nodded. "Not until you ask."

"Immortal or not, you'll grow old waiting for that." Her voice was low, as if *she* didn't believe what she said.

A rush of wind replaced her. Looking around the mountaintop, he knew that she'd done what he had decades ago...she'd taken off because she didn't know what else to do.

She still loved him, he was certain now. For himself, there had never been a moment since he held her in his arms on Koen's beach that he hadn't known that she was the only mate for *him.*

Turned on, angry, confused, Shani reached the roof of the tower and wandered across it for what seemed like hours. It wasn't, but she needed the time to seek her inner calm. How, after that confrontation? After touching him, after feeling his fingers on her thigh. *God!*

Did she remember that Cairine had a heated swimming pool on the floor below this one? Yes, she did. Before she tried to turn in to sleep, a leisurely swim in warm water might help her manage all the raging emotions coursing through her. In seconds, she entered a room where dim amber lights reflected off the water in a full-size swimming pool. Sighing, her eyes on the sparkles covering the surface of the pool, she knew it was exactly what she needed. She started to slip her dress off to do a few relaxed laps when a dark head popped up at the edge of the pool near the ladder.

The woman faced away from Shani, but turned toward her as she pushed her wet hair behind her and squeezed it back with her hands. Moving to the ladder, she looked up suddenly and saw Shani.

"Oh. Hi. I hope I'm not intruding. The lady who owns this place told us about the pool and I wanted to get a little workout before bed."

Grabbing a towel, she continued toward Shani.

Shani didn't recognize her, but she didn't need to. The woman was young, human, and looked a lot like *him*. This was Rodney's newfound daughter.

Scottie put a hand out to Shani. "I'm Scottie. I assume you are part of the team. I'm one of the newbs."

Shani responded with what she hoped looked like a genuine smile. "Shani. Pleased to meet you. The water's good?"

"Umm, yeah. Warm, and it's fresh. None of that awful chemical smell like at the city pool in New York."

"That's nice. Are you finished?"

"I think so. A couple of the newbies are getting together to take a hike after the sun rises. You're welcome to join us."

"No, I don't think so. I'm vampire."

"Oh. Should have guessed. You're gorgeous."

"Thank you. Well, enjoy your hike."

Nodding, Scottie laid her towel on a bench and slid a long shirt over the wet bathing suit.

She'd turned to undress for her swim, when Shani abruptly asked, "Are you the one who just found out who her father was?" *As if Shani didn't already know.*

"Yeah. That's the oddest thing about all of this. The mission thing, aw, it's weird, but I can deal with it. My power, that's always been there. But meeting my father, a man I've never known and never expected to, that's kind of a kick in the ass."

"Do you like him?"

Scottie was silent for a few moments, then nodded again. "Yeah, I do. He's a good man. If he had known my mother was pregnant with his child, I think he would have taken care of her. And me. But for whatever reason, he wasn't able to stay in New York and he didn't know I existed. I could hardly hold him responsible for abandoning me, could I?"

"No, I suppose not."

"Anyway, we've got a long way to go, but the fact that he came here, even knowing how dangerous it might be, says a lot."

"Oh, he's a brave man, no doubt. I've defended him myself in the past."

"You know Rodney?"

"Long ago. *Very* long ago. Well, I'll let you go. It will be sunup before I know it, and I should get this swim finished."

"Of course. Nice to meet you, Shani. I guess I'll see you after the party tonight."

"Party?"

"You didn't know? I guess our hostess is having a huge party to welcome everyone here before it all gets serious."

"That's nice. Be careful out there, Scottie, those mountain trails can be treacherous."

"I will. Have a nice swim."

Scottie moved through the door as Shani dropped her dress and shoes and slid naked into the water. *Figured.* She liked Rodney's daughter. Power moved through the young woman and left tiny vibrations on the surface of her skin.

Weaving into Scottie's aura, Shani read a gentle, honest woman who'd had a hard life. This, too, was unexpected. The water lapped at Shani's skin and tickled it along newly responsive areas.

Rodney was right. They were going to end up dealing with this issue between them sooner rather than later.

Eight

Exhausted from the all-night party the night before, Scottie was still dragging as she pulled herself together to meet the others in the banquet room on the 57th floor of the building. At least thirty people had already arrived, greeting each other, laughing, filling plates. Although she knew very few of them, she honed in on the table where Dani and Dylan sat. Even though the buffet was extensive, she grabbed a plate and sparingly chose just orange juice, bacon, and an apple.

As she joined the others, she looked around for her father, but he hadn't arrived yet. She noticed the stunning brunette she'd met at the pool two nights ago at a large table near the front of the room.

Vampires. They took a lot of adjustment. Powerful, physically perfect, immortal, with a strong sense of love and community. *What did she say her name was?*

Shani. That was it. When Scottie sought her gaze, she was surprised to see Shani staring at her.

Shrugging, she picked up a piece of bacon and bit off the end. "Must have made an impression."

Dylan finished off a 12 ounce steak and pumped his belly with both hands. "I know the vampires eat like this, but I am going to get fat if I keep this up."

"So stop," Dani barked, a typical sister's response. "No one told you to eat two 12 ounce steaks for breakfast."

"The food is too good. Someone needs to make me into a vampire."

Scottie grinned. "You want to suck blood for the rest of your life? I'm not sure getting to eat mountains of steak is worth it."

Scanning the room, his eyes moving from one hard-bodied, oversized vampire to the next, and then to the equally fit exquisite women, his gaze returned to Scottie. "Yes, I think it would be."

Her eyes moving over the same images Dylan's had, Scottie understood. These vampires were the absolute quintessence of masculine and feminine beauty. The universe had not failed them there.

She knew that her super-large and overly sexy father was something different within the vampire community. One night she'd overheard Chione speaking with another child of the moon in Zambia, and they'd referred to Rodney as a first blood hybrid. Scottie had been assured that her father was human, not vampire, but they'd also told her that he was human with *enhancements*.

Everyone in the room looked up when Chione and the woman called Cairine headed to the back of the room and stepped onto a dais, raising them so everyone could easily see them.

Chione began. "Please, everyone, continue to enjoy your first meal. As usual, we hold our meetings while dining so that we can multi-task, and so that we can linger on our meals. For those not vampire, you will learn quickly that we do indeed like to linger. Tonight, we begin to understand the task facing us, and it is astronomical in its complexity and devastating in its potential to do great harm to this world. It is why we gather, ten humans, ten vampires, and ten supernaturals, to protect this world. Crezia is our healer, brought to us through the grandest miracle I've ever seen, and she will be by our side as well. Donovan and I are here to channel your gifts, to guide you, where we can, and to do all we can to help you along the way."

She moved closer, raising her voice. "For over forty years, we've placed you in teams all over the planet. In that time, we've eliminated the awful possibility of global destruction from nuclear weapons. We've dealt with potential pandemics, and cured several of humanity's worst health problems. We have made it possible for most of the life on this planet to live well, and in peace. Of course, that wasn't enough. Populations continued to climb, so we took point there, too, and made sure that science found a way to house and feed nearly three times the people that this earth carried when these warriors were born about a hundred and thirty years ago. It's been exhausting, repetitive, and heartbreaking, but we've succeeded. Now, we face our greatest challenges, the time when all powers must come together, because it will take *all* of you to save this world. Please. Cairine will go over, in detail, what we face here in the United States. Listen and ask any questions you need to when she is finished. I, too, will be hearing the details for the first time."

With a nod, Chione left the dais as Cairine stepped to the center.

"While my team and I manage housing for the western half of the U.S., our most critical projects have been geological. Most of you are aware of Yellowstone National Park, located primarily in Wyoming. The hydrothermal features and dynamics make it a unique place to visit; geysers, hot springs, and geothermal vents create a fascinating, active terrain. But the reason we're concerned is about what fuels these geothermal events. Yellowstone sits on top of a supervolcano, so called because of the immense magma chamber that lies just beneath the park. In this country, two major faultlines, and two highly active volcanoes are monitored daily for activity. Yellowstone is the one we're focused on right now because it is one of the greatest potential threats to the nation and the world. Our specialized team of volcanologists, The Jedi Faction, named by my esteemed colleague Jackson, *you'll have to ask him why*, have been logging sudden and powerful movements, dramatic ground deformation, and a concerning increase in earthquake activity in the park. My fellow warriors, these are indications that a large eruption may be imminent."

Cairine paused to let the significance of that statement sink in. No one spoke as she looked around the banquet room. It was up to the people in this room to fix this.

"So that's why you've been called here. We don't have any absolutes, no set timetable, no defined game plan, no promises. We have two things that made me decide to bring the guardians to Yellowstone now. First, proven science; readings, reports, and measurements that show, indisputably, that this volcano may be ready to erupt. And second, a ripple, movement through the spiritual realm that something is beginning. Chione feels it, so does Talib, and I, with my limited reach, have felt its unsettling touch."

Again, Cairine waited before she revealed the extent of the danger. "This eruption has the potential for unbelievable devastation. The amount of magma contained beneath this park could blow unprecedented amounts of molten ash and pyroclastic material from the caldera. Between that and sulfuric gases, considering the density of populations surrounding the park and immediately east of the area, hundreds of thousands of people will die within the first 24 hours. Guys, this has the potential to be an extinction-level event. At the very least, the casualties will be unimaginable, and it will take the globe several years to recover from the effects of a volcanic eruption of this scale."

Chione returned to the dais and slid a hand around Cairine's waist. "We don't know if we can stop this, but we know that we must try. Tonight, though, we want to take you to the park and show you the site. We all need to see and feel the energy and power of this place. Jackson has arranged a multi-person transport vessel. We lift off in an hour, so bring a light jacket and be at the base of the tower by then with good walking shoes. While night is not the best time to see the park, the sky is co-operating tonight with a nearly full moon, so we'll still see much of the beauty of the area."

If being indoctrinated into the existence of vampires, supernaturals, and magic wasn't enough to knock a human off balance, the rest of Scottie's group took the news that they were going to be involved in trying to stop a major volcanic explosion in silence. Dani and Dylan followed Antoinette and Scottie back to the rooms they'd been assigned to and changed into clothes that would keep them comfortable and warm on this trip.

"Are you adjusting to this yet?" Dani asked.

Scottie shook her head. "No. I keep thinking that, if we survive this, how do we go back to normal lives? What comes next?"

"*You* won't go back to your old life. You'll go to France with your father. Nothing will ever be the same for any of us after this, but you've found family."

"I guess. Still, this is a bit more than anyone could handle well."

"We aren't just anyone. We're chosen, remember? We have powers that normal people don't have."

"True. Okay, let's go see this volcano."

Dylan tied off his boots and followed his sister and Scottie from their room. His eyes went to the guy they called Biker as he stepped out of his room. The man hadn't said a word all night. "Hey, you doin' all right?"

Will looked at the handsome young black man who'd tried to befriend him since all this began. "Fine."

Dylan knew it was all he was going to get.

Outside the tower, a sleek sky transport waited, now half-filled, as others climbed aboard. Shani looked around the group and noticed that Rodney was still missing. She didn't want to care, didn't want to ask, but she couldn't help herself. Trying to seem casual, she moved to the seats where Scottie sat speaking with the lovely Dani she'd met two nights ago when they first arrived. "Good evening, ladies. Field trip, eh? Scottie, where's your father?"

"I don't know. I haven't seen him tonight."

"He wasn't at the party last night either."

"No. He told me that parties are not his scene. Maybe he isn't used to being around people. I don't know, we're still learning about each other. You said you *know* him?"

"Uh, just passingly. Too long ago to matter. Well, I'll take my seat. You two be careful, this is all new to you."

No Rodney. Good, she wouldn't have to see him or think about him tonight.

Moving to the back of the transport, Shani dropped into a seat next to Eras. "Hey, 'bro. Looks like everything is getting real now."

"Yep. Danger Incorporated. This one worries me, sis."

"Yeah." There was nothing more to say, they all realized the stakes. If they failed, hundreds of thousands of people would die and the world as they knew it would be changed forever.

They couldn't fail.

Less than an hour after liftoff, they were on the ground at Yellowstone, wordlessly viewing the beauty of the region. The fly-over had been extraordinary, the landscape illuminated by moonlight some of the most incredible many of them had ever seen.

Cairine watched the rapt faces on her vessel. This transport could drop the top and she'd had the pilot do it as they approached so that their views were uninhibited by windows.

"This is the Yellowstone Caldera, one of Mother Nature's more active spots. Jackson or one of the other volcanologists can tell you more about its history, but what I know is that she's beautiful, and what lies beneath is power like we've never seen. The last time she erupted with the magnitude we are concerned about was over 160,000 years ago. We hope, we truly hope, that this sleeping dragon does not wake. Get out, explore, see if you can feel any of her magic. It's all around, and for sensitives like us, we can usually touch it in the air or through the earth."

Vampires, humans, and Totems wandered with reverence from the vessel, and still, twenty minutes later, no one had spoken. As Cairine had suggested, they walked on the land and lifted their heads to the sky, and something *did* touch them.

For the new human warriors, still adapting to their new reality, feeling the strangeness, a connection, an energy that slipped into them and around their minds and bodies, it was startling. What startled them most, *all* the warriors, was the tether that began in Chione and Donovan and moved from one to the next until they all felt a strange connection to each other. The tether was light, barely a touch in their minds, but it was there, indisputably tying them together. They did not stop, though, all thirty-one of the chosen warriors continued to move along the landscape until Chione called them back. "It is time to go."

All vampires feel the arrival of day, and it was coming.

Later, while the sun claimed the sky, Shani lay in her bed, pleasantly tired, the new bond to the others still touching her mind and heart. For the first time, she could feel the immensity of what the universe had put into place.

Nearly asleep, her mind already moving toward blessed unconsciousness, Shani kept hearing a persistent sound. Unable to process it, the sound pushed her awake and she recognized it. Someone was engaging the buzzer outside her door. Sluggish, she rolled up, looked at the monitor, and responded. "*Answer.*"

The twenty inch screen by the door came on, and Shani saw Rodney looking directly into the camera. *What the hell did he want at this time of day?*

No, she wouldn't let him in. "I am at rest. Please go."

"Let me in, for a moment, Shani."

"No."

"I have spent the day on the highest peak, and I must tell you something. You will want to know."

God, help her. *No, no, no!*

Shani sighed and stood to pull her robe on. "*Allow access.*"

The door slid open and Rodney came into her room, filling it with both his physical presence and the largeness of his personality. He had intrigued her from the first moment they met as adults, and if anything, her fascination had only grown stronger. Not that she would let *him* know that.

"I'm exhausted, Rodney. What do you want?"

It didn't help that his eyes moved from her face to her breasts, barely hidden by the thin robe, to where it cinched at her waist, a satin tie easy to pull. His eyes went to where it stopped just below where her thighs met. She didn't need empathic skills to know why his breath quickened.

"Raise your gaze, buddy, none of that concerns you anymore."

As if compelled, he lifted his eyes to hers and stepped closer. Shani stepped back.

Rodney smiled. "You can't back away enough. I've spent the day and night considering life, choices, consequences, joy, and pain. I hurt you, I know that, by refusing to take a young woman at the height of her sexual awakening. Your empathic talent was still evolving then, but you knew how deeply I wanted you. Anything I did back then, I did for you. Whether I was right or wrong doesn't matter now. I owe you an apology. Not because I was wrong, but because I loved you and I should have told you that I would come for you someday when the time was right, if you wanted me to."

Pausing, his eyes locked on hers, he moved forward again, just one step more. "So, Shani, I am sorry I hurt you. I would give anything to go back and make that right. It won't help, but you need to know that my pain has been just as great. I missed you every day of the past century, knowing that you would be with other men, and that I would have to live with that."

"Good. Is that all you have to say?"

After another step forward, he'd backed her against the bed.

"One other thing. It's a warning and a promise. We've both lived a long time now, and hopefully gained some insight into how our choices can fuck us up. And Shani, I never stopped loving you, never stopped needing you, so I'm giving you notice, now, that I intend to show you we were always meant to be together."

She could feel his heat. "It's too late."

"I've already declared how I feel about you. Shani, you're here, almost in my arms, and you want me. You need to understand that you have me."

As she tried to decide what to say next, to convince him of something that she did not believe, he took one last step, and raised his hands to her cheeks.

Rigid, Shani tried not to respond, but to have Rodney's hands on her after all these years, after revisiting those erotic feelings and memories over the past few nights, she couldn't stop the shiver and desire to pull him down and rip his clothes off right there.

Only a few inches separated his mouth from hers, and after hesitating only a second to make sure she wouldn't shove him away, Rodney kissed her so gently on the lips, she wasn't even sure they touched. His cheek on hers, she couldn't bring herself to leave that intimate touch, even if it was far less than she needed.

"I can't...not again..." she whispered. "You broke me so badly back then."

He pulled away to look into her eyes again.

"I will fix every rip, dry every tear. I would sell my soul before I'd let anything hurt you again. I promise, my love, that I know now, that even though I still think that I am too small a man to be worthy of you, I want you anyway. I will love you the way you always deserved to be loved."

His hands dropped to the tie of her robe, and he fingered the knot with one hand while the other slid along the edge of the satin, his knuckles brushing her bare belly.

"Don't say no to us, Shani. Give us a chance to find each other again."

She couldn't think. Her body scorched where he touched her, her mind reeled, her heart ached, and she admitted, she still wanted Rodney more than anything in her life.

But not yet. This was too sudden and she couldn't let herself trust it. He'd have to earn that again. For now, as much as she wanted to do exactly the opposite, Shani stepped around the edge of the bed, breaking his gentle hold on her robe. His fingers against her belly brushed harder as she moved away.

"Go back to your room. When, *if*, I decide to take you up on your offer, I'll let you know."

"I will, I'll go, but don't mistake me. I'm not asking for permission to show you that you love me, it's a done deal. I am going to make love to you in the most thorough way possible and do that again and again for the rest of our lives."

Arrogant. *And yes...!*

"You know the way out."

Flexing his fingers, she could see Rodney war with himself whether to try to convince her to let him stay or go as asked. Finally, he nodded and headed to the door. He didn't turn to her before he went past the opening, but she heard him say clearly, "I'll see you tonight," before he was gone.

Shani realized she had been holding her breath and released it in an explosion of relief and guarded joy.

Whatever happened next, she prayed that he meant what he said. Between her legs, deep inside her, twitching was so extreme, she thought she might orgasm, just at the thought of feeling Rodney there. It had to happen, now, she knew it. But on her own terms.

Once again, sleep took a long time to come.

Day faded into night, and everyone met for first meal again. Cairine watched the activity and smiled that, so far, it had all gone so well. Fia was filling a plate with a vampire-sized portion while Taylor laughed at her.

Brigitte had told her last night that she found the silent Biker fascinating and had decided that he bore more attention. Cairine watched her land heavily on a seat beside him at a distant table where he sat with a moderate portion of food. *Poor Biker*, she thought, *he has no idea what an intractable force Brigitte is.*

Eras had just come into the room, and when he saw her, he headed toward her. He'd tried to be attentive, but Cairine had found an excuse every time to retreat from wherever he was. The man spooked her. She'd told him several times that she was with someone, and it didn't seem to affect him.

"Good," he'd replied, the first time she told him about Otto. I'm glad you haven't been alone, but things are going to change."

Nothing seemed to stop him, so she spent most of her time running away. Jackson had laughed at her evasion of her first lover, but his advice was for her to confront Eras and deal with any residual feelings directly.

Did she *have* residual feelings for him? Of course she did. The burn still festered, and what felt like abandonment of their love had never quite gone away. That's why she was done. It was easier to not tear open old wounds. Otto loved her and he was an excellent lover. She couldn't, wouldn't, ask for more.

Like a man on a mission, Eras moved across the room fast, and, ready to duck out of the kitchen, Cairine noticed Shani grab her brother's arm. She redirected him to her table and forced him into a seat, then looked up at Cairine and smiled. Thankfully, Shani understood the situation and ran interference for her. Mouthing a *thank you* to Shani, Cairine still decided she was safer in the kitchen. As she moved to disappear, Chione and Donovan bee-lined to her when they came into the room.

Donovan greeted her with a smile. "Cari, we're going to try something tonight. What is the most isolated place on the mountain where we can form a large circle?"

"One of my favorite places is on top of Clancy's Peak. It's flat, high, and has one of the most beautiful views in the mountains. Right now, it should be lushly dressed in spring wildflowers."

"Excellent. Can you arrange for the transport again?"

"Certainly."

"Great. I'll make the announcement."

Brigitte looked up into eyes filled with suspicion, an unexpected reaction to her presence. *Everyone* loved her, especially attractive men. She was *built* to make men smile.

"So, I'm Brigitte. We've met a few times, but never really had a chance to get to know each other. You're Biker, from the American southwest."

He was as handsome as a vampire, and nearly as big. She supposed it was the earth magic he'd been granted as a chosen one. But he wasn't welcoming; no smile to her greeting, just a long stare, then he lowered his gaze to his plate and stabbed a big piece of ham to shove it into his mouth.

Brigitte stared at his mouth. *Sexy.* All sorts of things she could imagine him doing with it that did not involve food.

"Hi," he finally said, once the ham went down.

"You're not very communicative. I suppose it's the isolation you've lived with for so many years, eh?"

His eyes shot up again, this time with some hostility.

"So everyone knows all about me. I guess we're just tools for you vampires, aren't we?"

Pausing before she spoke, Brigitte leaned back. "How do you know I'm vampire?"

Will's harsh laugh was the first sign of real emotion she saw in him. "You're human, you can't know that. Unless you've asked about me."

"No. First, you're insanely beautiful. I've figured out pretty quickly that's a vampire thing. And you have the same odd energy that Olivia has. I've also come to identify that as vampire."

"Wait. You can read lifeforces?"

"Hell, I don't know what it is, I just know that something is different about vampires, and once I knew what it was, I can tell who is vampire."

Brigitte picked up a croissant and bit into it. "Well thanks for the compliment. And if you can read lifeforces, then you have a highly unique talent for a human. So what, specifically, *is* your talent?"

Cutting through another piece of ham, Will looked up, and Brigitte was surprised to see a genuine grin. "I guess we're making nice."

A sigh escaped as Brigitte leaned closer. "We're making nice, and from what I can see, we'll make very good *nice* together."

"Fuck, you vampires are good at getting your way. Okay. My talent is earth based. Olivia says that I can access power directly from the surface of the planet. I discovered some time ago that I cannot get very far from the ground without being pulled back to it."

"But you flew from Africa on a jet. And to Yellowstone with us."

"Because of Chione and Donovan. They carry earth magic and can *ground* my magic through them. Otherwise, I'm like a boomerang that shoots back to its starting place."

"Wow. Between all the warriors, we have a lot of incredible talent here. I think we're going to need it. Biker, here's the deal, straight up. You turn me on. I'm interested in seeing if we might be able to entertain each other while we're here. I guarantee you'll have sex like you've never had before. What do you think?"

His eyebrows raised, his smile widened, Will wasn't sure how to answer. "I like it, a straight up, straightforward woman. Yeah, I'm interested. So, if I read you right, this is strictly a *for entertainment only* arrangement, right? No strings."

"It's how I roll, so, yeah. I hope you agree, because I'm already imagining the main event."

"Wow. No performance anxiety issues *here*. I don't know if I can satisfy a vampire, but, uh, yeah, I'm willing to try."

"Smashing! Let's see how long tonight's little meeting takes, and perhaps I'll show you back to my room." Brigitte stood up, looked around, pulled Will across the table, licked his lips, and pushed him back hard enough for him to lose his balance. He recovered it just before he fell onto the floor.

"You're delicious, Biker boy. Can't wait."

Picking up her tray, Brigitte headed back to the table where Shani sat.

Taking a seat beside her sister, Brigitte looked over to see Shani staring at her.

"Really?" Shani commented.

"Just setting up my blood meal and entertainment, sis. What, you'd do him if you weren't falling back in love with Sir Hot Leather Vest over there."

At first, Shani didn't answer Brigitte, but after letting her eyes go to Rodney, who sat with his daughter and the human warriors, she took her hand.

"I don't want to, but I don't think I can deny him."

"Darling, you never *stopped* loving him. Give in, full-on, ass to the sheets, and let him make love to you until you can't walk. We may not survive this, so give yourself a gift and fuck the man who's been in your heart almost all of your life. It'll be worth it, I promise."

Quiet again, Shani nodded. "I know," she finally whispered.

The moon provided bright silvery light at the summit of Clancy's Peak, which was as perfect as Cairine had suggested it would be for their gathering.

Everyone came off the transport, dazzled by the view from this elevation.

The Final Five came off first and walked to the edge of the clearing to overlook the mountainside.

"There's magic here," Antoinette commented as she joined them near the edge of the ridge.

Chione came up behind her. "There's magic anywhere the earth meets the sky. It stirs the spirit, doesn't it? Come my friends, we will begin."

Donovan gathered the warriors and instructed them to form a circle. "Take a seat. I've warmed the ground, so it should be quite comfortable."

Dani looked at Scottie. "Warmed the ground?"

Will, passing, overheard her. "Donovan has earth magic. He can literally tap into the heat beneath the soil and bring it up. Touch the ground, you'll be convinced."

Dropping down, Dani placed her fingers on the grass, delighted to find it pleasantly warm to the touch in spite of the coolness of the air so high on the mountain.

"Wow. That seems impossible. I don't know what *we're* doing here. What do *we* have to offer people who can do something like this?"

Before he walked away, Will answered Dani's concern. "A great deal. It appears that all of us are more powerful than we know. Keep the faith, sweet chocolate drop."

Scottie punched Dani in the shoulder. "Sweet chocolate drop? Looks like brooding hottie has a thing for you."

"I doubt it. I saw one of the gorgeous female vampires talking to him at first meal, and they looked chummy."

"Oh. My new pop says that they are sex-machines. Still, Biker boy doesn't seem the type to give compliments and yet he just did. Of course, he's right, you're a tasty-looking morsel."

Dani grimaced. "Thank you, you're a kind woman."

"Honest. It's what I'm known for and what I get into trouble with. *Some* people don't *want* to hear the truth."

"Amen, sister. Let's go take our place."

Dylan followed, wondering how he could get in with a group of male vampires.

As Shani joined her sisters in the circle now forming, her eyes went across the center to the other side where Rodney stood with Scottie. She'd felt his eyes on her the entire night, but refused to return his gaze.

"Cairine, what is Rodney doing here? He's not a warrior."

"No, but he asked Chione and Donovan if he could stay and join our gatherings and they granted him full access to everything we do. Shani, Rodney's pretty powerful, you know that. To our knowledge, he's the only vampire-human hybrid that has ever existed. They feel he is meant to be here, that this may be his destiny."

Shani dropped her head back and looked at the star-studded sky. "Destiny." The word came out on a sigh. "The one thing that has plagued us all our lives. Once this is over, I hope it's a staggeringly long time before we have to hear that word again."

Cairine laughed. "I kind of agree with you."

Brigitte leaned closer. "Got a date with that new hot guy, Biker. I have to say, I'm pretty excited to taste him." Nodding several times, she twisted her lips. "In every way possible."

The women were laughing when Chione and Donovan left the circle and walked to the center.

"My warriors, please, sit down." Chione took Donovan's hand as they both sunk onto the heated ground and searched the faces of the chosen earth guardians waiting for them.

Chione's greeting filled the mountaintop, the melodic tones echoing slightly.

"Ladies and gentlemen of the three races, you are all here together, ready, for the first time. Most of you have been aware of your destiny for many years, and some of you are shockingly new to it. Those who have lived with this destiny for the past century have spent half of those years actively engaged in protecting this world. All the bullet points have been covered and we have arrived here tonight, capable of providing energy, food, water, housing and productive lives for the burgeoning population of this tiny planet. Your Grand Destiny was never meant to be a singular event. What the universe put into place a thousand years ago was a chance, a hope, a prayer that *this* world would survive when so many others did not. You've been guardians against the specific things that dominant species create that ultimately destroys them. Once the natural order of a world is compromised, so is all life. Your mission, this destiny, requires your shared magic. Some of you do not believe you have much to offer. Oh, my children of the earth, wait and see what you can do."

She stood and began a measured stroll around the circle. "This is why the warriors were chosen in trios, a triquetra of life-sustaining connections to the living planet."

Chione touched Eras on the cheek. "Vampires first brought from other worlds." Moving to Taylor, she took his hand and placed it over her heart. "Humans born of this world." With a smile, she released Taylor and took Su'ad's hand in hers. "Supernaturals which bridge all forms of life. Precious, all of you."

Continuing around the circle, she made sure that everyone felt included. "They brought you all together to stand heart to heart, mind to mind, spirit to spirit, and hand in hand. With those connections, the three races would make it through all to come and save the world. You are here to provide the shelter of the gods to this damaged world. Please, stand and take the hands of those beside you and we will see what we can do."

Rodney pushed up and addressed Chione. "Before you begin, may I speak?"

"Of course, Sir Rodney."

He grimaced and stepped into the circle, turning as he spoke. "I am not a chosen warrior, but I have spent most of my life protecting many of you. I have asked and been granted by the guardians of the guardians to be allowed to fight alongside you. I need to be here *for* you, *with* you. My talents are many but they are not magics given to me by the universe or the living earth. Yet I will give all I can to help you in your mission. If you will accept me, I conscript myself to this fight."

A round of applause moved around the circle, all in favor of Rodney's request.

Chione nodded to him. "Welcome, watchdog, to our battle."

"Thank you. I will step outside the circle now to watch you all burn bright."

Shani's eyes followed Rodney as he retreated past the circle and into the darkness beyond. Damn the man, he was doing it again. With his gentle nature, a body built for sex, a scent that she could barely control herself around, Rodney's habit of self-sacrificing bravery made him irresistible to her. She admitted that she wouldn't turn him down. The only thing she really wanted right now was for him to bury himself in her while she buried her teeth in him. God, all the years she'd waited to make love to the love of her life!

Did destiny play fair? Hell, no, but it wasn't too late to try again.

"Shani, are you paying attention?"

Donovan's deep voice intruded on her internal dialogue and brought Shani back to the circle.

"Sorry, Donovan. Yes, I am now."

"Then here we go."

Donovan joined Chione as she took Talib's hand in one of hers and Ife's in the other. Donovan weaved himself into the circle near them.

"Ready," he said to his mate. "Hand to hand, warriors."

Chione closed her eyes and sent out a wave of energy, low level, a tickle that went through everyone to bind their powers together. This would be the first time that this number of people merged their powers in one continuous thread.

"*Shu laka via Ghoss lorre*. It is our ancient language and means *connected forever in the eyes of the gods*. If we wish it so, we shall become *one*, and *one* shall become all."

No one spoke, the sacredness of the moment deeply felt.

Chione continued. "Moving earthbound things is easier because of the physical connection to the earth. Celestial magics can be tough. Tonight, we will blend earth and sky magics when we defy gravity and lift, as a single force, off the ground. To do this, we must deepen our connection. It is a matter of focusing and belief. To bend physics, we must work with it, not against it. It can be done, as long as we each reach for our powers and send them into the collective. Thusly…"

Chione repeated her shared energy, but his time, it carried first blood magics, and instead of a trickle, everyone felt a surge of power that created a hot glow where they touched.

"Wow," Scottie whispered, as Dani stared in disbelief and Will watched unimpressed.

"Now, it is your turn to release your magics. You may close your eyes if that helps you to focus, but all you really need to do is push your power out though each hand to the one you touch. And believe. You will feel the other's power too, as it goes through you. We shall begin."

Standing isolated from the group on a pile of large stones fifty feet from the circle, Rodney let his eyes roam from face to face, beginning with his daughter. He'd become accustomed to physical beauty because of all the years in the vampire community, but he believed now, as he always had, that beauty came from within. Luckily, he had good instincts when it came to people. He'd sized up the young woman he'd made, and found her rough, but kind of heart and honest; much as he had been as a young man who traveled the wrong path when he lived in New York City all those years impossibly long-ago.

Once his eyes landed on Shani, he lingered. God help him, she was the most beautiful thing he'd ever known in his life. Her spirit had mingled with his almost from the beginning, her touch electric to his lonely soul. He didn't deserve her now, any more than before, but he wanted her and he would be good for her. She'd never found her mate and now he believed...no, he *knew*...that he'd been hers all along. He'd screwed up back then...he wasn't going to let her go again.

Winds began to swirl around the clearing, slowly picking up speed until they began to wail. Rodney barely heard the collected gasps from the group as he watched them rise several inches off the ground. His own sigh of relief was lost in the wildness of air as they continued to rise. It appeared that the merge between all 33 in the circle had connected with ease and that they all had access to the power. Shaking his head, he lowered himself onto the rocks.

He still couldn't believe he had a daughter. When Koen and Tamesine revealed this truth, he'd expected them to laugh and pat him on the back for the success of their joke, but here she was, a part of him he'd never known existed. A gift from the gods he certainly didn't deserve, but one he would cherish forever. When Koen made him vampire later this year, he would talk with Scottie about the possibility of her joining him. He'd only just found her, he couldn't imagine losing her within the next sixty or seventy years.

A hundred years now sounded so paltry, the design of stingy gods. All that mattered to him, beyond making love to Shani, was that Scottie would agree to convert too. It was out of his hands, though, a choice only *she* could make. He'd already discovered that immortality wasn't for everyone.

The speed of the winds continued to rise and so did the group of warriors. Now, instead of gasps, he heard occasional thrilled cheers. A good eighty feet lay beneath them, a distance that could cause some serious problems if the magics failed. He had no concern, the vampires guiding this knew what they were doing, and he was certain that the first bloods were largely in control. This was a training exercise, and a chance to show the new recruits and the supernaturals that they had true gifts.

Rodney leaned back against a higher stone, this time with contentment. He was proud of his kids.

An hour later, elation and excited conversations filled the transport as it arrived back at the foot of Cairine's tower. Shani stayed with her sisters, using them to create a barrier to keep Rodney from approaching her. Even if she admitted to herself that she wanted him, and that she'd probably give in to him, she wasn't ready to face him on that level yet. Trust issues still loomed.

Rodney stayed with his daughter this time, though, and she was grateful. Tonight, all she wanted was to enjoy this accomplishment, celebrate, and share the night with her companions. Rodney, and all the craziness that went with him, could wait for another night.

Arriving back to the tower, everyone talking at once, they were happy when Cairine revealed that she'd arranged a party with second meal. They were ready to appreciate the unique world they now dwelled in, so they burst into the banquet room to bright LED lights peeking from behind walls of lacy fabric, and low volume dance music playing.

No one noticed when Jackson grabbed Cairine immediately and pulled her into the kitchen. She emerged moments later to search for Chione and Donovan, pulled them aside, and then all three went back into the kitchen.

Outside the kitchen, plates were being filled and alcohol flowed freely.

Brigitte kissed Shani and Ife on the cheeks and went to search for Biker, who they thought might be hard to find since he didn't join in with the others. She disappeared through the door and they watched it close behind her.

Ife shrugged. "At least she's getting some blood and sex tonight. I'm starved."

"Cairine says there are six people in the lower apartments who are blood donors for those of us who need it."

"Yes, that will do, but I'm also feeling sort of, peckish, in another way."

"You want sex too."

"It's been a while."

"Speaking to the choir, sister. Perhaps one of the feeders is handsome. You know Cari wouldn't be using them for sex, she has Otto, and she's committed to him."

"She *thinks* she is."

"Now, Ife, she's been with…oh, who am I kidding, the girl is madly in love with Eras and we both know it. Eventually, she'll realize it too."

"She will. Now, the idea of one of the feeders is intriguing."

"Ife, love, you could have any man you want. Just go to one of the local clubs, pick someone, and take him."

"I've never been comfortable with that."

"Really? You haven't, I mean, you don't usually just select a lover and do him?"

"I've never felt good about random sex with a stranger, yet I've never really found anyone I've clicked with either. I'm a mess, aren't I, Shani?"

Throwing an arm over Ife's shoulder, Shani winced.

"You and me both, my friend. You know what's going on with Rodney."

"He's here for you, isn't he?"

"He says he is. I don't know whether to trust it again. Last time hurt so badly, I think I cried myself to sleep every night for three years."

"I remember. Shani, he glows when he's near you, and you won't admit it, but your aura does too. I think you two have always been heading here, it just took a while to meet on the path."

Shani stepped away and snatched a large cinnamon bun from the table. "Look at you giving me advice on love."

"I never said I didn't understand love, I have just never found it."

Shani pushed back Ife's bright white hair and kissed her cheeks, one and then the other. "My beautiful sister, there is a perfect man waiting for you out there in the world. He's just traveling a different path, too. And like Rodney and me, you'll meet up with him soon and then, oh, glory, you'll fall madly, deeply, hopelessly for him. I can't wait to see you glow."

"You are the kindest woman I know. I hope you're right. I think I'm ready to be in love. I've watched it in others, and I want to feel that passion."

"Your love waits to cross paths with you, and soon."

"Ah. Meanwhile, look."

Her head swiveling in the direction of Ife's nod, Shani groaned. "I am not ready to deal with him yet."

"He's ready to deal with you. Go ahead, begin the journey back to him."

"Not tonight, Ife…"

A voice cut across all conversations. Suddenly silent, everyone looked up to where Cairine had stepped onto the dais again. Old style hip-hop music stopped abruptly. The expression on her face was not reassuring, and when they noticed Jackson behind her, she had all of their attention.

"I hate to upset this celebration, but I have news that cannot wait. You all know Jackson here and his place in my organization. He's just informed me that tonight, just an hour ago, we had a series of quakes located near region AD at the center of the park that measured 7.3 to 8.4, which opened up 7 new geysers. The seismicity isn't unprecedented, but it seems relentless tonight. His team measured significant deformation near the sites and 2 miles away, a serious carbon dioxide rupture. These are indications that the activity is on the increase, and is reason to suspect that we may soon face a full eruption. We still have no exact timeframe, and we're working on it, but at this time, we are all now on emergency alert. This could happen at any time. I hate to tell you tonight since we've had such an extraordinary one, but when I say we need to be ready to move, I mean at any moment from now until things either escalate or calm back down. So with that being said, can we get the music back on and see some dancing?"

While the music came back right away, the sense of joy and merriment didn't. Somber, lost in thought, concern, the relevance of Cairine's announcement, the expression on Jackson's face when she spoke, weaved throughout the gathering. Before long, everyone slowly broke apart and wandered back to their apartments. Tomorrow would be a new night, and time enough to accept the truth and prepare to meet the challenge. This night, after the magnificent visit to the top of the state, and the shocking reality of what loomed in the near future, or sooner, rest and recovery was what they all needed.

The staff quietly cleaned up afterward, stepping around Jackson, Chione, Donovan, and eleven vampire warriors born to this mission. Sleep would come for them too, but for now, a quiet discussion about where they'd been and where this would lead allowed them to believe that, while this would be their grandest challenge to date, that it would work and they would stop the destruction on this scale as they were meant to do.

Eras watched the woman he loved, her animated voice leading the discussion, and hoped he would have time to make love to her again.

Ife wondered if she would ever get the chance to know what true passionate love felt like.

Talib thought of his mate, Su'ad, who'd gone to their bed an hour ago, and hoped they'd have a chance to return to the forest they loved.

Shani touched Brigitte's hand and through their shared empathic connection didn't have to say a word; their hearts and minds locked on the importance of their power and how they must protect this land.

Caedmon pressed his leg to his mate's, and Crezia sent a healing wave through him, as she did every night since they'd found out that it was only her connection to him that kept him well. Her powers had grown through the decades to the point where they thought, aided by the others, she may be able to perform true medical miracles.

Fia and Bryson's twin link had weakened with their distance and now, faced with impossible odds, she smiled at her brother and sent a telepathic message to him. As children, they'd played with telepathy, mostly without success, but the skill had strengthened, and now, back together, the bond strong again, she sent him the message that this was a "piece of cake." Bryson smiled and tried to believe.

Maccabee watched his family and friends, and knew that no matter what, they all had to be well and happy when this was over. He was a warrior at heart, and while his power might not be the most useful, he'd fight harder than anyone and hoped that would be enough.

From her seat at the "head" of the round table, Chione watched her *guardians*. She had no doubt at all in their strength, commitment, and talents.

But they could use all the help they could get from the universe and the Mother Earth.

Nine

The doves waited on Cairine's balcony as they usually did, unaware of the danger that faced every living thing this side of Yellowstone. Four young doves had joined their parents, and while they made a bit of a mess on the edge of the tile, she didn't mind.

With a hot cup of cocoa, she lingered over the railing, watching a distant lightning storm scatter across the sky. This beautiful land would not be destroyed by the eruption of that sleeping dragon. *No!*

Otto had called and she'd warned him to stay on the moon for now. He'd had a break and was going to fly back for a few days, but she'd asked him to just trust her and stay where he was. He was a good man, he'd complied with no question.

"Penny for your thoughts."

Eras. She'd left her apartment door open in case Chione came by before they turned in. He'd always been an opportunist.

Cairine turned to face him. "Like you have a penny."

He moved closer, lifted her mug, sipped her whipped-cream-covered chocolate and handed it back.

"*No one* has a penny anymore. Still, I'd like to know how you feel."

"Okay. Hopeful. Worried. A little sad."

"Can I do anything to help? Relieve some stress?"

Staring at him, Cairine couldn't help but notice how strained he looked. He was thinner than a vampire should be, and while he was still nicely muscled, he looked gaunt.

"I should ask you that question. Eras, are you taking proper care of yourself?"

"Ugh, you sound like Bura. He's a bulldog caretaker. I'm good. He makes sure I eat and get the blood meals when I must."

"That isn't what I asked. Are you happy?"

The question motivated Eras, because he lifted the mug from her hands again and set it aside on the railing.

"At this moment, yes. Cari, we need to make love. You need to let me take you in your room and show you that we belong together and always have. I made a mistake, but I was a kid. I didn't know better. Back then, we all wanted to touch the world in every way we could, and for me, it meant fucking everything I could. I realize now that all I really ever needed was you."

Shaking her head, Cairine tried to move around him.

"No. I've moved on. I'm with Otto now…"

"Otto!" Eras spat the word before he pulled her to him, buried his face against hers, and spoke into her ear. "I'm sorry, but please, let me make love to you. I haven't made love to anyone since that summer we spent together in your little house here in the mountains."

A hard push answered him, but didn't budge him.

"You just admitted you have. To plenty of women."

His fingers moved along her cheekline and stopped on her lips. "No. I've fucked, but the only one I've ever made love with is you."

"No. Eras, you can't expect me to just drop my life and let you back in. There's too much going on right now, anyway. We have to focus on our mission."

"Which is why you need to let me love you. If this goes wrong, I can't leave this world without being with you again. Please, Cari."

She could feel him, his cock pushing against her belly. More than his words, to know that he was there, wanting her, just a zipper away from her, nearly undid her resolve.

Shoving him back, she moved a few steps away.

"You need to go cool off. Find the guys and take a run. Anything. But you can't be here."

He knew she meant it, and knew that nothing he said now would change her answer.

Dropping his hands, he walked to the entrance of the balcony. "I'll go. Yeah, a run's a good idea, but I'm not giving up. Ever. I love you, you beautiful, stubborn vampire, and I'll prove myself to you."

He was gone. Cairine's groan startled the doves, and they lifted up, their wings creating a whirr in the air, then landed back on the railing. She looked at the round eyes staring back at her.

"So what do you suggest? Do I undo my life to take him back? I don't get the idea he's the most stable person in the world. And yet."

She sighed and lifted a finger out to let one of the young doves step on. "I have to admit, but only to you guys, I have *always* been in love with that man."

The next night, on the roof, lounging in reclining chairs, Brigitte, Ife, and Shani, having blown off first meal, made plans to hit the local nightlife for food and blood meals.

"Talib clued me in to a fab restaurant with a club attached and it's just a few minutes by lift-car. It sounds perfect."

"We're with you, Ife. Cari has made several lift-cars available. I guess we need to let them know where we're going." Brigitte pulled her long hair up into a messy bun and stood. "I'm starving. I never got a chance to hook up with my guy since the nasty announcement last night. Maybe I can have him meet me there."

Shani pushed out of the seat to stretch. "I feel useless right now. Yes, let's go enjoy ourselves and get some blood. I've been running on a deficit for too long. My muscles actually ache."

Minutes later, at the base of the building, having added Talib, Su'ad, Eras, Bura, Taylor, Fia, and Bryson to their group, the three women took one of Cairine's roomier lift-cars and headed over the mountaintop to *Skyborne*.

Talib, feeling braver than he had the first time he'd flown with Cairine, leaned over the side. "Admittedly, I haven't traveled a lot, but this place is a good choice if it turns out to be our *final* night on the town. Great food, interesting company, incredible views…"

"Stop it, Talib. We'll be fine." Eras didn't quite believe it either, but his hope was powerful that he would have a chance to hold Cairine in his arms again.

"I keep telling my mate that the universe believes in us, so we must believe in us as well." Su'ad, as always, with the right attitude, slid her hand into Talib's, who enclosed it within the warmth of his own.

"Oh, wow, it's the only cleared area on top of this mountain." Shani watched as the car dropped onto a lit, organically designed landing spot in front of the entertainment complex owned by Cairine's friends.

"I see little bungalows. Look. Guess we know what those are for," Brigitte mentioned as she braced for the little bump when the car touched down. "I think this is going to be exactly what we all need. Dancing, food, sex, music, blood, sex."

"You said *sex* twice," Shani pointed out.

Brigitte grinned. "I know."

"Classic Bridge. We'll get a large table in the club and settle in until just before dawn. Cairine knows we're here if they need us."

Bryson led their group, his huge fit body and long blonde hair instantly grabbing the attention of numerous women in the busy club. He smiled, happy to be back in civilization again after so many years in Greenland. He'd adjusted to life there, he and Jessie had built a close relationship, but the chance to party and spend time with his friends was long overdue. Jessie had stayed behind with Jackson and Sally, fascinated by the scientist's work, but she'd been fine with him joining the group tonight.

Fia noticed that Taylor stayed close, annoyed, still upset about her loss of control in his office. He was a reminder that she didn't have a good handle on her impulsive, aggressive nature. The fact that he continued to try to convince her that they should get together pissed her off. She wasn't entirely sure she was right to keep refusing him.

"I should just fuck you and get it over with," she murmured, aware that the loud music would mask her frustrated comment.

Between Bryson, Eras, and Brigitte using compulsion, they cleared several tables and pushed them all together.

"Excellent. This is going to be an epic night."

"I just want to get some blood and a fat cock," Brigitte barked, compelling Shani to fake a gag.

"I see your guy. Look." Brigitte looked to where Shani was pointing.

In a corner, alone, with a tall glass, sat the object of Brigitte's fascination. "Biker."

Shani shrugged. "Sometimes it's meant to be."

As Brigitte stood to head over to meet the stoic human, her eyes went to the entrance of the club. Dropping her head to Shani's, she whispered, "Yes, you're right."

It was Shani's turn to follow her sister's gaze, her eyes landing on Rodney, who had just entered with Scottie, Antoinette, and the twin humans.

"Oh, hell."

Brigitte snagged a tall drink from a tray as a waiter moved past and took a long draw. "Sister, go fuck that man." Then she strolled across the crowded dance floor without spilling a drop of the drink.

Shani watched Brigitte straddle a chair at the small table as the man called Biker looked up. A slow smile let her know that Brigitte was likely going to get her blood and cock tonight.

Swiveling back to the entrance, she saw Rodney and his group clear a table and remembered that he had the ability to compel humans too. What the hell was she going to do? Already, just knowing he was in the room, her libido reacted, her body tightened, and the area between her legs began to spasm. She needed to get out of there.

"I think I'm going to do a little sight-seeing. It's just so pretty here. I'll be back in a little while."

"Would you like me to come with you?" Ife asked.

"No, sweetie, you need a blood meal and perhaps some time in one of those bungalows. Stay and scope out the local talent. I'll be back soon."

Shani didn't think Rodney had seen their group and she was pretty sure he didn't have the ability to read a vampire's life signal, so she hurried through the kitchen and hit a trail that led all around the edge of the mountaintop.

Lit with deep blue lights around the perimeter, they didn't interfere with the views that showed mountaintop after mountaintop as far as the eye could see. In the distance, a storm showed dark puffy clouds occasionally interrupted with lightning bolts. Because of the unsteady air mass, the air around *this* mountaintop felt a little electric tonight.

"So lovely," she whispered.

"It seems we've done this scene before, my lady."

Rodney. Close enough to feel his breath on her neck. His warmth, his presence, his *scent*, curled around her.

"How did you find me?"

"I once told you I could find you anywhere in the world. That has never changed."

If she turned around, her lips would be within inches of his. She shouldn't turn around. Breathing hard, unable to stop herself for anything on this earth, Shani turned to face Rodney.

His hands came up to hold her steady because she swayed. This close, alone on this stunning mountaintop, his breath touching hers, instinct took over, and she lifted her arms to pull him that final two inches.

"I didn't want this," she whispered as her lips touched his and he took over. All the lost passion, the lost years, hit them as Rodney kissed her, felt her quiver, her lips starved for his, and his tongue slid between them. The kiss heated to scalding in seconds, tongues battling for their place, as Rodney lifted Shani into his arms and held her as close as he could.

The kiss ignited her. Shani pushed out of his arms, shoved him hard enough to knock him to the ground, and raced down the trail away from him, from the club. Rodney regained his feet, unsure of what he should do, when he saw her stop and turn.

"You should follow me."

God, yes! Using speed faster than human, aware that he could almost keep up, Shani was well beyond the club now, so distant, the remaining trail was lit only by the waning moonlight partially covered by clouds at times.

Rodney stopped, scanning the trail, but she was gone. Searching as he moved forward again, he finally saw her leaning against a tree.

As he advanced closer, the moon slid from behind a dark cloud and illuminated Shani's face. Tears glistened on her cheeks. Maybe he had pushed her too much. Sorrow welled in his soul.

"Baby, if you want me to leave…"

"No. I've waited a hundred years to know how you would feel moving inside me. Don't disappoint me, watchdog."

Shani had worn a lacy sweater over a spaghetti-strapped hot-pink dress that hugged her body.

When Rodney had seen her in the club, his heart had threatened to break through his chest.

The lace sweater hit the grass as Shani pushed the spaghetti straps over her shoulders and the little dress slid down her legs to puddle next to the sweater. She wore nothing underneath. The moon's light slid over full breasts, fuller than they'd been when she was still human all those years ago.

"Fuck me, Rodney."

Shaking his head, Rodney moved to her and lifted her arms over her head to trap both her hands against the tree.

"Never. Every touch will be love, pure and hard-won, weathered by time, and finally, we're ready for it. What we do is as sanctioned by the universe as your gifts."

He lowered his mouth to take a button-hard nipple into his mouth and his groan of pleasure hit Shani in the gut and between her legs.

She wouldn't do this!

With a shove, aware she couldn't easily hurt him, Shani broke away from Rodney. "No slow and easy. No gentle foreplay. Not now, not after all this time. Not with where we've been and what we face."

She shoved him again and Rodney fell hard onto the wood boardwalk, his elbows striking with a thud as he tried to break the fall. He was breathing as hard as she was, but it wasn't because of the brutality of the fall.

His eyes followed her as she moved to stand over him, glorious, the wind whipping her dark hair, full breasts in his line of sight, her legs spread and a glimpse of heaven between them.

"Get undressed or I'll tear your clothes off you."

Rodney pushed from the ground. Using his vampire-like skills, he tore his clothes away and stood, equal measure, naked before her eyes. He didn't move again as she searched his body.

He knew she would find it perfect. Koen, Eillia, Park, and Tamesine had increased the blood they gave him daily over the years and he was practically a vampire physically. As heavily muscled as Koen now, he was nearly as big, everywhere.

Rodney watched her eyes linger on his cock and lifted it in one of his hands. Smiling, he ran his fingers down the length. "You want to take a ride on the Rodman's rod?"

Terrible, the old jibe he'd used as an arrogant human way back in New York. For some reason, this wild woman, calling the shots, brought back that silly humorous phrase. Yesterday and today merging…who they had been and who they were now.

"Yes. Yes, I do," she whispered. Shani gently pushed him down again, then lowered herself to sit on top of him as she leaned in for another kiss, her tongue aggressive and searching. She pulled away to bury her teeth in his neck as she lifted up and slid herself down on his "rod."

Rodney's arms went around Shani as she began to move. He thrust into her, but with the unbelievably erotic sensation of her teeth buried in his neck, he was unable to focus on just the feel of her as she moved up and down on his cock. The combination made him lose his ability to think, and it became about the connection of his body to hers, her mind to his, and his spirit to hers. Colors weaved through his mind and when he opened his eyes, they curled around Shani and reached into the sky.

Divine twined with the visceral as Rodney and Shani's spirits merged. The unusual tickling through their physical link drove Rodney past pleasure to ecstasy.

With each powerful stroke of his cock, skin on skin, heat on heat, he drove in and pulled out of Shani, the orgasm building with extreme friction until his entire body stiffened and the orgasm hit explosively. He shot into Shani, pumping over and over until he couldn't move. Eventually, his body dropped back onto the boardwalk as Shani continued to slide over him, driving herself down until seconds after he came, she tightened on him in an equally powerful orgasm.

Moaning, collapsed against Rodney's chest, she murmured, "Gods..."

They lay still, wordless, unsure of what to say. Finally, Rodney rolled over and curved his arms around Shani's belly to pull her to him.

"Shani..."

"Rodney, can we just...*not?* Just hold me."

He would give her the moon and stars, *anything* she wanted at her request. Her happiness and safety meant everything to him. Reaching for his jacket, he covered Shani with it and held her against him. This was all he ever needed; Shani in his arms, naked and satisfied.

Suddenly blowing out a deep breath, Shani pushed away and sat up.

He sat up as well, and laid a hand on her thigh. "May I speak now?"

Although she nodded, Rodney noticed she looked unsure. He spoke anyway. "That was as beautiful as I knew it would be." She didn't respond, didn't even lift her head. "Shani, are you all right?"

Finally, her head raised and her eyes met his. "I am. *This*, being with you...is unexpected. Rodney, I'd let the idea of ever being with you go. You had been my dream for so long, that when I finally released you, it took years to be able to actually feel happy again. Now, I just don't know how to accept this. It's too new. I need time, so we need to take this slowly."

Sliding forward, Rodney pushed her hair back and kept his hands on her face. He kissed her on her forehead, on each cheek, each eyelid, and finally her mouth. "This is your call, all of it. However you want to do this, is how we do it. If you need me, you call and I will be there. If you need space, I'll disappear until you want me again. But you must understand, I am yours until eternity passes or you no longer want me. You are mine, Shani, child of the moon, and I am yours. Forever, or just a day, whatever you desire."

She stared into Rodney's eyes, the gaze unbroken. When she spoke seconds later, she smiled suddenly, a kinder smile than he expected considering her conflicted emotions. "I remember the first moment I saw you on the beach that night. You were so enormous. Those long braids, muscles shown off by that obscenely sexy vest you wore. And when you touched me, oh, God, I wanted to feel every square inch of you. I was such an innocent back then, but I still knew that I wanted to explore this body."

Shani paused while her hand moved over his thigh, across the chasm between his legs and then to caress his spent cock. "I was too sheltered to truly imagine sex then, and yet you turned me on."

"You nearly got what you wanted that night in the forest in Patagonia. I wanted you almost bad enough to say to hell with everyone else."

"You had an iron will. Honestly, I wish you'd fucked me right there and let me know what we could have been together. I spent a lot of years wondering."

"I'm sorry, sweet lady. I may have been wrong, but I did everything for the right reasons."

"Yet it didn't turn out well for either of us, did it? I've never found a mate, and you apparently fucked women you didn't know and walked away."

"That isn't fair."

"I know it isn't. My emotions are still a little tender, sorry." Her hands moved to the long thick braid so like the ones she remembered. "God, you're built for sex. I just had you and I want you again, right now."

Her hand was still on his cock and it moved, beginning to fill again. "I told you, whatever you want."

"I do. But next time, I want us to be ready for each other, and to take our time. Are you okay with that?"

"Beautiful, I'm okay with anything you desire."

"Then let's go back to the club. And Rodney, I'm not ready to share this with anyone else, all right?"

Rodney pushed off the ground and reached down to lift Shani into his arms again. He swung her around, then pulled her close to kiss her. "Yes, my lady."

Inside one of the bungalows, Brigitte finished riding Biker. Barely able to breathe, he sucked in air.

"Holy fuck! That was…I've, uh, never experienced anything like that before!"

"Vampire sex. It's tough to go back."

"You guys must leave a lot of broken hearts in your wake."

Brigitte slid off him and dropped onto the bed.

"No. Usually we use compulsion to erase the memory. It isn't fair to leave people with unrealistic expectations. And yes, men fall in love with me all the time, they just don't remember that they do."

Will processed the thought. "Are you going to do that to me?"

She scooted over and rolled onto her side, her head propped on her hand. Running her fingers down Will's chest, over hard curves and muscles to his cock, now spent and nestled between his legs, where she tickled him.

"Would you want me to?"

"No, hell, no. I have no problem with remembering mind-blowing sex."

"Then I won't. You're different, you're part of the supernatural world now. I'd say there will be plenty more chances for you to have those unrealistic expectations fulfilled. Besides, I heard you can't be compelled."

"That's what they tell me. So, I measured up?"

"Ummm. You measured up." Her fingers began to move across the head of his cock and as it hardened, she smiled and leaned down to lick him. "Round two."

Later, walking into the club, Will watched Brigitte move among her friends, and charm strangers in her path. The beautiful vampire's personality sparkled, and good God, could she make a man smile. Unbidden though, he found himself remembering Olivia. He couldn't help it, he found himself wondering what it would be like to be with *her*. It wasn't likely he'd ever see her again, in spite of Olivia's cryptic last comment to him, but for some reason, he couldn't get her off his mind.

"A stiff shot of whisky is what I need," he commented to no one, and went to find a waiter. Here he was, with the moon in his hand, and he was asking for the stars.

He was leaning over the bar waiting for his drink when he saw Scottie's father enter with Brigitte's stunning sister. Will knew the look, they'd been together, and he could tell by their manner that it wasn't just wild sex. Something in Shani's eyes as she searched the room looked familiar to Will. Love, but not the kind that comes easy. He'd had that, once, and it had been his life. He hoped it turned out better for her.

Shani scanned the room for her sister. She needed to talk with Brigitte, and with one last glance back at Rodney, and a forced smile, she moved into the fray.

Brigitte was reaching for a glass of the special drink they'd tried when they arrived here tonight. Shani started toward her when a sound interrupted, but when she looked around to see where it was coming from, she realized that it was inside her mind. An odd tone and a message, not in words, but it was clear anyway…they all had to return immediately to the banquet room in Cairine's building.

Telepathy, when it wasn't her skill. As she approached her sister, Brigitte shook her head. "Shani, did you hear that? The message telling us we were to return to Cari's place?"

Still, her head moving to watch the other warriors, Shani noticed the same look of confusion. She nodded to Brigitte. "I did, but look around. *Everyone* did. Chione must be able to contact all of us now. This gets wilder every minute."

"Sure does. Well, then I'm going to take a stash of this shit because it is fucking amazing. By the way, so it Biker."

So they'd finally gotten together. *Good*, Shani thought. Brigitte had always been a sexual woman and the lack of good choices for lovers had made her touchy. Good that this new warrior might be just what she needed. And good that she and Rodney had connected. There would be time later to reflect on if that was really true. A hand to her belly let her know that she was pretty sure it was…being intimate with him after such a long time had shattered her painstakingly built wall against emotional chaos. With Rodney, chaos had come again in the most erotic way.

"We have to go." Shani reached for Brigitte's hand and led her past other members of the group, stopping in front of anyone they passed. "Come, we're leaving. Let everyone know," she announced.

She watched Scottie pick up her drink and start for the door. Everyone should have received the message except for Rodney, and she knew they couldn't leave without him.

"Scottie!" Scottie turned to Shani when she heard her voice, her eyebrows tenting. "Scottie, where is your father?"

Scottie shook her head. "I don't know. I was going to look for him."

"I'll do it. Go to the car with the others and I'll bring him aboard." Shani turned to her sister. "Bridge, get everyone on the lift-car, I'll search for Rodney. He wouldn't have heard the call. I'll be back in my seat long before you need to go."

"All right, sweetie." Before she moved, Brigitte stopped and laid a hand on Shani's arm as she looked into her eyes. "You did it. You had sex with Rodney."

"Later, sister."

"Holy shit. Yeah, later, details and more."

"Oh, hardly."

"I'll tell you mine, you tell me yours. Same thing."

"Get going, you pain in the butt."

Brigitte watched her sister disappear, aware that it wasn't the same thing at all.

On the boardwalk just outside the festively lit restaurant, Rodney watched the moon reflect off a big wading pool built just below the level of the restaurant. It featured contemporary open metal sculptures that depicted the natural world that surrounded the restaurant. It was crazy to think that this place was so popular, so heavily visited, considering there was no road access because of its elevation. Lift-cars had changed the world. He smiled. So had she. For him. Shani had changed his world.

Koen's love for Rodney and bringing him to the vampire world had given him the family he'd never had. Now, Shani was the home he'd always wanted. She was his heart, and he had a chance to win her back.

"Thank you, universe," he whispered to the sky, startled when Shani's voice interrupted.

"What are you thanking them for?"

He turned to face her, his eyes moist. "You. That I finally got to be with you. That we may have a chance. All of the above."

"The gods help us travel the right path, we just have to be wise enough to listen and go." She reached for him.

Tight against him, his scent broad-sided her and she wondered, if they really got together, how she would ever get anything accomplished other than sex.

"Rodney, we're leaving now. Somehow, Chione is able to use our minds like a message center, and we all received orders to get back to the tower. It isn't good."

"No, it can't be. Everyone else ready? Let's go then."

At the tower, everyone finally seated, a few with snacks or drinks, they were aware that this was serious. Something had happened since last night and they all knew what it had to be. The few conversations were quiet and brief.

When Jackson and Cairine entered the room, their faces told the tale. *Yellowstone was through playing nice.* Both stepped onto the dais, exchanged looks, then Cairine began to speak.

"I assume all of you realize why we've drawn you back. You were told that we must remain on alert, and sadly, things have continued to escalate. Everyone in the park has been vigilant, and now, we've a good picture of what to expect. It is the opinion of the scientists who have monitored the supervolcano for decades, and in Jackson's case, much longer, that the signs are too obvious to ignore. The likelihood of a major eruption is extremely high, so we must remain ready. Chione and Donovan have asked me to remind you that your jobs are simple. First, stay safe. We will be working in one of the most dangerous places on earth if this happens. There are no promises how this will go, even with our powers. We are all still in danger. So, remember that we are strongest together. No one goes anywhere alone, and for the most part, you go where you're assigned to go and do what you're assigned to do. Got it? Second, when the time comes to actively engage our mission, Chione and Donovan are in command. They are the guardians of the guardians, and they carry earth magic. To that end, their jobs are complicated. They are to guide, channel, meter, and focus all of *our* power. We must do all we can to help them."

Cairine stopped and looked at Jackson, who then stepped up beside her, a hand on her forearm. "Cari is right. We have an impossible task ahead of us, but vampires do the impossible remarkably well. What we will attempt to do is beyond-the-imagination fucked. We are going to try to stop the magma chamber from exploding into the sky to cover most nearby states several feet deep with molten ash that will kill pretty much anything it comes into contact with. The ash will travel on prevailing weather systems and cover most of the U.S. within days, then continue around the world to create what is called a volcanic winter. We have to control the release of sulfur dioxide, and the volume of the megablast. That magma chamber is only about 6 miles below the ground. However we're going to pull it off, we need to suppress the hydrothermal blasts and release the pressure in a controlled way to minimize damage. In other words, we've got a bottle with a stick of TNT in it, and we have to keep it from breaking the bottle and blowing it to pieces by putting our finger over the end. Or something like that. Sounds doable, right?"

Will stood. "But that *isn't* doable. I'm looking around this room at people who admittedly have extraordinary power, but no one can stop a geological event of this magnitude. If we try, there's a good chance none of us will make it through this."

Cairine nodded. "You're right, it's possible, but, Will, we have to try. The stakes are too high. Multiple thousands, perhaps millions, of people will die otherwise, and the earth will become a hostile place for years afterward."

"I'm on, I am, I'm just saying that, realistically, we can't expect to make it through this."

"Actually, we can," Chione said as she entered the room and headed to the dais.

TWO HOURS EARLIER

"Babe, why are we here? According to Jackson, this is ground zero."

"That makes it exactly where we need to be, Donovan. It's where we will be closest to the mother and her restless earth. I need to feel her, touch her, listen to her. So do you."

Chione took her mate's hand and led him to a soft spot on the ground, a six foot wide circle where the land looked like something had sucked it down from where it belonged by several inches.

"Here, my love, we shall kneel and touch the source of fire."

She wasn't kidding, Donovan thought, as he lowered himself to sit on ground that was warmer than it should be possible to be. He felt a hot rush on contact and tore off his lightweight jacket to pitch it away. Catching Chione's eyes, he shrugged. "Feels like the surface of the sun."

She smiled. "Not even close, but what lies beneath us could burn us just as quickly on contact. Place your hand here, clear your mind, and reach down to her. She doesn't like to give up her secrets, but she's bonded with us, and she knows we are only here to protect the life on her surface. Together, shall we?"

Chione took Donovan's left hand in her right and leaned forward to place it directly on the hot ground. Without any further thought, because he trusted Chione, he placed his right hand on the ground too, almost instantly transported to where Chione had guided them. Nowhere physical, he wasn't in the hellish magma chamber, but floating in a soft amber glow. From there, he could sense the heartbeat of the earth and knew, with no question, that this superheated viscous chamber filled with molten rock and gases was ready to force its way out of the ground.

This eruption was happening. Soon, and with no *realtime* way to protect the population. Their only hope was if the warriors could stop this from hitting the same catastrophic level that it had on its first eruption over 600,000 years ago.

God help us, his mind whispered, and somewhere in the soupy ether, a voice that was not a voice touched his mind and let him know...*she* didn't want it either. She wanted him and Chione to fix this.

"We will," he promised out loud. The connection to the planet spanned beyond her crust and out beyond the sky, Donovan shocked that he suddenly had a satellite view of the earth in all her magnificent glory. He wanted to weep, it was so beautiful.

Chione, he thought, *look at our world. Oh, God, look at this tiny place that holds us all and keeps us safe. We must do this, my love, we have no other choice!*

He felt her slide alongside him, and it wasn't her body either, just their minds, entwined, as they viewed this world that the universe had done so much to save.

And save her they would. Suddenly he was falling, falling, twisting through air that thickened and tried to stop him, until he felt the awful weight of gravity tugging him down and he knew he was back and aware in his own sluggish body. The spiritual journey was over.

Opening his eyes hurt, but he remembered that from the last time this happened. Spiritual journeys played hell on the physical form.

"Donovan?"

Her voice finally penetrated the fog, and slowly he sat up, aware that he was sweating heavily.

"It's coming," he croaked, barely able to speak.

"I know." Chione's voice was as controlled and melodic as usual.

Trying to laugh, but achieving a hoarse cough, Donovan finally stood, shakily, but he pushed upright anyway and held his own on two feet that felt like boulders strapped to his ankles. "You're better at this than me."

"Remember that, handsome. Let's get back and let them know what we've found."

After a nod, Donovan let his mate help him back to their borrowed lift-car. He had his pride, but he wasn't stupid.

BACK TO THE PRESENT HOUR

"Actually we can," Chione had answered when Will had asked if she thought they could survive this.

Chione walked through the room, her smile warm, fingers reaching to brush other fingers as she passed by.

Will had a moment when he admitted to himself that he'd follow that woman anywhere on earth.

Dylan wished he could find a mate as loving and lovely as their guardian. He'd never seen a connection like the one he saw between Chione and Donovan.

Scottie and Dani watched, overjoyed to be led by this impressive woman.

Antoinette just wanted to be with Chione to learn from her. While she knew that her personality was one of her strongest features, that she made people feel happy and calm, there were things the beautiful Chione knew that she didn't. Someday, she hoped to.

Chione stopped suddenly to wait for her mate, but Donovan threw a hand up. "Don't. I'll make it, but it may be a few moments. Go ahead, please."

She hesitated briefly, then joined Cairine and Jackson on the dais. "Hi, my lovely friends. Donovan and I have just come from the center of the park where changes are happening most rapidly. By the minute, the land around that area swells and sinks, and I would assume that the seismic monitors are going crazy right now. I do not know what the numbers might be, but I do not have to. We have been within the mother earth and we have seen that the magma chamber *is* rupturing, and that it will do so quite soon. Our job is cut out for us, but we have the power and capability to do it. The reason is simple; no other choice is acceptable. Too many people will die if the volcano erupts without our interception. We can help control the release, but while we still have moments of relative calm, we will discuss this further. Cari, tell your staff we will be working here all night and to keep the snacks and drinks coming. Now, my friends, let me describe what we're facing. It's beyond anything anyone has ever had to control before, but that we must control this event, there is no question."

Donovan stopped at a table just before he got to Chione. "I'm good right here, babe." He dropped into a cushioned chair and laid his head on his arms. He didn't move again for another fifteen minutes.

They worked through the next three hours until dawn threatened, and Chione wrapped it up.

"Go, sleep, and try not to let your minds wander and worry. We face something volatile and powerful, but we have great power to wield. I believe in us, and I'm not just trying to put a positive spin on this. We will prevail. Go. Rest. All return here tomorrow night at rising."

Brushing her hair until it shined, because it was a harmless, mindless thing to do to keep her from obsessing on the danger the warriors faced and the rest of the world if they failed, Cairine finished and carefully placed her hairbrush on the counter in her bathroom.

After so many years of doing the small things to fulfill their mission, making sure the earth could provide for all the humans who trod about on her, without destroying her, now the time had arrived to face the *grand* part of the Grand Destiny. They weren't ready.

She thought about the pain of losing any of these warriors. And the people, all the people who lived in the four states clustered around the park that would be killed too quickly if this supervolcano erupted.

Oh, God, it was too much to imagine!

Her entry monitor chimed and she looked up. Six a.m., past sunrise. Who was up and about at this hour?

Her shielding was in place so she walked out to the entryway. "*Answer.*" The monitor flashed on. *Eras?*

What the hell? "Um. *Allow access.*"

The door slid into its channel and Eras stood at the entrance. He didn't come in, just leaned against the opening. "Cari."

"What do you want, Eras?"

"I want to have a few words with you, but only if you want to. I need to warn you that it's about us."

"We've covered this."

"No, we haven't. May I come in?"

No! "I guess." Cairine stepped back as he entered, filling the room. He'd bulked up with two days of vampire-sized meals. When they'd been together, he'd still been human, and while he had been a muscled, fit young man then, now, he was as big as his father. As the leader of the children of the moon, Era's father Ahmose was one of the largest vampires she'd ever seen.

"Just, say what you feel you have to and go. I think we're all going to need our rest for tonight."

"Yeah, that's obvious. You know what else is? That we are supposed to be together. You're my mate, Cari, do you know that?"

"No, I don't, Eras. You're dreaming. Or thinking of another time. Anyway, you have no idea since we were never together as vampire. When we were human, we wouldn't have been able to tell."

"Look. I know you care about this Otto guy, but, Cari, we are facing a formidable event and there's every chance we might get hurt or worse. I can't die without knowing the truth. I believe we're mates, you don't think we are. It will take only a few minutes to find out."

Cairine smiled. "Just a few minutes? I would have thought you'd claim better stamina."

He was in front of her in seconds, his hands on her upper arms. "You need to test drive me to find out. I guarantee you won't be disappointed. Especially when we begin the merge."

It got too serious for her all the sudden. She wiggled free from his detainment and put some distance between them. "No. Go back to your room."

"One kiss."

"Not happening."

"One kiss and I'll go, no questions, no complaints."

"I'm not bargaining with you. This is my home and I call the shots."

"Fine. Let me ask you one last question. If something happens, if I'm killed in this battle, won't you always wonder if I was right? Vampires have to live with bad decisions for a long time, so what if I am the man you are supposed to be with? How will you justify choosing to never know?"

Bastard! He was right, she would never forgive herself if something happened to him. Whether it turned out he was mate or not, if he died during this fight, she would never get over it. Should she say yes? It seemed the only choice that she might be able to live with. Prove once and for all that he was wrong.

"Fine. A kiss. *One* kiss. No tongue. Then you go."

Moving too quickly again, Eras swept Cairine off her feet and carried her into her bedroom to drop her on her bed, then slid in beside her.

"What the hell?"

"You agreed. One kiss. You didn't say where it had to be."

Intimacy and intense desire overcame her anger and practicality. Suddenly, all she wanted was that fucking kiss, even if it wasn't enough to prove that they were mates, or to prove to herself that she was over him.

Eras rolled close, too close, his body hot against hers clad only in a satin gown that barely cleared her butt.

First, he dragged his fingers down her cheek and continued across her shoulder, along her sides, the fingers brushing too close to her nipple, and along her belly.

"That's not a kiss, Eras."

"Not done yet."

It was impossible to remain detached. Not only did every place he touched tremble, but it didn't escape her that this was the first time he'd touched her as vampire.

And he was right, her reaction was euphoric. Was it possible that he'd always been her mate? That they had wasted a century apart? And if he was right, where did they go from here?

He knew he had her. Eras moved his fingers along the edge of her gown, pleased to find that she wore nothing else underneath. *Easier to sneak in*, he thought, and although he knew he was pushing his luck, her body reacted to every place he touched. She hadn't moved to push him away yet.

He kept his attention on the side of her thigh, desperate to move his fingers inward and up between her legs. When she continued to allow him without stopping him, he decided it was worth the risk, so he pressed his chest tighter to her back and slowly slid his fingers back up Cari's thigh until he reached between her legs and felt her hand curl around his to stop it.

"Cari, you said one kiss."

"On the lips." By the way her voice sounded, Eras realized she was breathing hard. He slid one finger higher to touch her clitoris, knew it would be swollen.

"*These* are the lips I want to kiss."

She didn't push his finger away, she didn't answer him, but she didn't move either. Neither did he.

Her silence worried him; he didn't want to push her too far or hurt her. "Cari? I'll go if you want me to, or stay if you want me to. What do you want?"

No response. No words, no movement.

They lay for several minutes before Eras heard her sigh and felt her roll toward him.

"Stay," she whispered.

Cairine's arms went around Eras as he lifted his to pull her to him again. "I guess I need to know the truth."

"Cari, the truth is that I love you, and I think your truth is the same, but we've fucked this up."

"*You* fucked this up."

"Okay, yeah, I fucked this up. But I was a boy then. I'm a man now, I know where I belong, and that is inside of you."

He watched Cari closely as she rolled onto her back and smiled. "Then you better see to that."

"First, there's the matter of the kiss."

Eras stood and removed his clothes, then came up from the foot of the bed. Pushed up on her elbows to watch him, Cari's eyes sparkled. She wanted him as badly as he wanted her.

Growling, he slipped his hand beneath her buttocks and lifted her to his lips. "I'm a *really* good kisser."

He started along the inside of her thighs and nipped several times before he nipped just deep enough to draw blood. He'd had to; as much as he needed to be inside her, he needed to taste her. The moment that her blood touched his tongue, it removed all doubt. *She was his and meant to be his.*

Eras crawled up to her, and tore his wrist with his teeth. "Drink."

Cairine didn't hesitate, her desperation let him know she needed to know as well. She drew in the scent at first, then latched onto his arm, sucking hard. It was heaven to feel her tongue sliding across his skin.

"You understand now?"

Emotions were so deep, the revelation life-changing, Cairine had to concentrate to speak. "I understand. Eras, why have we waited so long?"

"Because you were right, I fucked this up. But I'm here now and forever. Don't even think you'll send me away."

"I couldn't. Can we discuss this later? I need to feel you."

"You're going to. I have to get to that kiss."

"Forget the kiss."

"Not *this* kiss."

Returning to the bottom of the bed, Eras's tongue continued between her legs, slow at first, giving her a proper kiss all along her slit before he tugged on her with his teeth. No puncture, not there, but using his vampire skill, speed and years of practice, he brought Cairine to orgasm, and held her close to him as she bucked against his mouth. Immediately, Eras crawled up her body again, and this time, she brought her legs up and across his back as he surged inside her, and stopped once he was buried deep.

"You're my mate, Cari. I have loved you from those early days on the beach and I never stopped."

Cairine took his face in her hands. "When you left me, I cried myself to sleep for six months, did you know that? I just couldn't imagine my life without you."

"I'm so sorry. God, baby, I can't make up for that."

"I'm past it. You were a child, I know that. So was I."

Eras began to move, his cock full and thick, and Cairine didn't want to talk anymore, she just wanted to *feel* him. Each stroke sent scatters of ecstasy through their bodies, the connection beyond any physical bond, the orgasm that built and splintered over them when they came final validation…*mates, finally.* Bright colors shot through the room, a frequent manifestation when mates merged in physical intercourse. Eras groaned in complete joy. *Mated.*

Later in the day, Cairine slid from her bed and stopped to watch Eras sleep. His huge body filled her bed, an arm thrown over his head, his legs wide. He was in a deep restful sleep and she was grateful she hadn't awakened him. Keeping the lights off, she slipped a robe over her skin in the cool air, then padded out to the galley on bare feet and ordered a hot cup of tea, keeping the lights off. When it was ready, she had planned to carry it back to the bedroom, but instead she slid down against the wall in the galley and sat there, her mind racing over the past several hours.

They'd made love. Finally, Eras was back in her arms and her life and they discovered that they were made mates by the universe. Now, though, facing this dangerous eruption, her heart pounded in fear. Would the universe let her have him back only to take him from her? How many of their team wouldn't survive this? She herself might not. Her loving family and friends, how could she go on if they didn't make it?

Poppycock, Chione would tell her. *You come with us and you fight to make a difference. Any sacrifices must be accepted, must be okay.* This was their destiny, good or bad, safe or not, they would fight until they succeeded or until they had nothing left to give.

"Stay well, my loves," she whispered into the darkness, and realized she must have little faith sitting here all alone when she should be resting in Eras's arms. Tears slid unchecked down her cheeks.

Ten

Jackson slouched in his chair, his expression somber.

Sally smacked him on the back. "What's up, bud? You look like the world's about to end."

He grimaced. "Funny. Breakfast?"

"Working on it. I've programmed in scrambled eggs and Texas toast, your favorites. Dude, relax, enjoy."

"I can't, Sal. This could be endgame."

"We won't let that happen. I'm going to enjoy my food and so are you. Time later to get all morose and apocalyptic. Nothing we do *now* is going to change anything, so we get something good to eat and take a walk. I want you to give me the tour. It's so pretty here in the mountains. L.A. just doesn't have these vistas."

The door to the communal galley opened and Jessie entered, followed by Taylor and Dean.

"Hey, the band's back together." Sally hugged Jessie. "God, girl, what's it been? Fifteen years? And Taylor, I gotta say, I'm impressed. You're shredded." Her eyes moved across Dean, whose body had also gone from fit to heavily muscled. She nodded to him. "Dean."

Dean's eyes followed her everywhere, and Sally was well aware why. The past several decades had been tough. Dean wanted to revisit their shattered marriage, and it wasn't going to happen. She was happy now in a stable relationship, with no reason to return to the toxic one she and Dean had devolved into before she called it quits. He was too intense for her, and while it had been twenty years since they'd been together, and it was possible he'd changed, she didn't want to tear down what she had with

Rick to try again with Dean. With Rick, they just had a good time, no trauma, no drama.

But, oh, hell, he looked wonderful. If she hadn't been with Rick for so many long, successful years, maybe she would have considered his plea. She would admit to herself, but no one else, that she would always love him; she just couldn't *live* with him. *God, though, he still looked like sex on a stick and a lost puppy dog, all at once.*

Sally turned to join Taylor and Jessie at the FP.

"Jess, you need to catch me up on what's going on in your world. How's Greenland? Any sexy fishermen to tell me about?"

"It's very lovely now that the temperature has moderated. The fishermen are mostly older men who I've known since they were kids. Bryson controls their memories with compulsion, so they don't know that. It's kind of hard to have romantic interest in someone you've known since they were a boy and is now in their seventies."

"Gotta agree. So no beau?"

Jessie continued to punch her breakfast choice into the FP unit.

Sally folded her arms and leaned against the counter.
"You know it's voice activated now."

"Oh. I'm so used to archaic machinery in Greenland."

"You didn't answer me and you've gone silent. *Who* is it?"

"I shouldn't say."

"Yes, you should."

Taylor had already finished and joined Jackson at the table, so the two women were outside of easy earshot.

"Who, Jess?"

"Okay. But don't tell anyone else. I don't want any questions. It's Bryson."

"Holy... Vampire Bryson? Fia's brother?"

"That's the one."

"Shit, girl, you have to tell me what it's like with a first blood."

"You're with a vampire. It's probably no different."

197

"I'm gonna say that's not true. We'll only know if we compare notes."

"Sal, we'll have a discussion some time, but not now, not here. And remember, I don't want this to get around."

"Are you not, I mean, doesn't he want anyone to know?"

"It's me. I'm not comfortable with everyone knowing. It's private, Sal, you know? Private."

"Okay. Of course, you know you can trust me, but I'll hold you to that discussion someday."

"Fine. So, what are we doing today?"

"Hiking. Jackson needs to get out of this building and out of his head."

"I don't need to get out of my head," Jackson's voice commented from across the room.

"We all beg to differ." Taylor popped up after grabbing his tray of food. "We eat, we hike, we remember the good old days." He paused for effect. "Before we all die."

Taylor's skills with the lift-car matched his boasts. He flew the car as if it were a high-winged craft, sliding across the landscape that they hadn't had a chance to see yet. Since all their Colorado travels had been with vampire companions, they'd only seen the mountains at night. Early afternoon sunlight was a welcome change. The car dropped onto a high ridge with a clearly defined trail, everyone thrilled to explore the natural beauty of these mountains above what would have been the snow line in the old days. Now, snow rarely dropped this low.

Taylor took Jessie's hand and led her from the car, while Sally stayed with Jackson, keeping her distance from Dean. She didn't want an awkward relationship with him, but she wasn't sure how to get from where they were now to where she wanted them to be. It didn't help that he continued to make it clear he still desired her.

"This path hasn't been used in a while. Lots of debris deeper in, but I think we can do this. The car has a flight stick and it can double as a scythe. I wish we'd brought snacks and drinks, I'd like to stay all day."

"Sal, we can stay as long as you'd like. Hopefully there's some fresh water up here." Dean was trying to be helpful, so Sally gave him a smile and tugged Jackson behind her.

"Come on, buddy. Let's get your mind off things of dire nature."

"Dire nature is my life."

"Not today."

The trail was rough, but the sun beamed, the air warmed, and the views were sensational.

Sally had stashed meal bars in her bag and revealed them at the perfect time as they sat on top of large boulders to overlook endless valleys between mountaintops. Relaxed, she leaned over to pat Jackson, who sat below her, on the top of his head.

"Feeling better?"

He turned to smile up at her. "Yeah, I do. It's just that Cari and I have been living with this threat for so long, the idea that it may be happening terrifies me. Merged, we're a powerful force, sure, but I know what we face and feel pretty sure that there's at least a significant chance we can't stop this."

Jessie peeled off a gooey stretch of caramel from a nut-covered meal bar. "*Don't* worry. Worrying about something before it happens just means you might have to live through it twice. Or something like that. My mama used to tell me."

"No way I won't worry. But thanks, guys, for giving me an afternoon with old friends. Those days in college seem like another life."

Dean lay against the rocks, soaking up the sun, his eyes closed, his shirt discarded on another rock. "Dude, it *was* another life."

Sally tried not to look, her eyes on the view, but acknowledged her failure when she closed them and then opened them on Dean. Yes, Shani's blood and the years had been kind to him.

A chirp interrupted the peace of the moment, and she watched Jackson stare at his fone before he answered it.

"Boogie, what is it?"

Jackson listened, then put the fone on speaker. "Boogie, repeat that."

The voice that came through was high-pitched and rushed. "We have a rupture. Southwest corner near the Geran breach. Security has the area blocked. The rupture, Jax…it's a big one. It's starting."

Jackson looked at his friends, then answered the unspoken question. "Start the evac, no details, we don't want a panic. Get the team on it and I'll be there within the hour."

Ringing off, Jackson pushed off the rocks. "Playtime's over. The vampires won't be able to come out for six more hours."

"They can channel our powers from inside. We need to get back." Jessie slipped off the stones, pulling Taylor with her. "How quick can you get us back to Cairine's?"

"Faster than I got us here. It might get a bit hairy, but I'm good."

"I'll contact the guardians. I'm going to try to use the communication link that Chione did the other night."

"You think *we* can do that?" Sally asked.

"I think we have to try. Taylor, try to ignore me in your head, just keep us in the air."

Taylor's piloting skills were up to the task. As he lifted off, focused, he felt a presence hovering on the edge of his mind. Nothing concrete, but someone there. Trying to phase it out of his mind, he knew what it was. Jessie, as she had warned. He tried to block her as she had requested, but the mind link was strong. Jessie's message got through. *Prepare, there has been a rupture in the park. Our talents will be needed when you rise tonight.*

She hoped that her plea penetrated sleep and that when dusk finished, they would all be ready to go. The message sent, all she could do was hope that everyone received it. Jackson had been texting the entire time, rallying the geologists and volcanologists that worked with him to keep a close eye on this threat.

He pitched his fone on the seat beside him. "We're so fucked."

"Jax, stop it. Believe in us."

"I'm trying, Sally, forgive me for saying this, but we're going to need more than a miracle if that chamber blows."

IN THE TOWER

The mind-linked message drove Chione from bed, her heart pounding. She looked back when she heard Donovan groan. "She reached you."

Scratching his chest, Donovan pushed off the edge of the bed, forcing his eyes open. The message interrupted the middle of their rest cycle, dusk still hours away.

"Um, yeah. It looks like things are going to get interesting fast now."

"It looks like. Go back to sleep, baby. I'll contact Cairine and make arrangements, then waken you again when it is time to act."

"No, love, I'll stay up with you."

"No need for both of us to lose rest. Once I find out if we need to intervene right away, we'll either have to *all* get started, or I can return to bed with you."

A sleepy groan came from Donovan again as he stepped up behind his mate and pulled her body against his. "How about we put each other back to sleep," he suggested, rubbing a growing cock against her buttocks.

"Regrettably, not now. If Jackson says this eruption can wait, I will accept that offer."

"Okay. I'll go back to bed. Alone. But let me know if you want to change that."

"You know I will."

Donovan stretched and dived back onto the mattress.

"You need me, you call for me."

"Promise. I'm going to get dressed."

"Be careful, Chione. Whatever you do, don't go near the daylight."

"I'm not that incautious."

"You're that dedicated, and I could see you risking it."

"Not without you by my side."

Donovan smiled as he snuggled into his pillow. "That's what I mean."

"Sleep well."

Taking the stairs quickly, Chione arrived in front of Cairine's apartment door and pressed the chime to announce herself. The door slid open at once to reveal Cairine waiting.

"You received Jessie's message," Cairine stated.

"Yes. It appears we all did."

"How do we handle it? We can't move from here for nearly five hours."

"The rupture isn't dangerous enough yet to require intervention, but we need to be in place and ready. I'm waiting for Jackson, who will update us as soon as he has all the reports from his staff. If we have to be present before nightfall, we'll send those who can go. The humans and supernaturals will travel to the area for proximity and we will give them all the support we can from here. Our talents are stronger together, but that isn't an option until tonight."

"No. I'll help co-ordinate, anything you need. The transport is on stand-by and my pilot is staying with it. If we need to go, she's waiting to take us at a moment's notice."

"Thank you, Cari. Until then, everyone needs to do the same. I'm sending out a message that all the vampires should feed. They'll need the power." Chione dropped her head. "The timing could be better."

"I'll say."

Eras's deep voice came from the hallway that led to Cairine's bedroom. Chione's eyes followed his voice to see him leaning against the wall, clad only in his undershorts. Her eyes shot to Cairine, who shrugged with a shy smile.

Chione nodded. "Good. That's one more thing put right. For now, you two go back to what you were doing. If I need you, you'll know."

Chione left and the door closed behind her, leaving Cairine standing in the middle of the room.

"Well, that happened." Eras came up behind her and turned her around so he could pull her into his arms.

"Cari, you're all right, aren't you? You don't regret letting me stay with you?"

Her answer wasn't verbal. She leaned into him and buried her face against him, feeding her arms around his waist and holding on tight.

Love overwhelmed him, his desire to protect his woman, to assure she was happy, Eras just held her, his chin on top of her head. "I love you to the moon and back."

That did it. The phrase that they had used when they were human. Ten decades past, and he remembered. God, so did she. The tie was strong, the love stronger.

"I love you to the moon and back too." She felt his arms tighten.

It was done. He'd won her back because she knew they belonged together. When faced with his devotion, his kind, gentle nature, the beautiful history they had, and a physical bond forged by the universe, Cairine submitted. *This man was hers, and she was his.*

Done. *Mates.* Unless either one of them was lost in this horrible battle. *Unless sacrifices would be demanded.*

God, she was going to drive herself crazy with all the *what ifs!*

Cairine stepped back to capture Eras's gaze. "I no longer have any doubts. You are my mate, and I am yours. We don't know what this battle will bring, so, Eras, I want you to make love to me as if it might be the last time."

Eras shook his head. "No. I already did that a century ago, and I'll never do it again. I'm going to make love to you like it's just the first of many, each better than the time before."

"You've acquired a velvet tongue."

He reached for the cock that filled out his underwear and rubbed the tip. "You have no idea."

"Okay, yeah." Her eyes dropped to his tenting shorts. "Come with me and bring that with you."

As she turned to face the hallway, Cairine slid her robe from her shoulders, and Eras followed the most perfect ass he'd ever seen into the dark.

TWO FLOORS ABOVE

Shani lay across her bed, a hand moving over her breast, down her side, over her belly to where her legs met. Dragging her fingertips through the moistness there, her eyes closed, her memory returned to the moment Rodney's cock had entered her, a dream ripped from yesterday, fulfilled too late to matter to the young human girl who had wanted him so desperately.

It wasn't the same as she had expected. Of course it wouldn't be; neither he nor she was the same as they had been so many years ago. Erotic, yes, his body turned her on more than ever, but the tenderness, the deep loving soul of it, was more than that young girl could ever have understood.

He had loved and missed her all that time. The ache in her belly, in her chest, brought tears to the experienced woman she was now.

Now, here in Colorado, they faced one of their ultimate trials. Vampires could survive nearly any death, but not humans. In spite of Rodney's first blood talents, he was still human, and he could die a forever death.

"You can't come," she whispered.

The problem was, he'd never agree to stay behind. Compulsion would likely not work, but it was her best option. She had to try.

Sitting up, she kept her eyes closed and searched for him. She'd taken his blood so it would be simple. There. Her heart beat quicker at merely the *thought* of going to him.

Without bothering to dress, she grabbed a robe and tied it around her waist. She was only going to do the deed and come back to rest until the sun dropped. Sooner, if all hell broke loose. It was the reason she would not wait until tonight; this volcano could erupt at any moment.

One floor above, third door to the left...*knock, knock!*

Seconds passed that felt like hours, showing Shani that just the *thought* of him heated her up.

"God, I'm hooked."

The door slid aside and Rodney stood in front of her, naked but for skimpy shorts. He wore a pleased smile that shook her where she stood.

Shani didn't know how this would turn out in the end, but she knew how she wanted it to; he would submit to her compulsion and she would go back to her room.

"Is everything all right?"

"No, but it will be." She entered the room and turned to face him as the door slid shut. "Rodney, would you look at me?" Classic line before compulsion command. He'd recognize it, but he had no reason to suspect anything, so he raised trusting eyes to hers.

It wasn't necessary to touch him, but she needed to, and moved closer to slide a hand up his chest. He felt so good she nearly abandoned her intention and threw him on the bed waiting in the corner of the room. No, this had to be done. "Rodney, you will stay here in this apartment when we leave tonight to go to Yellowstone. You will not engage in the battle at all."

His gaze didn't waver.

"Do you understand?" She needed to confirm that he was under her command.

Still, he didn't respond, he just kept his eyes steady on hers. Suddenly, he burst forward, lifted her into his arms, placed her on the bed, and lowered himself beside her.

"What in the name of the spirits made you think to try to compel me to stay out of the fight?"

Fuck. *Okay, it didn't work.* She couldn't compel him. *Damn vampire blood cocktail!*

"Rodney..."

"No, I don't want to hear it. I actually understand why you tried it, and I appreciate the attempt to protect me, but I'm here for the entire battle, come what may. All that is precious in my world is here, and I could never stay here, safe, while you are all out there risking your lives to save the world. Shani, you *are* my world."

"You're human, need I point that out? You're really fucking breakable."

"It has come to my attention on occasion."

"Then let me…"

"If you want to do something for me, I do have a problem that needs attention on *this* occasion."

Yes, she could feel it against her hip. Neither wore enough clothes to keep anything apart, and the insistent pressure brought only one response.

The shorts were gone, and her right hand was on his cock, moving along the smooth skin and hot, firm shape.

"I didn't come here for this."

Rodney pulled the tie loose from her robe to reveal the fact that she'd worn nothing else.

"Yes, you did."

His hands warm, the fingers moving across her skin tracked down the same area she herself had touched earlier with fantastically different results. Shani gave herself over to Rodney's talents, because he was right. This, him, every part of him, was *really* why she came here today, she just hadn't wanted to admit it.

When his fingers reached between her legs, they slid along her inner thighs, tickling her, until they moved into the moist channel and slipped along her clitoris. At that moment, he lowered his mouth to nip at her breast, before his tongue slid around the curved shape until he reached a nipple and latched on. Shani closed her eyes to immerse herself in Rodney and nothing else, in what he was doing to her. The looming threat was relegated to outside her mind.

"This time, I'm going to take my time and make love to you exactly as I dreamed about many times. My Shani, in my arms, beneath my tongue and teeth, and between my legs."

Rodney slid to the bottom of the bed and concentrated on his job, to lift his head one more time, and whisper, "My Shani," before he lowered his head again to bring her to just shy of an orgasm. Instead of finishing, he moved up to lie across her, nipped her belly and breasts again, and then pushed into her. Shani was ready, her body responded instantly, and she clamped down on the intruding organ.

Yes, the swirling lights showed their connection, and they were beautiful, but he needed only one thing. He wanted to hear her scream.

Using skills he'd gathered over all the years he'd missed her, he drove in and out, ecstatic to feel her, aware that she liked it when he pulled all the way out and slammed back in. Shani met his thrusts with equal force, and their orgasms blew at the same time, wrapped in sparkling lights as they came harder than either of them had ever done.

Neither moved for a long time, breath ragged from the intensity.

Rodney finally turned to Shani. "Will you drink?"

"I need to. The stronger we are, the better the chance to succeed."

"I don't want you to drink from anyone else. Please, use me anytime you need to."

"You know what will happen."

"Bring it on, my lady."

SAME FLOOR, ANOTHER ROOM

Still half asleep, he answered the chime, saw who was there, and gave access. The door slid aside.

"Biker."

"Hey."

"Can I spend the rest of the day with you?"

"Uh, yeah. Sure."

Will stepped aside to let Brigitte into his room.

She looked around as if assessing the décor, well aware the rooms were pretty much the same.

"Nice. Homey. A little impersonal."

As he hit the key to close the door, he turned and leaned against it. "You seem like a woman with something on her mind. Care to clue a guy in?"

"Yes. I don't want to be alone. I went to my sister's room but it was empty. I know where she is, she's with the love of her life."

Brigitte dropped against the wall opposite Will, mirroring his stance. "I know we're not in love, but I think that, here, at the eleventh hour before we engage in something that might, you know, *kill* us, that being *with* someone is better than being alone. What do you think?"

Deliberately slowly, Will came forward and took her hand. He led her to his bed, slid his jeans back off and pitched them on the floor, then reached for Brigitte. Equally as deliberately, he removed her clothes, piece by piece, and when she was naked, lifted her in his arms to lay her on the bed and came down with her.

"I think it's a fine plan."

"I have to feed. Care for a little fuck and suck?"

"Outstanding. It's like sex on steroids. No, better than that. I don't really have the words to describe it."

"Pretty much." Brigitte paused. "Thank you. This whole *we all might die thing* is such a buzzkill."

"Preaching to the choir, beautiful."

"Let me begin." Brigitte crawled to the bottom of the bed, took Will's cock in her hand and led it to her mouth. "I think I'll start here."

ONE FLOOR BELOW

Bryson had fallen back asleep when his door chimed. Groggy, because vampires never did well during daylight hours, he smiled and hoped it was who he thought it was.

Using vampire skills, he slid the door open from the bed and nodded as Jessie came through.

"Hi, gorgeous."

Jessie grimaced, just like every other time he'd ever called her that. He meant it, he thought she was absolutely beautiful, but she habitually defaulted to self-deprecating humor when it came to her looks. He planned to change her view.

"Bry. I heard Chione say that every vampire should drink. You need to be healthy for this. Plus, I'd like to stay with you today."

He pulled back the sheets and patted the bed.

"You never have to ask, all you have to do is come to me. I always want you, Jess, you know that."

Jessie sighed and began to remove her clothes as she walked toward him. God, that vampire was good to her.

"You know, I finally do believe it. You *really* love this ginger-haired, freckled geek. The most sexy man in the world, and *you* love *me*. It's like a fairy tale."

"Here's your fairy tale. Get over here so I can drink from you and pound you into this bed."

"Awww, just like in Cinderella."

Bryson grabbed her and spun her beneath him.

SAME FLOOR, DIFFERENT ROOM

Crezia and Caedmon finished a round of extreme sex.

She rolled off him to suck in oxygen, trying to recover her breath. "Ummm. This mountain air seems to have stimulated us. We get better each time, have you noticed?"

"Yep. I was there."

She smacked him. "Such a brat."

Caedmon grinned as he rolled off the bed. "Want some vodka?"

"Bring the whole bottle."

As he reached the galley, Caedmon stumbled, stopping to massage his thigh vigorously.

Crezia saw the incident and pushed up on an elbow to watch him grab the bottle of *Pincer Shanghai*. "Sweetie, we need to recharge your batteries before tonight."

"I know. Lately, it seems like it happens quicker."

"I just wore you out, that's all."

Caedmon sat back on the bed and handed the vodka to Crezia. She lifted it to drink right from the mouth of the bottle.

"Yeah... I've been meaning to talk to you. It's fine, but I think I'm having trouble again. I really am working through your magic sooner than I used to."

"Then we do our healing sessions more often. You are not reverting to your previous human disability."

"I'm sure I'm not, but I'd welcome another session, especially with what we face tonight."

"Come, we'll begin right now."

Caedmon turned the bottle up, took a lengthy draw, and wiped his mouth with the back of his hand.

"Okay, let's do this."

Sitting cross-legged on the bed, Crezia and Caedmon held hands as they synced their respiration.

Comfortable and familiar with this spirit merge, they moved easily into that realm where Crezia could harness the strongest levels of her healing power. It had grown almost exponentially since it first manifested with Caedmon, and now she could heal almost on a mythic level. It disturbed her, though, that she couldn't permanently heal Caedmon. It seemed that he needed frequent sessions with her magics to renew his strength and wellness. While she would do that for him forever without complaint, her concern was that if something happened to her, what would become of him? They'd been inseparable since they mated just after their conversions, and the idea of him becoming disabled again broke her heart.

When she'd mentioned her concern once, he'd taken her face in his hands and simply said, "Then you'd better not ever let anything take you away from me."

After touching her magics and transferring them to her mate, they pulled free and slowly lifted from the bed.

"Better?"

"Oh, yeah. Tingly, but in a good way. I love feeling that electricity running through my muscles. Thanks, Zia. Now, I can take on that little volcano."

"*Little* volcano? Ugh, maybe I gave you too much!"

"Come here, wench!"

He had no trouble *catching* Crezia following a brief chase, after which they ended up back on the bed.

SAME FLOOR, YET ANOTHER ROOM

"Fuck! *What?*" After two mind-link messages, Fia had been trying to get back to sleep, but now her doorchime interrupted.

Crawling from her bed, she looked at the monitor, wiping a blurred eye that didn't want to wake. *"Answer."*

When she saw who it was, she groaned. "What now? *Allow access.*"

Whisking open, the door slid into the wall.

Standing, arms crossed now, legs wide, she yawned. "What do you need, Taylor? You know it's still daylight."

"Yes, and we have a crisis, right?"

"Got the news. Need the rest. Now, what is it?"

He wandered deeper into her room, the opposite direction from where he needed to go. Leaving the door open, Fia followed him. "Taylor, I want to get back to sleep."

"I know, but all the vampires are supposed to feed, and I'm here to help."

No. Oh, no, that would not happen again.

"I've already made arrangements with one of Cairine's feeders down below. Thanks, but you can go."

"I've perfectly good blood. Why do you fight me so much on something so simple? You need blood, I'm happy to donate. What's the big deal, Fia?"

"Taylor." His name came out in a combination of exhaustion and frustration. *Because you turn me on? Because you're my friend and I don't want to fuck you? I don't want to lose you?*

"You're my partner and friend, I don't want to *use* you. Cairine says all of her feeders are good people and easy feeds, so thanks, but no thanks."

"Fia, you are the most exasperating woman I have ever met! I don't see how getting the blood that you need from me is using me. I'm offering, for fuck's sake!"

"And I'm politely declining. You need to get some sleep too, Taylor. Chione said that if something happens sooner, the humans and supernaturals are going in without vampire back-up. Go, get your rest. I've got this covered."

"Fee..."

"Taylor, we have worked together for over four decades. What makes you think you can change my mind on this?"

"The voice of illogic sounds really logical again. Fine, but, hey..." Taylor stopped speaking and walked to the door and turned. "Be careful out there. You'd look nice with a suntan, but I don't fancy seeing your skin fried like a hunk of ham."

"Ugh. For a brilliant man, you suck at analogies. Go sleep. And Taylor. You should get a girlfriend."

Taylor walked out and stopped in the hallway as her door closed behind him. She didn't hear what he said as he walked away. "That's what I'm *trying* to do, wild one."

ONE FLOOR ABOVE, ONE LAST ROOM

Sally settled in, the televid on, muted, her favorite comfy pajamas warming her cool skin, a tall glass of ice-cold milk and a bowl of chocolates on the nightstand.

"Well, if this is your last night alive, it's the perfect date."

Tuning the televid to a classics channel, she looked up the third season of an old show that had remained a favorite even after a century.

Scooting down against fat pillows, she reached for the bowl of chocolates.

"Hello, David," she whispered, as the credits began for the television series Dr. Who, and her favorite actor in the role. She'd seen this season of the show dozens of times, and yet every time, it felt fresh and new. *That* was quality programming.

Just as the show began, her door chimed.

She didn't bother with the formality of checking to see who might be there, it had to be Jackson.

"*Allow access.*"

Her attention back on the screen, she said, "What up, Jax?"

"Wrong college buddy."

Sally's head spun toward the voice she would have figured to be the last one she'd ever hear in her room.

"Um, Dean. I'm sorry, I figured it had to be Jax. What do you want?"

"Some comfort? A human connection on a night that might be our last. A connection with *you* because of all we've meant to each other over the years."

"Dean, it's been decades."

"I know, I've counted each one. Look, Sally, I'm not asking for a chance to get back together, or for a booty call, or for anything other than a little kindness. I'm tired, Sal, and I'm lonely. I *miss* you. I miss *us*."

He was breaking her heart.

"Come here."

Dean hesitated before he walked over to her bed to sit on the edge.

"Why don't you stay here with me? I've cued up Dr. Who, and I've programmed all manner of great comfort food, so you're welcome to share. But that's all I'm offering."

"I'll take it, gratefully."

"Okay, scoot in, but keep quiet."

"The Tenth doctor?"

"Is there any other?"

"I remember that the only answer to that question is *hell no*."

"Good. Then I won't have to retract my invitation. Go program in some strawberry chocolate ice cream. I'll keep it on pause."

Dean walked to the FP unit, happy to know that she remembered his preferred ice cream flavor. That she had accepted his company at all made him, for this moment in time, one of the happiest men on earth.

Eleven

"Time?"

"Time. Jackson just updated me. The rupture is a big one, but the lava stream and gas emissions are contained. For now, it's managed. However, he says he just received reports of more land deformation in six other spots around the park. It's definitely beginning. We should get on site as soon as possible."

"Okay, I'll shower and dress."

"Shower, Donovan? We're going into a place where we'll likely be covered with ash by morning. Or worse."

"There was a time I would have laughed at that myself, but I'll be quick. I like rocking this long bang, but my hair needs a quick wash."

Chione laughed. She hadn't forgotten that the first time she met him, his head had been shaved. He had been every bit as sexy without one hair on his head as he was now with a full mane that flowed past his shoulders. Her mind traveled back to that rocky start in South America and how perfect her life had been since then.

She lifted her eyes to the heavens with a prayer.

"Please let us gain dominion over this eruption, tame the beast, and all go home safe after saving the world. It's what we do, Destiny, so help us win."

Fifteen minutes later, Donovan came from the bathroom.

"You smell so fresh," his mate commented. "Everyone's ready, so shall we join the remainder of the team? We're meeting in the banquet room."

"Let's do it." Donovan grabbed Chione as started past him and pulled her close. "I love you madly."

She knew what he meant. "I love you gladly."

"Let's go save the world!" Donovan swept Chione into his arms and blew down the stairs.

The banquet room was busy, but eerily quiet. Chione and Donovan entered and all eyes moved to them. They continued to the dais, where Chione stood and silently surveyed all the faces.

"What a somber lot. Look, what we must do during the coming days is unprecedented. Will we succeed? Will this massive bowl of superheated rock and ash cover the states and damage the globe? Maybe. But with *us*, maybe not. That's what counts, that we do all we can to keep this under control. Our biggest task is to keep going. No matter what, we do all that we can do. The universe has chosen all of us, so it must have faith in us. You realize what it had to do to put us all here, yes? To bring our healer Crezia, it had to resurrect a vampire who died over 6000 years ago. That's a lot of *faith*. So, yes, we are worried, and yes, we are scared, but what hero ever wasn't? It's how we stay alive. So, when we link, all we have to do is reach into ourselves, into the deepest part of our souls and spirits, and let the magic flow. Donovan and I will do the rest. Primarily, what we must do is help the chamber vent its gas and pressure slowly, so that it doesn't blow its contents up into the air to cover everything in its path. As I requested, everyone is wearing lightweight durable clothing, comfortable, protective boots, and long hair secured, right? Then let's fly."

Jackson was at the door and led the thirty-one chosen warriors with various skills, two guardians selected by the Mother Earth herself, and one dedicated man who loved them all.

The transport made short distance between Cairine's tower home mid-way up the Rocky Mountains and the center of the Yellowstone Caldera in Wyoming. Surrounded by mostly stone and soil, the trees cleared away some time ago, they noticed that a series of powerful solar lights had been placed beginning at the perimeter of the area and spiraling inward.

Chione nodded. "Great plan, Cari."

"It was Jackson's idea decades ago. We knew that if we ever faced this threat, we would manage it at night, so lights would be helpful. My Jackson has been the perfect partner. You couldn't have given me a better friend and associate."

"It was sanctioned. Apparently, you and Jackson were always meant to be paired, as all of you have been. It has been up to each of you to find out why."

That comment brought several heads around to consider partners over the years, good relationships and bad. Bura looked toward Eras, who chuckled.

"Yeah, Bura, we all know why you got *me*, you unlucky bear. The man has kept me straight for forty years. If he hadn't been there, I might be working in fast-food service long before now. And fucking *that* up."

Laughs went around the cabin of the transport, a welcome respite. Seriousness returned when the transport landed, and everyone walked out onto the hot ground.

"Holy...I guess there can't be any doubt now. This place is an inferno."

Jackson explained. "The pressure from the magma chamber is penetrating the surface at multiple points. So far, only one big rupture has occurred, but we're tracking about twenty smaller ones. It's likely only a matter of time before we start to see bigger breaches and, God help us, the possibility of the *big* one."

"We stay in contact," Chione called out. "The mind-link will always reach the group, except, of course, for you, Rodney. Stay with someone at all times. We're going to walk the caldera within the local area and see if we can pick up any vibrations. Sometimes the Mother speaks to us. We just have to be quiet and listen when she does."

For the next two hours, the group wandered silently along the rough ground to see if anything relevant or useful came to them. Mostly, the heat melted resolves, and although they were all relieved that, at this point, the ground seemed stable, no one believed it meant that they were out of danger. While the earth didn't seem to *speak* to anyone, their link through Chione and Donovan to the earth let them know that this was inevitable. *When* was still the question, but this volcano *would* blow if they couldn't stop it.

Some distance from the others, Will wandered alone. His connection to the ground held ties that the others could not know. He felt her tremble. Having removed his shoes for closer contact, beneath his bare feet, tiny vibrations led him to places where the surface moved, dropped or lifted, what Jackson called land deformation, it was happening all around them in tiny fractures. Will didn't need a link to Chione to know that this was real, and that if they pulled this off, stopping this eruption, it would be a universal miracle indeed. Though he didn't believe they could do it, he hoped, *prayed*, that he was wrong.

Brigitte waved at him from where she tracked the area with her sisters. He'd grown fond of the lovely, sexually inexhaustible woman. It was clear to him that the vampire was way out of his league and that when this was finished, she'd return to her extraordinary life and he'd go back to the desert.

Funny how life fucked with you, even when you were trying to stay off its radar.

Rodney scoped the landscape with Scottie and her team of humans, but he kept searching for Shani, already addicted to her again.

While he *was* breaking down her resistance, he knew what a brilliant stubborn woman she was, and it wouldn't surprise him if, in the end, she decided they should not continue. For Rodney, because he knew it was the wrong choice, he'd try until his final breath to make her understand that they were real and meant to be. He'd fucked up, and that was on him. So now it was up to him to fix it.

While Cairine and Eras weren't ready to make any declarations yet, everyone who knew them had no trouble figuring out that they were together again. Quick glances, bright smiles, *accidental* bumps against each other, the clues were impossible to miss. Shani and Brigitte tried to pretend they didn't see the moments, but eventually, they couldn't help themselves.

"So, Eras has filled out quite well as vampire, have you noticed?" Brigitte pointed out what she knew Cairine had most certainly already *noticed.*

Playing it cool, Cairine *um-hum'd.* "He's vampire, of course he has."

"You wouldn't have any insider knowledge?" Shani asked.

Cairine stopped and stared at the two women with earnest innocent eyes. "Okay, okay, like you don't know. Shani, you just cheat. You're trying to get me to admit it, so, yes, Eras and I are exploring our relationship."

Brigitte looked at Shani. "Exploring? Is that what the kids are calling it these days?"

"Must be. So, how are the *explorations* going?"

"We'll know more at a later time. Until then, we're keeping things under wraps. Honestly, my friends, this has startled me and I don't have any idea if it will work in the end. I'm happy, but I'm worried at the same time."

"We're sure it will go beautifully. You and Eras belong together." Shani hugged Cairine.

Brigitte made a point of capturing Shani's attention.

"You might want to see to that advice for yourself."

"Rodney and I are a different story."

"Not that different. Love is love, and a mate is a mate."

"We'll see."

"Understated, but true. Okay, let's do our job, ladies."

As they continued to check the landscape, broken into groups of three or four, Chione, Donovan, and Will felt the movement, powerful, beneath feet connected to the earth like no other being had ever been. Waves of heat and motion, the feel, the sense, the magma, boiling, ready, the three earth-connected warriors knew two things; it was coming, but not tonight.

Chione sent out a mind-link to everyone so they would know that tonight, *this* night, they could go home to recover from a night fraught with unimaginable possibilities.

"It's all right for now, my warriors. We will still be called, but we can go home and let our minds and spirits relax so that we will be ready when the day does arrive."

With no reason for immediate deployment, the team allowed adrenaline spikes and mental lists of regrets a chance to die down as they contemplated getting back to Cairine's building to their apartments. Another day to sleep, eat, fuck; to do everything a person might want to do for pleasure.

It turned into a blow-out party. Cairine watched her guests consume most of the alcohol she'd stockpiled over the past few years. Her chefs had been instructed to keep the food coming, and they had. Music filled the banquet room, creating a frequent loop of hilarious drunk people dancing like there was no tomorrow. No one was immune to the frivolous fun.

As dawn loomed, the vampires always aware, they retired to the kitchen seeking somewhere quiet to talk.

Fia led the way, joined by stragglers every few minutes until almost all the vampires were collected in the kitchen, alone together, for the first time in a long time. She perched on one of the electric stovetops.

"Bry!" Her brother, just entering, joined her and pulled himself up on the same counter.

"Eh, sis. I'm sorry we haven't had much time to catch up. I've missed you."

"Same here." Fia looked around the room at her friends and family. "I have an idea. Let's all go home to France after all this is over. We'll swim in the Mediterranean, eat Koen's food, and just pretend we're eighteen again with no trauma in our lives. How does that sound?"

"God, I'm on for that." Eras heard Fia's suggestion as he entered. "We were all so unseasoned then."

Cairine sat on one of the barstools, her feet propped up, drinking a local beer. "Even if we go back, we still can't actually *go back*, Eras."

He approached her, stopped, looked around the room at his friends and family as they watched him, shrugged, walked up to Cairine and pulled her into his arms. "No. I'm more interested in going forward, anyway."

"And the cat's out of the bag." Shani held up her glass in a toast. "About time, kids. You were smoking back on the beach even then."

Everyone offered congratulations, thrilled to see them together again. All Shani could think of was that Koen's house, and especially that beach, reminded her of only one thing…sex in the sand with Rodney. She remembered clearly that she'd wanted to drag him down there back then. That sweet innocent human girl had no idea what the next century would bring. *Although…*

Her eyes went to Cairine, smiling at everyone, a little uncomfortable with the attention, but obviously happy. Could she and Rodney get there?

"Bed time. I'm losing stamina. I'll see you tomorrow night." Shani hugged everyone in the kitchen, opened the door to the still raging party, and as she passed through, she searched for Rodney. He wasn't there. She could use her tracking, but she didn't have to. Reaching the entrance to her apartment, she nodded to herself. There he stood, leaning against the wall outside.

Shani drank in the sight of him. His hair was longer than before, not by much, but it brushed his buttocks, twisted into long braids just like it had been that night on the beach. He wore the tight black pants, his generous penis visible in a mound that wet her right there, and God, he was wearing that sleeveless matching vest. He hadn't changed much in appearance from the man that young girl had wanted to discover her sexuality with. This was like Cairine and Eras. They were made to be together. The universe must want this, because there could not have been a better time, a time of greater need, than right at this moment.

Smiling to herself, her head down, she walked up to the door, spoke, "Disengage," and put a finger out to hook the top of the vest to pull him in.

"Fuck me, watchdog. Fuck me hard."

She was in his arms blindingly fast and up against the wall. Her legs went tight around his waist, and she ground herself against him. "Fast, hard, uncontrolled. I want to know what you're like when you need it, when you've lost it, when you have to have it."

Their clothes were gone and he had her on the floor, his cock the last thing she saw before he drove into her so hard, so fast, she gasped.

Rodney didn't slow down.

"You *know* what I'm like. Do you remember that shaft of sexual need you sent to me in the Patagonian forest? I was standing there with the others, you used your power to send all that young desire at me like a fucking arrow. I barely made it through that day!"

All the while, as he reminded her of that moment, he pounded into her, her heels on his back, the rawness, the need, the lost years, ecstasy reborn, and when he came, she felt *his* orgasm as well as her own, powered by the relentless intensity of his strokes. She'd had sex with a lot of men through the years since she and Rodney had been apart, but never anything like this…never this primal.

The moment they came down from shared orgasms, their bodies spent, they couldn't move after Rodney dropped off her onto the floor. Several long moments passed before Shani spoke.

"I guess we're doing this."

Rodney closed his eyes. *I guess we're doing this.*

It meant she would give this relationship a chance. In the generous years he'd been granted by Koen, this moment was the one that he felt he'd been waiting for. Tears welled, then spilled. He was an emotional man, always had been, and that this perfect woman accepted him left him humbled that she could love him.

Suddenly he felt her arms around his shaking body, her hands twisted in his hair, tears covering her cheeks as well.

"Rodney," she whispered. "You have to know I could never have stopped loving you. I knew the moment you picked me up on the beach that day that we were special. It took us a few thousand days to get here, yeah, but hey, we've finally made it."

"You know you've made me the happiest man in the world, right? Whatever happens in the coming days, nothing will touch that."

Rodney pushed off the floor and lifted Shani in his arms. "I love you, my moon child. With every breath I take, I will devote my life to making you happy. I intend that you never cry again unless it is with joy."

"Rodney..." She buried her head against his chest as he lowered her onto the bed, the sound of his strong heartbeat beneath his warm skin one of the most beautiful things she'd ever heard. Yes, as he said, no matter what happened, for this moment, life was as it should be.

JUST BEFORE DUSK

Shani shot up. *No! It was happening!*

Shaking, it took a moment before she leaned over to waken Rodney.

"Rodney, wake up. The volcano, it's ready. I have to go."

He came awake slowly. She smiled as he rolled over to face her, exhausted. She *had* worn him out last night.

"I'll get dressed."

"I suppose I can't convince you to stay here."

"No. You and Scottie, all my kids, will be there, and so will I. Trust, my love. We've just found each other again, nothing is going to separate us."

"You have more faith in fate than I do."

"I have to. We are stronger together."

"If you believe it to be so, I'll do my best to believe with you, but, keep that promise. I can't lose you now."

"Never. Is it night?"

"In less than half an hour, it will be safe for vampires to leave this building."

"I'll be ready within ten minutes."

She watched him as he entered the bathroom and remained frozen on the closed door. When Chione sent through the mind-link a few minutes earlier, she'd considered leaving him asleep in bed, but she knew it was a breach of trust, and if they were going to try to build something, it couldn't begin with that. Shani admitted that if it were she in the same situation, she would insist on being there just as he did.

When the door opened again, he emerged, naked, wet, drying off with a huge towel, his cock partially erect. Her eyes went to it, then up to his face with a questioning look.

"I was thinking about you while I cleaned up. That's all it takes. If we had more time…"

"Stop. I might be convinced to tell them to go on without us."

In front of her instantly, Rodney had her against the wall, her arms held there too, as he attacked her with an aggressive kiss. She battled back, her arms pulled loose and curled them into his braids, pulling on them. Seconds passed before Shani did exactly what he wanted her to do, she gently pushed his head to the side and bit, sucking hard to pull in blood that ignited when it entered her mouth and merged with hers. *Her mate.*

As she drank, he lifted her into his arms and held her close to his body while she finished the sudden blood meal.

Sealing the wound, she slid down and dropped to the floor to kiss the tip of his cock and run her tongue around the head. "Tonight, if the chance presents."

If he'd been horny before, the touch of her tongue to him fired him almost beyond thought.

Keep it together. You've a fight coming. Time for that later.

Rodney pulled it together. He was nothing if not focused and results oriented. This must remain priority. So instead of taking her to his bed, Rodney reached for his pants.

Outside, the humans and supernaturals already on board, the vampires converged on the transport and took their seats.

"All aboard," Donovan called out, and the craft lifted from the earth. He turned to the group of hastily collected warriors. "So, Jackson's been up for several hours, in touch with a round-the-clock crew in the park. Two more vents opened up overnight. Another group of earthquake swarms measured between 6.0 and 8.5. Chione feels that the magma chamber is reaching critical and ready to blow. So we're going to stop it." He turned to his mate.

"Your turn, babe."

Chione stood. "We paired you in trios by your natures for the past four decades. You worked alongside one each of the other two species to maximize your strength and bond with each other. Now, though, as a single unified force, it doesn't matter how you're placed. We need to maintain physical contact at first, we're strongest that way, but as this unfolds, it's going to be harder and harder to stay that way. As we come off the craft, stay close, and do as I command. If I say hold hands, take the hand of the nearest warrior."

"So, we're no longer paired like we were, human, vampire, Totem?" Ari asked, seated between Fia and Taylor.

"It just isn't important at this point. We're powerful as thirty-one, all together, that's all." She paused as she looked around the cabin at the beautiful faces she had loved since all this began.

"One last thing. If we try, but it seems like it's going to blow anyway, I'm going to send out an urgent message to return to the transport. If I do, do not hesitate, get here as quickly as you can. If this fails, there's no reason for you to die with it. We'll do everything we can to protect you."

Sober, adjusting to the reality that loomed, the passengers fell silent. There was nothing more to say. Everyone knew all there was to know for now.

"We're landing," Cairine announced.

Showtime.

Twelve

Buckling, the earth felt her surface pushed around like soft clay, the ground lifting and dropping as it responded to incredible uneasiness below. Sulphur dioxide poured from four new openings, breaches forced by pressure so great, they split the land like it had been stabbed and ripped. The chamber of fire bubbled and begged for escape, and although the earth flinched at the destruction it caused, it couldn't stop it.

Chione was right...*the sleeping dragon was awake and on the move.*
"Stay together if at all possible." Her eyes slid across the faces, worried for people she loved, but especially, her gaze stopped at Donovan's face, the love of her life, mate forever, and then Talib, her own son, brought to her and Donovan long past when he should have. Gifts, *treasures*, in a life with so many. She couldn't lose anyone here, but these two men were her life.
"Let's ride," Donovan barked as he led everyone off the transport. It was hotter than hell, which fit, since, right now, the place looked a lot like hell would. He could see at least two of the hydrothermal vents Jackson had told them about, spewing superheated water and gas into the sky.
"Oh, baby, how are we gonna do this?" he commented, calmer than he felt, as Chione walked up beside him.

"With the greatest of care." After a few moments, she continued. "And a whole lot of universal help and luck."

The guardians of the earth stepped from the transport, one after the other, and began to line up. Aware that he had no earth-given talent to contribute, Rodney took his place behind them as sentry, an objective point of view should they need it.

Although Chione had said that they did not need to stay in the pre-assigned groups of vampire, human, and Totem, they gravitated toward that pairing anyway. Eventually, thirty one strong, the line was tight, fingers interweaved, confidence and resolve apparent, they were ready to face this threat.

"Bring it on," Fia yelled, grateful for this chance to save so many people that would otherwise die. She realized that there were no promises, but without them, many thousands in the adjacent states wouldn't have a chance. She looked to her right and saw Taylor waiting, his hand outstretched to hers, and took it, because more than anyone, he was the one who could keep her focused.

"All you have to do is tap into me and Donovan, and we'll do the rest." Moving ahead of the line-up, Chione took Donovan's hand and led them forward.

Jackson called out. "These vents aren't too dangerous yet."

"But the major eruption is waiting." Chione turned and stopped. "What we must do is help the earth release the pressure without forcing the magma up. We're going to attempt to help Mother Earth do that so that we control the catastrophic expulsion of ash, molten rock, and gases. It stands to reason we won't be able to stop it all, but if we can keep this volcano from an eruption like it has seen in its past, we will save a lot of people."

Hand in hand, arms raised, they showed they were prepared and dedicated. Chione had never been more proud of them.

"Thank you, my soldiers. I feel that we are near the center of the magma chamber. If it blows, it will be here, so it is time to begin."

Donovan, holding his mate's hand, led her around until he took Maccabee's hand at one end of the circle, nodding in appreciation when Talib, at the other end of the circle, closed it up by coming around to take his mother's hand.

Now complete, the circle connected everyone to everyone else, as Chione reached out, using Donovan and every other earth warrior's mind, spirit, and magics, to touch the abyss beneath their feet.

As if transported, they all felt blasts of suffocating heat, the air blistering scorched skin, followed by a sudden assault of pungent acrid odors filling their nostrils, sulfur burning them, and their eyes seared like liquid fire filled them. They felt entombed deep inside the earth, scalded, charred so badly, they could not survive.

Chione's voice came out of nowhere, like she was suspended above, out of the inferno they'd been dropped into. "Forbear. You are not on fire, although you think you are, this is just our connection to the land beneath our feet. Feel the power of what nature has built, what drives the earth. Touch her, know her, accept your ties."

The idea of touching this Tartarean world terrified the warriors, but they reached out anyway, faith in their guardians and in themselves. They could feel their own magics swirling around them, the power at their fingertips, and trust that this must be done.

Panic suddenly set in as they felt their way through the red and black colors writhing around them...*it was ready and it was coming!*

Collected voices broke through the mind-link, hushed moments later as Chione and Donovan guided the powers that twisted around the circle. They felt control return and a sense of wonder that the earth responded to their guidance. Cracks began all over the park, twenty feet apart, fissures to reach through the fracturing landscape as Chione and Donovan created tears in the ground to release pressure built by shifting plates far below the continent.

It's not enough...it's not enough...

Acknowledgement came through the group that they couldn't stop it all, not all, that eruptions would happen, controlled mostly, some not, but the big one, the apocalyptic one, they still had a chance to release it slowly, or slower, or guide it...*something perhaps!*

They were still connected by mind and hand when the ground beneath their feet began to rumble, to shift, like a roller coaster ride, rough and moving fast, up and down, heat shooting forth.

Run, the ground will give! The message came through the mind-link, not from Chione, but from Will, who pulled free of his companions. He moved around the circle, yanking on everyone's hands, screaming, out loud, *"Run! This area is going to explode!"*

With a terrifying blast of heat and force, the ground shook and moved, the rumble deafening.

Rodney, watching from behind, saw the tremors and heard the real-time belch, already behind Shani and Scottie, grabbed their hands and pulled at them. Still processing what was happening, they resisted, but he overpowered them and dragged them from the area just moments before the ground opened and the dragon breathed.

The gas came first, igniting the surrounding air as pumice and ash blew as high as they could see. The warriors scattered, humans and Totems carried by the vampires at speeds they couldn't move, clearing the chasm before the eruption worsened.

Choking, forced to the ground, Jackson, trying to shield his eyes, looked up at the pyroclastic plume carried away from them by wind and the direction the eruption faced.

"It's not the big one," he tried to tell everyone, but his voice couldn't carry far between the coughs and gags.

"Clear the area, go back to the transport," Will commanded. "There's more to come."

"We can contain it," Chione told him.

"I don't think we can."

"Will, believe. If we don't try, the death toll will be staggering."

"We can't do it!"

Chione grabbed Will's head and entered his mind using force she hated, but there was no time for delicacy.

"Stay with me," she whispered, and carried him into her spirit self to show him the combined power of the warriors from her point of view.

Watching the endless power fill the skies in this spirit realm, Will was speechless.

Chione's spirit body blocked his view.

"*This*, Will, is what we have, what we wield. But we need you. You are the strongest bond we have to the earth and all that lies beneath. Stay. Fight. You were made for this!"

She was right, he could see it now, and more than that, he felt it, he knew it. They had to fight for the innocent.

"I give you all I can until I have nothing left."

He felt himself land on the ground, already covered with ash and stone, the heat rising by the minute. Lifting his eyes to Chione, who stood over him, he asked, "What do we do?"

As the plume heightened and widened, she reached for Will, and linked to all the others to once again access their collective powers. First, a critical message.

Get out of the area. Our proximity has contained the first blast and kept it from reaching devastating levels, but our job is far from over. Go to the transport and stay ready to go. We're winning, but barely. Keep the faith and stay safe.

Ash was so thick now, she couldn't see any of the other warriors, and that included Donovan and Talib. She knew they were safe, that all of them were, but there was no promise that they would stay so. Getting them away from this spot was the right choice. Will and she were the only ones still near the rupture.

What now? Will questioned. *I know that we are linked on a level beyond that of the others. What do I do now?*

Chione answered exactly as he expected. Will wondered if they were syncing well beyond the tether provided by the mind-link. He felt as if they were almost merged with each other and with the living planet.

We stay the course, here, at ground zero, and weave our magics to vent the pressure and guide it outward instead of up. If we can keep the release below ground, we may be able to stop this from repeating its history.

Will was by her side for whatever they needed to do. As long as the others were clear, his risk was unimportant. If he could go out on a win, it was worth it all.

"Look at me, a hero after all," he whispered into the rumbling air as it became more and more toxic by the second.

Another explosion signaled the next fissure, the sound traveling to his ears from the direction where he thought the transport must be. He felt Chione's stab of fear as she realized the same.

Across the field, the warriors scrambled to reach the transport, but visibility had dropped to less than a few feet. They could barely see the person next to them, let alone the safety of the vessel that might be able to get them out of there.

The mind-link let everyone stay in contact, but no line of sight on the transport. When the next eruption blew somewhere nearby, no one had any idea where it was or how near. Heat soared but did not give any useable information to those lost in the ash-created fog.

Rodney had forced Shani and Scottie from the first blast and hoped they were close to the transport, but now, with everything shrouded by ash, he felt directionless.

"Shani!" he screamed into her ear, his grip on her arm punishing. "Can you sense anything?"

"The others, but they are just as confused as we are. Chione and Will are heading *into* the center of the eruption, not *away* from it!"

"Gods help them! Are you still channeling your powers?"

"We are! All of us are! I can't leave her! Get Scottie out of here!"

"Not without you! Shani...!"

"*Go!* I'll be fine!"

Shani turned to Rodney to pull him close. Her lips to his ear so he could not miss what she had to say, she whispered, "I'm going to Chione. You get the others out of here and safe. I'm vampire, I'll be fine. I love you."

Rodney grabbed into air thickened by the ash, but she was gone. He screamed her name into the charcoal blackness but received no reply. Scottie's wrist remained clasped tight in his other hand. All he could do now was trust that the universe would guide and protect her. It had great reason to do so.

He turned toward the opposite direction he felt Shani run. If she was running *to* Chione at the center, he needed to take them the other way. "Come with me," he called to his daughter. She didn't fight him like Shani. He could feel the tightness in Scottie's hand; she was really frightened. He wasn't, not for himself, but for the others, yes, he prayed he could get them to safety.

Twenty feet from where Rodney wrestled with his choice of action, Jackson led Sally, Jessie, Dean, and Taylor to where he thought they might be safe. He forged ahead through impossible conditions, but the only thing he knew with any certainty was that if the eruption continued, this was *not* where they wanted to be.

"Sally!" Jackson held onto Jessie's hand, and hoped she had Sally's. "Jess!" He waited, but either she didn't hear him call her name, or he couldn't hear her if she answered. *This was so fucked!*

The transport was likely in this direction, he was pretty sure he had that right, but it could be east or west of where they were so the chances of actually finding it were slim. What he hoped was that they might find a vehicle and could try to drive out of the immediate vicinity enough to clear the ash.

Chione had been right, their magics and proximity had stopped or at least delayed the worst case scenario eruption where the magma chamber blew its top and spewed staggering amounts of ash, molten rock, debris, and gas into the air to cover and burn everything in its path. Their journey into its core had shown him, all the warriors, the depth and volume of the chamber, and it had been greater than their science had calculated.

If the supervolcano erupted without their intervention, with all the force and volume it was capable of, this would be exactly what they were terrified it would be…an extinction-level event that would take a long time, if ever, for this planet to recover from.

Jackson took comfort in the fact that they may have changed that outcome, but none in the fact that he and his magics-filled companions were still in mortal danger. He had to hope that Sally, Taylor, and Dean were still with him.

Eras had moved himself, Bura, and Cairine from the site before the biggest blast. He'd seen his vampire friends move other humans and Totems away as well, with full expectation that everyone was safe. Except for Chione and Will. The mind-link made it clear they were moving toward the devastation, not away from it. When he felt Shani heading toward them, too, he kissed Cairine, and bolted. No way Shani was going into this alone. He felt Brigitte move alongside him.

One for all, all for one, he heard her say within their mind-link. Brigitte knew he felt the same way. He loved his sisters passionately, he would never let anything happen to any of them. Plus, their father would kill him, a *forever* death, if he did.

Ife joined them on the run, the ash no problem to finding her siblings life signals.

They reached the place where they felt Shani and Chione's signals, and found Donovan and Talib already there. Seconds later, the remaining vampires arrived, Cairine among them. She lifted her voice over the sound of rushing wind.

"You didn't think I wouldn't come?"

Eras shrugged. "I hoped!"

"We're stronger together, here, where we're needed."

"It's true. Supervolcano, you are going down!"

Cairine laughed. "It *is* down!"

"It's going to *stay* down!"

For the moment, the ash cleared, just enough that they could see each other, clustered around Chione and Will.

Overjoyed, Chione spoke to her vampire team. "Our work is cut out for us, but we are powerful enough to meet the challenge. Mother Earth loves all her living children, but her worry now is for her own biology. What we call geology is merely that which inhabits or drives this planet, and right now, she is helpless to stop this."

Shrieking and rumbling from below pushed immediacy, so, relieved to still have proximity and contact, Chione and Donovan linked the vampires, threaded their powers through the human and supernatural species still nearby, and sent their magics beneath the earth to continue their attempt to harness the increasing pressure that intended to blaze from a newly opened massive crack that pushed through the ground.

Fearful, but confident, they felt the crack widen and watched more ash burst out, the air thicker and hotter than before. Eyes, throats, and nostrils burned as the sky went black again.

Some distance away, Jackson hunkered down next to a tree, Sally and Jessie on his sides, and Dean beside Jessie. He hadn't been able to see or speak to Taylor since they took shelter here, worried that something may have happened to him.

The conditions were worsening.

Beneath the ground, liquid rock bubbled incessantly, forced to the top of the chamber by pressure born of ancient constructs of dynamic motion. Massive slabs of planet-forming stone fought for position, and the chamber, caught up in its competition, boiled over.

As its insistent contents pushed upward, there was something...*what?*...holding sway over that which it should not be able to touch. The contents could destroy mountains, and yet a barrier appeared that tried to bar its way. The battle for dominion ensued. Molten rock continued to push up, up, and out.

The vampires, hand to hand, focused on a deafening explosion that blasted rock so near their location, the hot stones rained down on top of them with, and even their first blood talents couldn't stop the hot missiles that tore into their group. They dropped together, shielding each other with hands and magic. Bryson and Fia went to the ground, but as Bryson threw himself on top of his sister to protect her, a scalding scatter of large rocks hit them, pounding their heads, and they both lost consciousness.

No! Chione's mind couldn't control the outcry as heat and ash broke the surface; the threat the largest yet. *Was it coming? Were they failing?*

Suddenly, Chione felt a new force rise and push against the tearing earth.

Redirecting her energies, threading it through her mate, Crezia channeled the merged powers to overcome the chamber's push, but felt a sudden enormous surge, beyond her, beyond the others, as her healing powers merged with Scottie's powers designed to support life. Somehow, that specific blend of talents boosted all the others to create and sustain a horizontal block that pressed from above the magma chamber to force the flow outward. Instantly, small openings popped up around the periphery of their position like slow leaks. Yes, ash flew, yes, gases surged, but the fissures were small and posed no catastrophic danger.

The chamber had to release the building pressure, its plume, but not in one life-destroying flow. Crezia and Scottie's talents touched the earth, and together with Will's unprecedented earth magics, they took back control from the fiery caldera.

Now, pulling from the earth, each warrior power-pushed their skills, blasted past nature's imperative to obey physics...and obeyed *them* instead.

It was no longer a case of *if*...Chione and Donovan now only guided the powers, the warriors were actively pursuing management of the volcanic force.

The vampires gathered near the center reverse-flowed their own powers to the highly effective team of humans and Totem counterparts. The realizations arrived that the strongest powers were vampire, but the strongest *connections* were human, due to their earth-born bond with the planet, and the Totems, who embodied both human and animal life forces, also earth-born.

Although the ash still blinded them, now that the threat of annihilation was unlikely, most found comfort in the warmth and darkened air.

Some distance across the breaking landscape, beneath a large old bent tree, Jackson held Sally's hand like a lifeline. The sounds of crackling and earthly upheaval made it difficult to hear, the ash hanging in the air like hot smoke limited vision to mere inches.

"Sal! Is Taylor beside you?"

"No! I don't feel anyone within reach!"

"Jessie's on my right and she says Dean's beside *her*!"

Sally's heart skipped. "So Taylor's missing?"

"It looks like! I tried to use the mind-link, but there's no response."

"Shit! That's worrisome! Do you think he's… *No!* I won't go there, I can't!"

"Taylor's fine! I have to believe it!"

There was nothing else to say. Jackson drew Jessie and Sally closer. If another breach *did* open up, where would they go from here to be safe? Visibility was almost at zero. The situation was not unlike that of a mine field; you couldn't know if the next step would be your last.

Sally tugged aggressively on his hand.

"Let's finish this! We've been with the first bloods since before they were vampire, we *have* to have more to contribute! Focus! Feed your powers, let's win this mother!"

Circling, hands to hands, Jackson, Jessie, Dean, and Sally, went to the white room they had been taught to go to in order to enter the spirit realm. Usually, they needed their vampire companions to do so, but Sally believed, passionately, re-ignited to this mission, to each other, with so many lives at stake, they could do much more than they had been so far.

"We wouldn't have been around from the beginning," she told her friends. "We wouldn't have been placed in exactly the right time to travel this path with our vampire friends for all these years. We *must* have more to give!"

Her belief was so powerful, it transferred to the others and, just as refocused as Sally, they reached deep, and when they felt as if they'd reached as deep as they could, they pushed on, and found more. Stunned at the depth of their ability, they found themselves channeling the magma and pressure alone, moving toward the outward crevices, creating new pathways for the magma to flow, pressure lessening as they continued.

Sally knew, *knew*, that this was making a difference, their contribution what it was always meant to be. They just had to find it. In the midst of it all, she reached into the realm to search for Taylor. Still, he did not answer.

God help them, to lose someone they loved...

No, fates, destiny, all responsible for this, don't let this happen!

It was out of their hands. If Taylor was gone, then destiny had chosen his path; it could and *might* happen to any one of them. Stay true to the mission, she reminded herself as she went back to work.

It is truly working, Chione thought as she sent the message to everyone. The level of power coursing through this region, from her warriors, the tether to Mother Earth, was impossible. *And yet it was.*

Dozens, then hundreds, of vents opened to siphon off the pressure of millennia, to cool the molten rock enough to convince it to stay in the ground, to meet the demand of extraordinary people who the universe had trusted with magics unheard of in all creation, to fix this and protect this small world.

Catastrophe may yet come, *but not tonight.*

In clusters around the center of the magma chamber, the group of vampires, two broken groups of humans, and a united group of supernaturals merged their spirits, magics, and lifeforces to aid the mother of the earth in saving the world. They'd fixed most of the critical issues facing the planet with a burgeoning population, but to tackle a geological event of this magnitude, and succeed in stopping an eruption like this, the warriors felt euphoria as they stayed on task, and controlled what was uncontrollable. For now, anyway, thousands upon thousands were safe, and they could rest at the end of this mission.

Above and below, the universe and the living planet accepted that their chosen warriors had won the fight.

Pushing against the geology that pushed back, and lost, Sally pressed both Jackson and Jessie's hands. Tonight they would drop into their beds to sleep for days; she knew that all their energy reserves would be depleted.

But look what we've done, she fed onto the mind-link. *Look what we've done!*

Finally, a timeframe later, they had no idea how long, a ripple moved through the warrior link that the danger was over. The eruption had been contained. Hundreds of bubbling, venting, crackling breaches had opened up, and remained open, over much of the thirty miles of territory that defined the mouth of the caldera beneath the ground. The vents would continue to burn for some time to come, but they were no more dangerous now to the surrounding populations than any other single breach.

Belching fiery air, and sometimes ash and pumice, they still posed no national or even inter-state danger.

Unlinking, and moving apart from each other, Jackson and his friends stood unsteadily, blinking, as the ash cleared just enough to see the local landscape and marvel at the damage the vents had caused locally. To stop the worst from happening, they'd shredded this area.

"I, uh…wow. I have no words for what we just did."

Sally nodded at Jackson. "Yeah, I'd agree. Um…"

She looked around, her eyes moving across one puffing crack after another. "I still can't sense Taylor."

"We have to find him." Dean watched Sally closely. "Are you all right?"

"I'm fine, Dean."

"We should pair up for safety. Sally, why don't you come with me?"

She agreed. "Sure." Her eyes went to Jessie and Jackson. "You guys be careful."

"This area is still volatile. Other portals could open, so watch where you're stepping and listen for any sign of a new breach. Contact us if you find him."

Dean took Sally's hand as he led her away, but she pulled it loose a few minutes into the search. "You don't have to baby me, Dean. I can do this."

"Yeah, Sal, I know that, but you heard Jax, it isn't safe."

"I heard him. We should stay close, but you don't need to hold my hand." Worried she'd hurt his feeling, she laid her hand on his forearm. "I appreciate it, but I'm okay."

"I won't apologize for wanting to protect you."

"I would trust you with my life. Honestly, you're sweet, but I'll be careful."

Carefully was the only way to move through the radically revised area. Jackson was right, it *was* dangerous. So far, no one had found Taylor.

Jackson reported to Sally and Dean that they'd come upon the Totems, all ten present, and they all spread out to help search for Taylor as well.

Shooting a message to the vampires, Sally enlisted their aid too, and the search widened. The fact that he hadn't responded to any of the messages they'd sent out through the mind-link wasn't encouraging.

"After all we've been through, I can't imagine losing one of us. To finally get to this point, to succeed with impossible odds, I hoped we'd get to go somewhere isolated, just the five of us, and spend a few weeks living like normal human beings again. Just for a few *normal* weeks. I want to swim in the sea and drink margaritas in a skimpy bikini and watch the sunset. With my besties. God, what if Taylor is dead?"

"We have no idea what happened to him yet, so let's not go there. Right now, I can't get the idea of you and that skimpy bikini out of my mind."

Sally stopped Dean. "You know I love you, don't you? I never stopped. But we aren't lovers anymore, and I don't expect we ever will be again. Dean, we're friends with a past, but I don't want that to hurt us. I still want to stay your friend through whatever comes. Can we do that?"

It took a few moments for him to respond. It wasn't like he hadn't already gotten that, but letting go of a dream wasn't easy. "Sure, Sal. I mean, yeah, I know you're with that Rick guy." His eyes went to the murky sky with a bitter laugh. "Just hoped you'd drop the dick and give me another chance."

"No, Dean. We tried. It didn't work before and it won't work now. And Rick's not a dick."

"Huh. Then, I guess I'll look for a sweet hottie when we get to our post-battle celebration."

"Good plan. So, we need to get back to finding Taylor so we can book that flight."

"They're okay," Crezia sighed with relief after sending her magic into Fia and Bryson. "Head injuries from the heavy strikes, but I've started the healing."

Reassured, the others watched as Fia roused and looked up at their worried faces. "What?" she barked, and winced.

"She's fine," Brigitte laughed.

Sitting up, Fia put a hand to her forehead. "Ow. Bry's okay? Is everyone else okay?"

Chione nodded. "As far as we know, except that Taylor is missing."

Brigitte's head shot up. "What? I've taken his blood, I can find him."

Twenty minutes later, using the mind-link, Chione sent a message to everyone that Fia had used her blood connection to Taylor and that he'd been found, buried beneath a mound of ash. He was unconscious, with multiple burns, but Talib gave him blood, and he'd roused, coughing and choking from the ash, but he was alive.

Sally slipped into Dean's arms without thinking about it, tears tracking down her ash-covered face. "Oh, thank God!"

She needed the comfort of his arms, and they felt so good to her, but when he didn't let go, his face buried into her hair, his arms tightening, she pushed away to detangle herself because she didn't want him to get the wrong idea.

"Everything's all right. Let's join the others at the transport."

Dean got it. He stepped back with a smile. "Yeah, lets."

She'd hurt his feelings once again, she knew that. Sally led them, moving quickly, wondering if she should say something. Distracted, she didn't notice the softness of the ground beneath her feet, but when a burp pushed a huge bubble of hot ash underneath her right foot, she lifted the foot and started to move backward. At that second, the ground began to give way, and she screamed.

"*Dean!*"

He surged toward Sally and grabbed her hand to pull her free from the moving earth when it began to crack.

Sally could feel it collapsing beneath her feet.

"No, Dean, go back!"

Dean continued to pull her, but she knew the ground was going. "Run!"

Trying to pull her hand loose, she also shoved against Dean, but he was relentless. He suddenly thrust his weight onto the unstable ground and lifted her, then threw her into the direction he'd leaped from. Sally crash landed, her full weight shoving her face-first into inches of ash. It knocked the air out of her, so when she tried to breathe, she inhaled the ash, choking, struggling to both breathe and get up to help Dean.

Determined, she crawled across the ground to see Dean falling into the earth.

"*No! Oh, God, no!*" Her screams were lost in the violent cracking as the breach opened wider and she saw Dean's face as he disappeared into the slit.

Her mind screamed as she pushed closer...*have to get Dean, have to get Dean!*

But as she crawled toward where she'd last seen him, the breach continued to widen, her choking worsened to the point where she couldn't breathe at all, and she couldn't see him anymore.

Hands came around her waist and lifted her, pulled her away from the fractured land.

"*No! No! No! No!*" Sally kept repeating the only word she could think, because this couldn't be true...*couldn't be true! Dean couldn't have fallen into the earth!*

"Sally! *Sally!* Stop fighting me!"

Jackson's voice broke through the crackling sounds, but she didn't hear what he said. She saw several figures moving around the area where Dean had disappeared, but she went into another coughing fit so extreme, she couldn't draw a breath, not one, and thought that she was dying too. *Okay, it was okay, because Dean was gone, and it was right that she went with him. He couldn't go alone, not along that dark path of the unknown. She would go with him, yes, that was right. It was good.*

Sally lost consciousness, her last thought that she had to find Dean. He was on the final journey and she had to find him.

BACK AT CAIRINE'S TOWER

"She's still out."

Jessie pulled the blanket higher to just below Sally's chin. "She feels cold."

"Yeah. So do I."

Taylor sat on the other side of the bed, his hand beneath the blanket holding Sally's still hand in his.

Jackson walked closer, his eyes as wet as Taylor's.

"Yeah. We just came from the hottest place on earth, and yet we can't get warm." He sipped a cup of hot coffee. "I don't know if we ever will again."

Cairine and Chione came through the open door.

Placing her head against Jackson's, Cairine let her eyes go to Sally. "She'll be all right. Crezia's blood has exponential healing properties even compared to mine."

"Thank you. I think the ash had burnt her lungs. If it hadn't been for vampire blood, she'd be dead now. Too."

"Crezia said her lifeforce was nearly gone, so yes, we nearly lost her. Now, though, you know she'll fully recover."

"Thank the spirits," Chione said, her eyes on Sally's prone figure. "It was a hell of a fight. We still never thought we would lose anyone."

No one had a response to that comment. The silence in the room spoke more than any words could have.

Chione went to Jessie, Taylor, then Jackson to use her *impression* touch to help them find some peace.

"I'll see you tonight. Try to rest. You've earned it."

Cairine followed her out. That night, in chairs and on a pallet on the floor, Taylor, Jackson, and Jessie stayed in the room with Sally. They wouldn't leave her for anything, because they all knew that the moment she finally woke up, she would need them.

It was dark. No, there *was* light, dim, not direct, but the room wasn't completely dark, no. Sally looked around. Ginger red hair filled her line of sight when she turned her head to the right. She smiled. *Jessie.*

She put a hand up and smoothed the frizzy hair down. Jessie stirred, then lifted her head. A slow smile widened until she reached for Sally. "Hey, you. Glad you're back."

After a slight nod, Sally's eyes moved around the room where she saw Jackson slumped in a chair at the foot of the bed, and Taylor with his head on the other side of the bed as Jessie had been. Her eyes shot back to Jessie's, tears welling, the unspoken question answered when Jessie's eyes filled too.

"I'm sorry, Sal. He's gone."

Sally closed her eyes. She was right the first time when she woke. It was very dark in the room. There would be no light in her world again for a long time.

Thirteen

Rodney pulled Shani closer and just breathed in her scent. That she was here, in his arms, that his daughter was safe, and that the world was okay, at least for now, allowed him a sense of peace he'd never known.

They could rest, and live their lives. The worst had happened, they'd succeeded in stopping it, and they had survived. Most of them, anyway. He still felt awful that they lost the gentle man that Shani was close to, and that she was hurting. He'd never really had a chance to get to know him well.

But it was a new night, and there was much to celebrate. He didn't think that Dean would object to their joy that they had saved so many and stopped the horrible volcanic winter that might have come. They deserved a hero's reception. Cairine had told him that her chefs would prepare a feast beyond measure for the victorious warriors.

A muted groan let him know that his mate awakened, and he shifted his gaze to see her searching his face. "We made it," she whispered.

"We made it. Soon I take you home with me or I come with you, whatever you want. But wherever it is, we go together, right?"

"Yes. We go together." She paused. "Can you believe what we did?"

"You stopped a volcano that could have destroyed this country and half the world." Rodney grinned. "You guys rock."

They had. *All* of the warriors had. Right now, it was taking everything Shani had to try not to think about Dean's death. He'd been a part of her life for so long, the idea that he would never be there again brought too much sorrow to imagine. For the loss of his companionship, his incredible smile and silly jokes, his lame attempts at flirting, and all his possibilities...gone now forever. She turned to Rodney.

"Make love to me, now, just so that I can feel."

"You will never hear me say no to that request again."

AN HOUR LATER IN THE BANQUET ROOM

The party was in full swing when Shani led Rodney into the room. Music reverberated off the walls, the clatter of plates and raised voiced enough to almost overtake it.

Several couples were trying to dance to the music, glasses of wine or some other alcohol in their hands.

"We missed the beginning," Shani complained.

"We had our own celebration. I liked it better."

Had she blushed? Rodney had taken his time and truly made sure that she was satisfied. Scottie signaled them from the other side of the room and he tugged Shani with him.

"Scottie, you've met Shani?"

Her eyes moved across Shani, dressed in what looked like lace doilies she'd seen in old photographs, and nodded. "Oh, yeah. Hi again."

Hesitating, Rodney pulled Shani to his side. "We're together."

"Together? You're with a vampire? Well, you've certainly traded up."

"Shani and I have known each other for a century, but we just redeveloped our relationship this week."

"Oh. Well, congrats. I guess we'll get to know each other better soon, right?"

"I hope so. It appears the three of us have a lot to learn about each other. I look forward to that time together."

"Okay. Well, Pop, you two enjoy the party."

"That went well," Rodney commented after Scottie walked away.

"I think you need to spend some quality father-daughter time before you bring me into the equation. Maybe you should take her home to meet Koen and the gang before we move forward as a family."

Rodney turned and lifted Shani into his arms, beginning to dance around the floor. "Family. I love the sound of that."

Several tables away, Scottie took a full bottle of Kentucky whisky and dropped beside Dani and Dylan, her eyes on Rodney and Shani.

"Your dad's in love," Dani commented.

"Ya think?"

"Yep, I think. They glow, I should know. You okay with that?"

"Well yeah. I'm new to this, but even I know he had a life before he met me. A *long* life."

"I wonder what will happen to us when this is over."

Dylan, swiping a long sip from Scottie's bottle, wiped his mouth with the back of his hand. "Or *if* it's over. It can't be just this one thing."

Dani shrugged. "No, I agree, it probably isn't. But at some point, it has to be, right? I mean, we deserve a life, right?"

Scottie stole the bottle of whisky back from Dylan.

"You bet your ass, and we're going to get one. I suggest that you two and I hit a southern port and veg for a few months."

"What about the rest of our team?" Dani asked.

Scottie's eyes went to Antoinette, who had been hanging with the vampires almost the entire time they'd trained and worked together. "Not her, I don't think we fascinate her enough. She's got a real thing for the vampires. Good, let her enjoy them." She searched for Will but he was nowhere in sight. "And the Biker dude...nah, he puts a harsh on. The man has some serious issues. But you and Dylan, I really think we could have some good times."

"I'm in," Dylan agreed, trying to reacquire the whisky, but Scottie grinned and chugged the rest. "Whew! Holy shit, I should have let you have it. What's the alcohol content in that anyway? I'm buzzing like a bee on a real dandelion."

Laughing, she and Dylan decided to arm wrestle to see who was going to go get the next bottle, when someone slid into the seat beside hers. Scottie looked up, surprised that it was the dark-haired vampire who she'd merged with when they were fighting to control the volcanic pressure.

"Hi, I'm Crezia."

"I remember. Scottie."

"Yes, I know. We have something to discuss."

"We do?"

The strikingly unique white-haired vampire took the seat across from Scottie and Crezia.

"Did you ask her?"

Scottie looked from Crezia to Ife. Keeping her attention on Ife, she leaned in. "Ask me what?"

Ife smiled and touched Scottie on the arm, the alcoholic haze lessening immediately. "Scottie, I have been working for almost fifty years to replant and revitalize the lungs of this planet. That's what the Amazon basin was called ninety years ago when it had a healthy system of rivers and tributaries and a vast rain forest that housed animals, insects, and plants found nowhere else in the world. I've worked a huge team of specialists, and myself, to exhaustion and we're losing the battle."

"I'm, uh, sorry, but what does that have to do with me?"

"Us." Crezia tilted her head. "Do you have any idea the value of what you and I can do together?"

"Um, sure. We just saved the world."

"We did, so let's go save it again. Between my powers and yours, I think we can help jump-start the rain forest. I'm in if you are, and Scottie, you're going to want to be in. The adventures wait for us, but more important is the fact that we can protect something that is irreplaceable. This volcano was dangerous, and I'm thrilled we stopped it, but now I crave the chance to do more. What do you say, Scots, are you up for another impossible challenge?"

"Wow. I mean, I appreciate the challenge and maybe, after a while. For now, I just want to let loose and party with my friends."

"We *all* agree on that. How about we come back tomorrow night and we talk?"

After Scottie nodded agreement, Crezia and Ife left, but the idea that she might be able to save the rainforest stayed in her mind. Who was she kidding, she was *so* in.

"Dylan, dance with me." She grabbed the handsome, beefy young man she was becoming increasingly fond of, and pulled him to the impromptu dance floor on the edge of the room.

Fia looked over the group of partiers, but knew that she would likely not find Taylor. God, what he must be going through. She knew he had remained close with his old college friends, and to lose one in such a terrible way had to be inconceivable. She knew how she'd have felt if one of her family or friends she'd grown up with had not made it out of that mess alive.

And she wondered if he would come back to France with her. The thought that he wouldn't suddenly seemed unacceptable. Going to work each night and *not* finding his smiling face waiting? The idea made her world colder.

"Please, Taylor, come home with me," she whispered as she snatched a bottle of *Angel's Envy,* and headed to the roof. It had an unbelievable view and that's where she needed to be right now.

Eras watched Caedmon dancing wildly with Crezia, embarrassingly so, and loved every second of it. His best friend and Crezia were two halves of a whole, inseparable, and in love like no one he'd ever seen before. They seemed to fit as if the gods built them to be so, and he couldn't be happier. Bryson and Mac were playing a game of electronic cards near one of the tables on the side of the room. Both men lived in such isolated places, they would need some time to reintegrate into enjoying noise and crowds again. Keeping each other company was a great start.

He'd watched Cairine leave the hall earlier and he knew where she headed. She'd carried a couple of bags and a heavy tray with her to take to Jackson and his college friends as they dealt with Dean's loss. He loved her more with every passing second. There wasn't a chance in this world he'd ever let her go again. He would become the man he always should have, for her, for himself, for his legacy.

Besides, he knew something that she didn't...Chione revealed to him two nights ago that she'd had a vision, and in it, Cairine walked along a beach with a dark-haired child. He knew without question it was his.

In search of comfort, of fulfillment, perhaps the connection that a sexual contact created, even briefly, Brigitte had gone in search of Will. She found him, half an hour into the search, beyond the edge of the mountain that supported Cairine's tower home. He sat on a stone wall someone had erected just before the ridge dropped several hundred feet. His legs dangled over the side, his head forward. It was clear that he needed to be alone. This event had overwhelmed him and he wasn't dealing with it well. There were people who never adjusted to the supernatural world, and here he was, one of the most powerful humans who'd ever lived, trying to find his way through it all to come out on the other side, well and whole.

She left him undisturbed because she didn't think that he needed to deal with her tonight either. Mostly because she was seeking the same thing he was, but in a different way. Perhaps some time in the future...

Daylight arrived, softly lit as it often did, in pale pinks and liquid blues streaked with white clouds. The vampires had gone to rest for the last day here.

Cairine's shields closed, she turned to Eras, who brought her a mug of hot chocolate with frothy whipped cream piled high.

"*Merci.*"

She sipped her chocolate in silence as he sipped his herbal tea, then looked up suddenly. "Are you leaving with the others tonight?"

He was surprised that they hadn't discussed this already. "Yes. I'm going home and when I get there, I'm making arrangements for someone to take over my duties. Actually, Bura and I had been working on some ideas that would make the crops more independent, stable, and disease-free. If we can do that, then Bura and our crew can handle most of it by themselves. I'll just check in on occasion and fly in for emergencies. Then, my love, I'm coming home to you, here in Colorado, which is where I belong."

Cairine kept her gaze on his, nodded, then took another long sip from her mug. Setting it down on the table, she stood and headed into the bedroom, stopping at the opening of the hallway. All she said was one word.

"Good."

That simply, it was settled, and as Eras cued the lights to darken to maintenance only, he knew that he was home.

IN SHANI'S ROOM

Shani held Rodney, aware that she wouldn't hold him again for a while. It had been discussed and decided that after her entire lifetime without a father, Scottie deserved his undivided attention. This adjustment was going to be tough, and the young woman would need ample time and Rodney's presence to do it easier.

"Shani, I can't..."

"You can," she'd told him. "She is your daughter and she needs you. I can't imagine if I'd never known my father. She just met you, and to throw me into the mix, you two getting to know each other, you and I getting to know each other for who we are now, and she and I trying to figure all this out…it's the wrong way to do it. I'll still be there when you two work out your kinks. We know we belong together now, we can wait another few months. You surely get this."

Silent, Rodney had pushed out of bed, paced, naked, and she hadn't been able to take her eyes off him. Finally, he'd crawled back in and pulled her to him.

"I know. Fuck, I know. But how can I go even a few days, let alone months, without holding you?"

"We'll sneak in moments here and there, but Scottie has to be your priority."

"I love every breath you take, every move you make."

"Old love songs? That's beautiful, thank you. You know I feel the same. Now get over here and *show* me how much."

NIGHTFALL

The transport stood ready to take everyone to the airport, the pilot ready to wait through a lot of hugs, tears, and promises before they were ready to go.

Finally, those flying to other countries were packed and in their seats. As the transport lifted off, the pilot wiggled the wings and used a lighting system to spell out the words *bye-bye* across the bottom of the craft.

Cairine stepped back to join Jackson and Sally, who waited behind her. Sally had decided to move in with Jackson for the time being.

"I'm rudderless, Jax. I don't know what I want or who I am right now. Can I just stay here and work with you?"

He'd agreed without hesitation, and Cairine had pulled her into a tight hug to make sure she knew how much she was welcome.

Dani and Dylan were staying too, but only for a few weeks until they began classes at the *International Science Academy* in Chicago.

After they finished specialty classes in geology, they would return to Colorado to work with Jackson and Sally. Scottie had planned a trip to Mexico for them, but they felt certain that the trip would never happen. Scottie had been preoccupied with the proposal from Crezia and Ife to help redevelop the rainforest in Brazil, and they were pretty sure that, in the end, she wouldn't be able to resist.

Dani turned to her new friends. "So, what do we do for excitement around here?"

Jackson shook his head. "Ha, ha, funny, funny. You mean other than diverting a global catastrophe? How about we take you to an Asian-inspired buffet downtown Denver?"

"Aw, tugging at my heartstrings already, buddy. Lead on." Dani's smile was wide as she grabbed her brother's hand and followed him back into the tower.

IN THE DESERT SOUTHWEST

As soon as the whole shitstorm was finished, Will bought a cheap old bike and headed back to Tequila Flats.

Now, arriving in front of his desert home, he stopped and leaned against the bike for a few moments.

So, save the world, then go back to your useless existence. Valuable. Worthless. Homeless, because this had never really been home.

Where did he go from here? With what he knew, with what he'd done, with what he *could* do, what kind of a future awaited? He did know one thing. He couldn't go back to living the way that he had, ignoring his connection to the planet, drinking until he couldn't think or feel, and most of all, existing alone with only sand and sunsets in his life.

Finally, he pushed away from the bike, went into his home to throw a few things into a backpack, dug up his stash of cash, pushed the bike into the house, and swung his leg over his classic Harley-Davidson.

There was still a lot of road out there, and surely, hopefully, one of them would lead him somewhere he belonged.

ON THE FLIGHT TO FRANCE

Rodney lowered himself into his seat beside Scottie.

"I know you've met Koen and Tam, but let me introduce some of the others you're going to meet. They can be a little overwhelming, especially Koen's brother."

"That's great, Pop, but, uh, I kind of have to break some news to you." Scottie paused.

"What news?" Rodney worried immediately that she was going to tell him she couldn't handle this magic and supernatural shit and didn't want anything to do with him or his family.

"Yeah, um, see, I'm not going to be staying with you in France."

Gods help him, that his daughter had no wish to get to know him after all. "Scottie, I know that the vampire world can be difficult to accept, but you'll find that they are wonderful people. You'll love them, I promise. Please give this a chance. Give *me* a chance. I am your father and I want you in my life."

"What? No. Oh, no, Rodney, that isn't it at all. I'm going to go to South America with Crezia and Ife to help them to reseed the rain forest. With my ability to accelerate the growth of any type of plant and Crezia's healing talent, Ife feels certain that we are what she needs to finally permanently restore what has been lost in the Amazon. Pop, I'm not spurning your vampire world, I'm embracing it."

Relief flooded Rodney's mind and heart. "Thank the gods! I was certain you had been through enough, and I could understand if you had, but I am so grateful that you are comfortable with your talents and the others in this community."

"Oh, shit, yeah. I love this stuff! When I was growing up, my talent was weird and creepy and people stayed away from me in droves. Now, I know how powerful I am and what I can do with it. I'm stoked, Pops! I can really help this planet to heal. This is the best thing that I've ever...well, of course, there's finding you, but we'll have time, I promise. I kind of think this comes first, though."

"It's critical. May I tell you I am proud of you? Had I raised you myself, I don't think I could be more pleased with your heart and the fact that you care this much. Thank you, Scottie, for coming into my life."

"Sure. Uh, yeah, well, I always wanted a dad, and now I got one. Um, when we get to hang out, I kinda already know I'm going to love you."

It was a big admission. Rodney felt his chest squeeze and could only do one thing after that; he hugged Scottie and told her that he felt exactly the same.

"At least you'll get to meet the members of my household before you leave. I'm pleased you're coming home with me, even if it is only for a little while."

ON THE FLIGHT TO ZAMBIA

Antoinette watched all the people on the plane as they relaxed, ate, drank, laughed and joked with each other, took naps, happy to be heading home.

They were all so beautiful. Perfect specimens of unique humans with extraordinary powers, extreme lifespans, and eternal youth. She wanted, needed, *must*, get a chance to study them, to *know* how they worked, to see the DNA.

Ever since she'd been a child, Antoinette had always known that she was special. Her gift had just seemed normal to her then, because to a little girl, it *was*. She'd had no idea that other people did not have the gift.

Still, she'd gone through her life, through the rebellious teenage years when all she wanted to do was find out how things and bodies worked, when she'd gotten in trouble for frequent trips to science installations, often after-hours when she'd broken in, to frequent sexual encounters to see how the human body needed that stimulant, to the days when she finally broke too many of her family traditions and was exiled. This, *this* was her reward.

Chione had graciously accepted her plea to return to Zambia to live amongst her people after the mission.

Antoinette was ready to find her place in this world and here, with the children of the moon, she was sure she had.

TWO DAYS LATER IN JAKARTA

Could there be anything on this earth much harder than walking into the home of someone you cared about after they died? To see, to touch, things that they'd left behind, abandoned forever, because they could never come home again?

Dean's apartment was as neat as a pin. Everything in place, even the kitchen, no spot on the counters, no crumbs on the table, nothing.

Shani wandered into his bedroom, tears sliding silently as she picked up a photograph that had to have meant the world to him. It was a 3-D capture of him, his hair blowing wildly around his head, and Sally, laughing without a care in the world, her hair as crazy in what must have been a stiff wind. They looked happy and in love, and she was sure that was why he kept it there by his bed.

He'd still been deeply in love with his ex-wife. She would have to ask Sally if she wanted it.

On an all-glass table near the window of the room, a large aquarium lit in pinks and blues held tiny fish with iridescent blue and red stripes. She'd never known he had pets. Above the tank, an automatic feeder perched to dispense just the right amount of food daily. Fish, who would have guessed? With a gulp, Shani realized she'd never asked. It made her heart hurt.

"I'm sorry, Dean."

All his things, precious to him, lying where he'd left them, where they waited for his return. Soon, the items would be nothing more than something carted away or taken to resource reclamation to be recycled. There was a supreme sadness in that, in viewing the remnants of a life like this.

Vampires knew two things more than anyone else in the world. Loss was inevitable, you had to learn to accept it with grace. And it didn't hurt less each time you lost someone.

As she finished, carrying the photo of Dean and Sally, she noticed a leather-bound book lying on a shelf just inside the door. Her fingers slid along the smooth leather as she picked it up and looked at the title. It was old, a book of poems, the author identified as a former priest. Father James Kavanaugh. She spoke the title out loud.

"*There are men too gentle to live among wolves.*"

The pages yellowed and well-worn, it was apparent he loved this book. Just a glance at the heart-felt prose touched her.

"My friend, I hope there are no wolves where you are."

Tucking it under her arm, she took it too.

Fourteen

IN BRAZIL

"Whew hoo!"

Scottie had never felt so alive, so vital, so stoked! This was what it all meant! "Zia! It's absolutely spectacular! Come up! You gotta see it from here!"

Crezia laughed, watching her new friend risking it all by swinging out over the new planting field on a rope at least 40 feet off the ground. "Get down before you bust something by crashing to the ground!" she called up.

"Ha! You can just *fix* me! But look at our incredible success!"

She wasn't wrong. They'd planted twelve hundred indigenous trees eight days ago, and using the combination of Crezia and Scottie's skills, they'd suffused the ground with healing earth magics and Scottie's powerful growth magic. Lit by low-level solar powered lights, the field was already a small miracle.

Crezia felt the same wild thrill that Scottie had, their tiny seeds were a remarkable six inches tall and healthy. While she'd love to see them from up high, her more subdued personality kept her on the ground.

Watching Scottie swing perilously high, screaming in joy, she admitted that it looked like a lot of fun. Could she?

"Get up here!" Scottie had landed on the thick tree limb she'd used for her take-off. "For God's sake, you're vampire and a healer, what the hell could happen?"

Scottie was right. It was just Crezia's super-cautious personality that was holding her back.

Why not? It was new times, with new experiences, so what the hell...*she was going to fly!* Her vampire skills put her at the top of the tree with Scottie in seconds.

"Girl, you'll love this. And the view, looking out over all our tiny babies from all the way up here, is worth the trip."

Just below the two women, Ife walked out to the perimeter of the field, her hands on her hips. "Oh, Spirits, how beautiful. No matter how hard we tried, we could not get this hard-packed, nutritionless soil to grow anything well enough to rebuild our lost paradise. And look at this! You ladies are my heroines!"

"They're amazing." Caedmon had come up behind Ife, his eyes on the field of young trees. "It's all been worth it, to protect what we have and to reestablish this lost treasure. So many beautiful creatures here are gone forever."

"That's true, but we've the DNA to bring some of them back. Not all, sadly, but we can reverse much of the damage and now that the vampires are on the front lines protecting this land, it should stay that way."

"We'll need a new generation someday."

Ife looked at Caedmon, so tall and strong by her side.

"We'll get one. The universe seems to be pretty good at this."

"So the Amazon is going to thrive again in the future."

"It looks like it will, thanks to merged magic. I think that Scottie and Crezia may be here for a while. Are you okay with staying?"

"It's hotter than hell here, but it was colder than I liked in Siberia, so, yeah, I'm ready for the change." He looked up at the lone mature tree in the entire area. "I *know* she is."

"You two are perfect mates, Caed. I'm happy for you."

"Thank you. I recommend it. No one in your life yet?"

Ife's eyes went to the moonlight-sprinkled river and the horizon line beyond it.

"I'm afraid not."

"He'll come."

"We'll see. So, Caed, that looks like fun up there. Care to challenge me to ride that rope swing? We used to swing out over much higher ones at Victoria Falls."

"Hell, yeah!"

IN JAKARTA

Another scorcher sent Shani to the private pool behind her home. The work had been exhausting tonight, so all she wanted was to slip into cool water with a tall glass of local wine and close her eyes.

The area was private as was most of her living space, so she dropped her clothes on a chair and carried a stemmed glass to the pool. Once she lowered herself into the water, she reached for the wine, and, pressed against a wood rack, letting the water's buoyancy support her.

It felt right, the water lapping sensuously around her body, her skin responding to the caresses with arousal.

It had been three weeks since she'd spoken with Rodney, just after they'd boarded their respective planes to return to their homes. Between missing him and *wanting* him, combined with the unsettling absence of Dean, she'd made it through that time in a persistent state of melancholy. Dean would never be back, and she wasn't sure how long it would be before she held Rodney again.

"You're just lonely," she whispered to the trickling waterfall across from her.

"Would you like some company?"

Startled, afraid she was dreaming, Shani twisted around in the water to see Rodney squatting just above her on the aqua tile that surrounded the pool.

"How are you...why are you...*are* you here?"

"I'm here. To stay. This being apart, it wasn't working for me."

"But what about Scottie?"

"Scottie wants to get to know me, but not yet. The girl has a wild streak and a chance to continue using her magics to repair the Amazon, so she's in South America with your sister."

A few moments passed as she realized what this meant. Shani's eyes shot to Rodney's. "Then get your clothes off and get in here so I can attack you."

She watched him stand unmoving where he was and then back up.

"How are you wearing that leather here? It has to be nearly 90."

"Leather works everywhere. It breathes."

He had decided to torture her. Shani crossed her arms on the tile as she watched him take his time to remove the sleeveless vest and fold it carefully to place it on a deck chair. As usual, he wore no shirt, so she feasted on his thick chest and bulging arms as he released the snap at the top of leather pants that fit like a second skin. He kept his eyes on her as he peeled them off over his hips, his cock popping free as he tugged them over his thighs.

She raised her eyes to his. "You can move like a vampire. Get in here. Now."

He smiled…and lingered. He'd made the mistake of moving too close to her. Shani surged up out of the water and grabbed the waistband of his pants, still at thigh level, and pulled him off balance into the water.

Rodney resurfaced coughing, and went back under because his pants still locked his legs together.

Shani realized his struggle and dove beneath to free him from the soaked leather.

And stayed.

While Rodney treaded water, his eyes rolled back when he felt Shani's mouth close around his cock.

"Gods…" he groaned. How many times had he dreamed of this?

Staying under, Shani worked him from the tip to the base, over and over, her tongue still hot beneath the water, brought him to orgasm and he shot into the water as he reached for her and pulled her back to him, his arms around her.

"Shani. My turn."

His head disappeared beneath the water as hers had, and she curled her fingers around the wood panel on the side of the pool, and held on. He'd pulled her legs up and over his shoulder and lifted her until he rose above the water level, her crotch just at the waterline. She watched his eyes glitter as he used vampire-level skills to bring her to orgasm too, her body stiffened and lifted to meet his mouth again as she came back down from his skilled tongue.

Sighing, her eyes searching his face with a languorous smile, Shani hooked her feet around Rodney's neck and pulled him to her. After a long deep kiss, she bit his neck, drawing sensuously on his blood. Giving over to the intense eroticism of her lips on his neck, her teeth beneath, his blood, hot, moving into her, he was stunned when his hardened cock jerked and he came again. *From just a blood draw!*

Once she'd finished feeding, Shani moved back and supported herself against the panel, nearly orgasmic herself. "Welcome home, my love."

"So, um, let's do that again sometime soon. That was…indescribable. Honestly, I don't have the words."

"You don't need them." Her gaze locked on his with purpose. "It's a mate's response to feeding his vampire. There is no doubt, you were always supposed to be with me. I was always yours."

"Good thing we've fixed the order of the universe, then, isn't it?"

Both completely beat, they dropped into Shani's bed, uncaring that they were still wet, and fell asleep in each other's arms.

A few hours later, Shani wakened sharply, and sat up, her hands on her belly. Rodney felt her burst upright and sat up, reaching for her.

"Shani, are you okay?"

She didn't answer at first, then rose from the bed to pace, her fingers moving across her belly, splayed wide, then brought together as she walked back to him, her eyes shining. "I can't believe this, but, Rodney, it appears that you are Shoazan."

"What?"

"I can feel her within. It looks like you're quite fertile, my love. I think it was from our first time together on the mountain in Colorado. You've made another daughter."

Rodney was thunderstruck.

IN PARIS

Taylor caught Fia just as she had stepped to the front of her cottage to pull her shielding. Daylight approached.

"Taylor, hey. What did you need?"

"I need to tell you something."

"Okay, but quickly, buddy."

"Yeah, I know." But he still didn't speak.

She leaned against her door jamb. "Tonight would be nice."

"Fia, I came back with you for two reasons. Our work here is vital. We're accomplishing important things. That hasn't changed. But after losing Dean the way that we did, so abruptly, that *did* change some things. The other reason I came back was you. We've danced around our attraction for years. I know you won't admit it, but for whatever reason, I'm not enough for you. I get that, okay, but I can't keep doing this. We get no promises as we travel through our journeys in life, and I kind of want someone to travel mine with me. I'm ready for a partner, and I know you're not. So, Fia, I love you, but I'm leaving."

Fia wasn't shocked...and yet she was. There hadn't been any secret that Taylor was crazy about her, but she'd hoped that they could return to their humorous, combative relationship. She couldn't imagine her life without Taylor, but she couldn't commit to what he needed from her. He was her best friend, he couldn't be her lover. She fucking *sucked* at maintaining that kind of relationship.

"Taylor, rethink..."

He placed a finger on her lips. "Stop. It's done."

"It's nearly daylight, I have to go in, Taylor, but please, stay until tonight. Please. Let's talk about this. I don't want you to leave."

"I don't *want* to leave."

"Then don't. Stay until I rise tonight."

"Fee..."

"Please."

After several moments, Taylor nodded. "I'll think about it."

"Okay. I have to go in, but I'll see you tonight. Right?"

"We'll see."

Fia closed herself behind her UV shielding, dropped her clothes, and crawled into her bed. She felt sick to her stomach because she already knew he wouldn't be here when she rose tonight.

THE FOLLOWING NIGHT IN COLORADO

She met him on the roof. In her long lifetime, this was one of the hardest things she'd ever had to do.

He looked devastated.

"Otto, I love you, you know I do. This was never planned, you know that too."

"Yeah. You told me about Eras after we got together, that he was your first. It's true that a man can't fight that kind of history. Plus he's vampire, like you."

"That's not it. You have always been more than enough man for me. But it turns out that Eras and I are suited as mates and that's something extraordinarily special for vampires."

Otto slid his fingers into Cairine's hair and kissed her forehead. "It's special for humans too. Well, you've been the best time of my life. I have to thank you for that."

"Otto, I can purge your memories if you'd like. It'll make it easier."

"No, Cari, please. I would really like to remember you. *Us*. I can be trusted with your secret, you know that."

"I know. Of course. I like that our time means so much to you, too, but Otto, please find someone to love. You're an incredible man."

"I will. And I'm sure she'll be smashing." He brushed Cairine's hair back before he turned to go, his eyes shining with moisture. "She just won't be *you*."

Cairine watched a man she truly loved walk to the exit to her roof and disappear behind the closed door, aware she may never see him again. She had made the right decision, but she would really miss her space cowboy.

Sad, she went back to her apartment where Eras waited.

"How'd he take it?"

"He's upset, but he understands. He's a good man. You would like him, Eras."

"I probably would have. Go on into the bedroom, I'll bring you some coffee."

Shaking his head at the incongruity of life, Eras headed to the galley to get Cairine her favorite vanilla coffee. He'd just passed the entrance to the apartment when the doorchime signaled that someone was outside.

He glanced up, surprised, because it was just after rising. "*Answer*."

The monitor lit up. *Taylor?* He should be in Paris.

"*Allow access.*"

Taylor came through the door, two bulging bags at his side. "Hey."

"Hey. I thought you went home with Fia."

"I did, but I'm finished with Paris. Eras, do you think Cairine would mind if I stayed here for a while?"

"No, of course not. You can take one of the apartments next to Sally and Jackson."

"Cool. Thanks." Taylor didn't move.

"You remember where they are, one floor up?"

"Yeah, I do. Um, Eras, I have a request. You can think about it if you want, but you're my first choice and I hope you'll be okay with it. I wonder if I can get you to do me a little favor. I want you to convert me. I want you to make me vampire."

IN ZAMBIA

It was another glorious day in the village. The gardens burst with blooms, butterflies and bees scattered over the vast variety of choices for sweet nectar. It was one of the few places on earth where the nectar gatherers were abundant, free of cages or controlled environments.

Chione watched them fly from bloom to bloom as they were made to do by Mother Nature. She was grateful that, at least here in the protected village, nature remained inviolable and essential to their lives.

She sat on a cushioned bench as she prepared to deliver one final mind-linked message to the earth's guardians. They were all over the globe again, as they were meant to be, but for now, their mission was over. This was a time of rest.

My friends, I reach out to you one last time before I release you, for a while, from your duties as born protectors of this world. You have succeeded beyond all expectations. This mission was to do all we could to make sure that the life on this world could continue, despite their own bad choices and natural disasters. You've fed a population that would have been unsustainable without your help. You've provided them a working base for healthy food, potable water, energy, disease control, and resource recovery. Now, I understand that there is a real chance that we can bring back the rainforest in the Amazon. You are all such a blessing. I want to tell you that the powers-that-be, and the living planet, wish to thank you. You are free to live your own lives, but remember, we still live in the days of awe, when anything can happen, and there will be a time, someday in the future, when we may need your talents again. Until then, live and love well. Goodnight.

"Beautifully said, gorgeous."

"I have an idea. Why don't we go and try to make another baby."

Donovan took Chione's hand and led her back to their home. They still lived in the same type of yurt they had since he joined the community. "Come with me."

THIS TIME OF AWE IS FINISHED...FOR NOW

HOWEVER...Another tale continues
SIX MONTHS LATER IN CORSICA

He had been traveling for over a hundred years, staying sometimes in a secluded place for months or years on end, immersed in its beauty and solitude, eating, drinking, and sleeping as he contemplated the meaning of life. Other times, he journeyed into human-packed cities, to *feel* everything he possibly could, to seek his lost connection to humanity through food and sex.

It never worked. Soon, he returned to the solace of silence found in aloneness.

Standing on the edge of the Mediterranean Sea, his eyes closed, he finally opened them to watch the sun set over distant mountains. *West, toward home.* Toward old friends, and a life he'd walked away from so long ago, his memories had begun to fade.

Good. That's what he sought. What he wanted. What he *needed*. Memories that cut him to ribbons were finally wrapped in the fog of time and distance.

Sighing, he admitted…it was far past time to go home. The pain had eroded into sweet thoughts and regret that faded when life made him sit up and pay attention.

It didn't mean he no longer missed her, it just meant that she was no longer part of the life that lay ahead of him. She had been gone over a hundred years now, and although he'd lived through all of what had seemed like endless days, there were moments that felt like he'd just seen her yesterday. Those were the days he locked himself away.

It had been several years since he'd slid into that pain and let it consume him.

Yes, he was healing. For a long time, that seemed like a betrayal to the love of his life, that he could allow himself to move past the pain and consider the possibility of living his life fully again. But there it was…*his life waiting for him, and he, ready to do so again.*

The tide gently flowed over his feet as he wandered along the sands barely within the water's reach.

It wouldn't be the same. Not just because she was long gone, but it had been well over a century since he'd left, and even in the extraordinary lengths of a vampire's life, a century brought many changes. It had to the world around him, he'd been aware of that, but only peripherally. The world hadn't touched him much in all those years.

Vaz fingered the fone in his hand. It held one number. Park, Bernie's best friend, still in southern France with her family and the community they'd built there. He should call her and let her know he was coming. He should commit to it.

But a second later, he dropped the fone back into his pocket and kicked at the water. *Soon, but not today.*

For now, the future of this wonderful world is safe. The guardians remain on duty so we don't mess it up too badly. For now.

It is obvious from the final pages that life moves forward, and that there is always a chance to love again. Thank you for staying with the First Bloods through this part of their journey. Come back for **When Day Is Done**, *Vaz's story.*

If you enjoyed this book, please take a few moments to leave a brief review. It's amazing what that simple thing will do to help keep a book series alive. I appreciate each and every one of you for traveling the slow path with me and these beautiful, great-hearted vampires.

Sign up for notifications of new releases at clquinn.com *or on my Amazon author page.*

Thank you, Charlie

Made in the USA
Monee, IL
06 August 2024